A Lady In the Dark

I felt myself being hurled by the force of the door as it flew open. I screamed and stumbled backward against the high poster bed that I had slept in as a child. A tall man rushed toward me, his visage taking on an eerie cast as the light from the flickering lamp made dancing shadows across his face. I screamed again and pulled myself up onto the bed.

This was no ghost, I saw, but flesh and blood, someone who had entered the house uninvited and was now moving toward me....

LADY OF THE SHADOWS

PAULA PAUL

BERKLEY BOOKS, NEW YORK

LADY OF THE SHADOWS

A Berkley Book / published by arrangement with
the author

PRINTING HISTORY
Berkley edition / July 1992

All rights reserved.
Copyright © 1992 by Paula Paul.
This book may not be reproduced in
whole or in part, by mimeograph or any other
means, without permission. For information
address: The Berkley Publishing Group,
200 Madison Avenue, New York, New York 10016.

ISBN: 0-425-13341-9

A BERKLEY BOOK ® TM 757,375
Berkley Books are published by The Berkley Publishing Group,
200 Madison Avenue, New York, New York 10016.
The name "BERKLEY" and the "B" logo
are trademarks belonging to Berkley Publishing Corporation.

PRINTED IN THE UNITED STATES OF AMERICA

10 9 8 7 6 5 4 3 2 1

To Brenda because sisters are special

and

with special thanks to Rob Cohen

LADY OF THE SHADOWS

Chapter 1

SHE danced before me, suspended in the air as she moved, never touching the ground.

She was Galveston. The island city of Texas in the Gulf of Mexico. My birthplace. I had chosen to return by ship from New York rather than inland by rail, and as the ship drew near to land, I saw that it was the glistening play of the last light of the evening upon the waters that made the buildings on the island appear to be floating above the ground. The movement of the surf provided the illusion of her swaying dance.

I felt the warm semitropic breeze caress my face as I stood on the deck of the steamer *San Antonio* and watched the harbor as it seemed to grow nearer and nearer.

"There she lies," an elderly gentleman said, his eyes on the distant shore. "The Queen City. Queen of the Gulf."

I smiled to myself at my fellow passenger's remark. Although I had seen the gentleman on board during our journey, I had not been introduced. I did know now, however, that he was Galvestonian. None other would have been likely to use the sentimental nickname Queen of the Gulf. I had no sentimental feelings for the city, as beautiful and strangely mysterious as she appeared, but that she was my home I could not deny. I was bound to her by the tangled roots of my personal history. I'd been born there twenty-eight years ago, in 1861, and I had spent my entire unsatisfactory and often unhappy childhood there. My mother, Anne D'Arcy King, whom I had hardly known and who had died when I was only two, was buried there. So was my father, the indomitable, the powerful John King, whom I had known all too well. So, too, was my brother, Anton, only recently buried there.

I was returning to Galveston at the request of Anton's lawyer, William Hienz. He had said my presence was necessary for the final details of disposing of Anton's estate, since I was his only living relative. Because my journey from New York required eight days either by rail or by sea, prudence required that the funeral and burial be held before I arrived. Anton's funeral, I had no doubt, had been well attended. In spite of the fact that I, his sister and only living relative, could not be there, he had many friends.

"Excuse me," I heard the gentleman beside me say. "Allow me to introduce myself. I am Thomas Sealy." He handed me a card, and I glanced down to see the words *Thomas Sealy, Esq., cotton factor* imprinted upon it.

"Thank you," I said, "and I am Laura King."

"King? Any relation to the late John King?"

"My father. You knew him?"

"Of course. Everyone in Galveston knew John King. I knew his son, also, although I never knew there was a daughter."

I made no reply, but it didn't surprise me that no one knew. I'd been away at school since my childhood, and my father hardly remembered I existed either.

"Please accept my condolences on the recent death of your brother," Mr. Sealy added.

"Thank you," I said without emotion.

"We'll be in port soon, Miss King," Mr. Sealy said. "Will you allow me to help you with your bag?" He pointed to the small cloth valise I had set at my feet.

I gave him a smile. He was truly a gentleman. "That's very kind of you," I said, "but no, thank you. It's small, and I can manage quite well."

"It is small, indeed," he answered, returning my smile. "And it's unusual for a young woman to travel with such light luggage. My own daughter requires two trunks full of frocks just for a weekend at her cousin Mattie's." He leaned forward, shaking his finger to make a point. "But then, I always say, the prettiest of you don't need elaborate wardrobes. It only distracts from your beauty."

I felt myself blush at his inference that I was pretty. I had never thought myself so, and in all my twenty-eight years I had never been told I was pretty. I was certainly too tall to be fashionable and not quite plump enough. My hair, I thought, was my best feature. Although it was an unremarkable shade of brown, it at least was thick and had a healthy shine. But that was not enough to make one pretty.

"Your eyes," Mr. Sealy said, as if he had read my thoughts. "Such a deep and sparkling blue, and the ivory skin of your face—ah, forgive me. I see I've embarrassed you. My enthusiasm at being home again makes me too talkative, I'm afraid."

"Don't apologize for that," I said. "Enthusiasm for anything is too often a rare quality."

"Not rare if one's home is Galveston," he said, his eyes twinkling. "Will you be staying long?"

"I'm afraid not," I answered. I didn't bother him with the boring details of my reason for returning. Attending to whatever Mr. Hienz had found necessary for me in regards to Anton's estate would be my last duty to the last of my family. I would be returning to New York and to my teaching duties as soon as it was over.

I had no illusion that Anton had left any great fortune to me. I did not expect to inherit either the family business or the Shadows, the family home, which my father had built near a cove, which he had renamed Shadow Cove. In his will my father had left everything to Anton, and Anton would not have been inclined to leave it to me, I was sure. Papa had left me enough money to finish my education and the admonition to find a suitable husband to take care of me. It had always been his contention that women had no place in business.

To my father, daughters were no more than a nuisance, an unlucky roll of the dice. Anton had followed Papa's pattern by ignoring me for years. One of the few times he had communicated with me since Papa's death was on the occasion of my twenty-first birthday, when he had expressed concern that I had not yet found a suitable husband and, I sensed, consternation at the thought that he might be expected to care for me as I advanced in years since I obviously was destined to be an old maid.

As if to underscore the urgent need for me to find a suitable husband to take care of me, Anton had informed me several years ago when I turned twenty-five that if he had no offspring at the time of his death, he would leave the bulk of his estate to charity. That, my egocentric brother seemed to feel, would assure him a place in the annals of Galveston history as a great benefactor. I suppose he had illusions of some monument being erected in his memory. Of course, dying at the age of thirty had not been part of his plan.

I was not bitter at the prospect of not inheriting the family estate. I had long ago accepted my secondary position as the female offspring, just as I'd accepted that my brother had been my father's favorite. Anton was Papa's great pride and hope, his one chance at immortality, since he thought he could infuse him with his own invincible, overpowering, and hard-driving spirit.

Anton had indeed inherited my father's energies, but he had expressed them, more often than not, in raucous revelry, leaving the business to run itself, which apparently it did, since Anton was never without money to spend on himself and his friends. The telegram I received informing me of Anton's death said that he had spent the night he died in the company of comrades.

Knowing Anton, I thought I could read between the lines. No doubt it had been a night of merriment with plenty of drink and boisterousness. Anton had left his friends for a walk on the beach, and his body was found the next morning, his demise laid to drowning, so the brief message said. Again, reading between the lines, I surmised that Anton had been drunk when he took his walk and that he had stumbled and fallen into the sea. My brother was an excellent swimmer and would not have drowned had he not been rendered incapable by drink.

In spite of the fact that I had accepted my own fate and position in my family, news of my brother's death had nevertheless filled me with a kind of melancholy and longing—a longing for what had never been. As a child, I had idolized my older brother. I had admired and was even a little envious of his charm and his ability to make friends so quickly. But we had never had the closeness I desired. Oh, Anton had seemed rather fond of me for a while when we were both young children. He would call me Lauretta, a pet name I'm told my mother had used, but that period of attention was short-lived; as he grew older he became interested in other things, particularly girls his age, and he became as adept at ignoring me as my father always had been.

"Are you all right, miss?" Mr. Sealy asked, peering into my face solicitously. "You looked suddenly so unhappy—

distraught. Has the journey been too much for you? Could I get you . . . ?"

"Oh, no, please, don't worry," I said. "I'm quite all right, thank you. I'm just a little tired."

The elderly Mr. Sealy smiled politely and turned away, watching the shoreline again. As I moved my eyes toward land, I saw the towering lighthouse and the outline of the masts of vessels lying at anchor in the bay. I could not help but remember the first time I had watched that shoreline from aboard a ship. It was shortly after my sixteenth birthday, and I was leaving Galveston.

My father had decided to send me off to a boarding school in New York. Papa seemed relieved to have found, at last, some decent way to dispose of me. Anton, I believe, hardly knew I was gone. He didn't even come with Papa to the ship to see me off. Once I was gone, I heard from Papa only occasionally—stilted, dutiful letters, inquiring after my health and my needs—but I received not a single word from Anton during that time before Papa's death. I returned home to Galveston only for a brief time each summer, and then, after Papa died, not at all. By that time I was nineteen and had been accepted as a teacher at Mrs. Swathmore's Academy for Girls, the school from which I had graduated. Now, nine years later at the age of twenty-eight, I was returning for an unhappy duty, but when I left again in a few short weeks, it would be never to return to Galveston again.

"She docks in five minutes!" a deckhand cried as the ship was steered skillfully into the harbor. As we drew closer, the illusion of the city's dancing magic gave way to reality. I could see the rough-hewn boards of the buildings along the waterfront, and I could smell the shore, a mixed aroma of rotting fish, oleanders, and steaming, salty air. The vessels that lined the piers were more clearly visible now, and I knew that many of them were from the West Indies and Mexico as well as from European ports.

As I looked down at the water below me, it was not the blue-green hue of the Atlantic I saw, but the muddy brown of the gulf, full of the black mud and silt of the great rivers of the Southland that emptied themselves there.

Other passengers crowded around me, leaning on the rails to search the shoreline for signs of the carriages and coaches that were to meet them. It would be William Hienz who would meet me, but I did not know him and therefore had no idea what he looked like.

When at last the ship was docked, the other passengers scurried about, eager to be on shore. I let them all leave ahead of me, partly because I didn't wish to be caught in the rush and partly because I felt a reluctance to step ashore into what had once held so much unhappiness for me.

"Do enjoy your stay," Mr. Sealy said, giving me a pleasant smile as he prepared to leave the ship.

"Thank you," I said, returning his smile.

He tipped his hat in a gallant gesture, then turned and disappeared into the crowd of people leaving the ship.

Eventually I had to disembark also, and once on shore I found myself in another crowd of people. I searched the sea of faces, looking for the unknown William Hienz. There was no one, however, who appeared to be looking for me.

In time most of the crowd had dispersed, leaving no one around me except for a few sailors leering at me and making me feel decidedly uncomfortable. The wool gabardine suit I wore added to my discomfort. It had been appropriate and practical for the cold March winds of New York, but March was already summer in Galveston, and even though the sun had set by now, it was not yet dark, and the air was as hot and stifling as midday. I felt my face flush, and the tendrils of hair that escaped the net of my small feathered hat had grown damp. The starched cotton shirtwaist I wore beneath my jacket would be stained with perspiration, I was certain, since I could feel a veritable rivulet between my breasts.

Trying to forget my discomfort, I picked up the small valise I'd carried with me when I boarded the ship and stepped inside a building bearing the name of the ship's company on which I'd booked passage. Perhaps Mr. Hienz would be waiting for me there. Looking around anxiously, I soon realized he was not there either. I experienced a moment of dismay, but a spinster on her own has to learn to be resourceful. There was but one thing for me to do, and that was to hire a carriage to take me and my trunk to Shadow Cove. Surely I would be expected there. And yes, I did have a trunk, in spite of Mr. Sealy's impression that I had just my small valise. The valise held only some personal belongings for my toilette.

Lady of the Shadows

I had several minutes' delay as I waited for stevedores to unload my trunk from the ship, but while I waited, I looked around for a carriage to hire. I spied one driven by a young black man, looking oddly formal in black coat and trousers and a bowler hat.

"Yes, miss," he answered in reply to my inquiry. "My carriage is fo' hire, and yes'm, I know the way to Shadow Cove, and the way back, I reckon." His manner of speech startled me. The accent of the southern black was overlaid with a strange cadence that hinted at something foreign and mysterious.

"How much?" I asked. I had by necessity developed a habit of being concerned for every penny I spent, and it was even more necessary now, since I would be foregoing several weeks of my salary while I was in Galveston.

"Twenty cents," the young man said. He was already hoisting my trunk to his carriage, seeming to know that I had no choice but to go, whatever the cost. I had expected that lifting the trunk would be more trouble for him because of his slight build, but as if he knew some secret principle of leverage, he soon had the heavy trunk loaded.

We drove away from the bay and the harbor toward the gulf side of the island. We passed the financial district on Strand Street and crossed the residential area where the grand houses of bankers, shipping magnates, and import and export merchants, such as my father had been, were located. Many of the houses seemed to have grown even grander since I'd last seen them. Before long we had reached the edge of town, and my driver headed the carriage along a lonely stretch of road running parallel to the beach.

Flat coastal plains stretched out into the growing darkness all along Galveston Island. It was a monotonous flatness, but marshes of sea grass, tall enough to hide a man, interrupted the monotony now and then. A wind, blowing off the black gulf waters, made the grasses bend and bow, as if in a frenzied ritual, while they whispered hoarsely to the earth and sea.

The gulf answered the whispers with its own eerie voice. The sound of the gulf had always been vaguely subdued and haunting to me. Even when the tide was up or when a storm had whipped the waters to a fury, the sound was not the clear crashing noise of the surf upon the northern shores, but a mournful, wailing cry, as if each wave had been privy to unknown, haunting terrors.

The wind blew harder as we drove away from the city, and as the road wound now and then close to the shore, I could feel the salty spray hitting my face. My driver pulled his hat down nearly to his eyes and, bending his head and hunching his shoulders, gave the reins an extra flick, pushing us onward into the gusts. The marsh grass bent double in the wind, then straightened again to shake itself at us in a defiant gesture.

I kept my head down against the wind until I was aware that we were rounding the familiar final turn, and I raised my eyes to see the Shadows looming in front of me, casting moon shadows into the night. How familiar, yet strangely unfamiliar, my childhood home looked to me now.

My father had built the house to suit himself, and, as with almost everything else in his life, he'd used little restraint. It was a massive house, rising to four levels and with turrets and spires and wooden towers abounding. A wide veranda swept across the front, facing away from the sea. The veranda had once been my favorite play area, and I would daily cart my dolls and doll carriages and other bits of maternal fantasy from my room to play there until Letty, my nursemaid, forced me inside for supper. The veranda was empty now, however, except for an old cane-bottom rocker I did not recognize, bobbing back and forth in the wind.

The turrets, once painted a bright white, now were a storm-weathered, dingy gray. Even the palm trees and willows that had dotted what was once the large expanse of lawns in front now looked tattered and worn as they shuddered angrily in the wind. It was those trees, casting long shadows across the plain, that had given the house its name. I noticed, too, that the tall marsh grasses had been allowed to encroach upon the grounds, giving the house a wild, untamed, and uninhabited look. It was a house I no longer knew.

My driver stopped the carriage at the rusting iron gate at the end of the front walk. "This is her, miss, the Shadows." He had to shout to be heard above the sound of the wind.

When he'd helped me from the carriage, I walked toward the gate. It was not locked, and it creaked and groaned on rusty hinges when I pushed it open. I moved past the matching stone lions at the base of the steps leading up to the veranda, then climbed the steps, holding my skirts to keep them from sweeping into the mud and grime that had collected there. Boards on the old veranda creaked, sending a cry into the night as I walked toward the door. Reaching for the large brass handle, I tugged at it, and the solid resistance I felt momentarily stunned me. Without really thinking about it, I had expected the massive double doors to be unlocked for me, as they always had been when I was a child. But that was foolish. This was not my home now, but the house of my dead brother.

My stunned realization soon gave way to anger when I remembered William Hienz's promise in the telegram that he would meet me at the dock. Where was he? And why hadn't he at least arranged to have the house unlocked for me? He could have asked the servants to see to that. I assumed there had been servants. I couldn't imagine my brother living alone in these massive quarters.

The driver had by now managed to pull my trunk from the carriage and was dragging it, thumping and bumping, up the stairs to the veranda.

"Trouble, miss?" he asked, seeing that I was struggling with the door.

"I'm afraid the doors are locked," I said. I couldn't see his face in the darkness, but I could well imagine it must be showing chagrin. He would be thinking he would have to reload my heavy trunk to take me back to town in order to find a hotel room. "Please wait," I said. "I'll try the back door and then open the front for you." I hurried down the steps, not giving him time to protest, and once again ducked my head into the wind as I turned to circle around the house. I had little hope that the back door would be open, but desperation drove me on. I had to find a way to get inside, because I could not afford a hotel room.

It was such a large house that a trip around it could not be made quickly, and my walk was slowed even more because of the darkness. I had to struggle through the jungle of tall grass, my shoe heels sinking into the mud. I tried to stick close to the house so that I would not become lost in the grasses. There were several obstacles in my path, though. I stumbled across an overturned lawn chair first and fell to my knees. Standing again, I tried to brush the mud and water from my skirt. I struggled onward, only to run into a wall jutting from the house. The wall was part of an addition that had been made since I left, so I had not expected it. Slowly and carefully I inched my way around the wall until I knew I was at the back of the house. From there I could see the moon reflecting on the sea and hear more clearly the sea's constant keening.

My father had built the house at what he'd thought was a sufficient distance from the water's edge to eliminate danger from flooding in a storm, yet he made sure it was close enough to the beach to view the great expanse of the waters from any of the windows at the back. He loved the sea with the same passion he loved money, perhaps because he knew the sea was so important to his prosperity.

At last I touched a feature of the grounds that was familiar to me—the walls of the stone walkway leading from the house to the kitchen and smokehouse. Very soon my fingers touched the damp boards of the narrow back door. Once again I tugged at the latch, and once again I was met with sturdy opposition. The fact that I had expected it was no comfort to me. In absolute despair I placed my arm against the door and leaned my head, facedown, against my arm. I had no idea what I would do. I had fully expected to stay in the family house the few nights I would be on Galveston Island.

Suddenly I was startled out of my moment of despair by what seemed to be the sound of footsteps coming from inside the house. Feeling my heart pounding in a wild rhythm, I lifted my head to peer into the narrow window beside the door. I could see a light inside, and it was moving toward me. My instinct was to run, but cold fear kept me paralyzed and anchored to the back step. I heard the rattle of the latch on the back door as it was unlocked and released. Just at the moment my blood finally warmed enough to allow me to turn and run, the door was opened. A ghostly illuminated face appeared before me, and I screamed, trying desperately to run but too paralyzed with fear to do so. In the next instant I saw that there was no need. It was my carriage driver who greeted me, holding a lighted lamp at his eye level.

"It's all right, miss," he said in his unusual voice. "No need to fear me."

"How did you get in?" I asked.

The young man shrugged. "I done it before. Mr. Anton hire me many a time after a night with his friends or with the . . ." The man paused, interrupting himself as if he had been about to say something he shouldn't. "And many a time he lose his key," he said. "He tell me to work my magic." He laughed, throwing his head back and rolling his eyes toward the ceiling, letting the light from the lamp he held reflect on his dark face. "My magic," he said again, as if the very words both pleased and amused him.

His strange laughter made me uncomfortable, but the howling wind was no comfort either, so I stepped inside the house. The carriage driver locked the door after I was inside, then hung the key on its hook next to the door in a manner that suggested he was quite used to doing it. He turned to walk toward the front of the house and gestured for me to walk beside him while he held the lamp to light the way for us.

"You is Mr. Anton's sister," he said. It seemed more of a statement than a question. How had he known that? I wondered. Had Anton mentioned me to him? I doubted that he had, since I was certain Anton seldom if ever thought of me. It was more likely that since the driver knew Anton, he knew of his death and merely surmised I would be a relative come to settle his affairs. "You has his eyes," the young man said. "How many times I see those blue eyes glarin' at me from where he sittin' atop that fine white horse. How he loved to ride! It hard to believe even death can keep him from ridin' Sir Blanco."

"What an odd thing to say," I said.

The driver laughed again, and the sound of his laughter was unsettling to me. If I could just get my trunk inside, I'd send him on his way. "If you would be so kind—"

"Yes," he said, interrupting me as if he'd read my mind. "Yo' trunk is inside."

"Thank you." I turned away from him, trying to appear calm and self-assured. "If you will take it, please, to the second-floor room immediately to the left of the landing." The driver set the lamp down to do my bidding. I picked up the lamp and held it to light the way for him as he moved my trunk up the back stairway. The door to my old room was unlocked, and as soon as the trunk was inside, the young man turned toward the stairway again. I followed, down the stairs and to the door, still carrying the lamp. The young man reached for the door but turned to me before he opened it.

"My name is Felix LeFeu," he said. "I come if you needs me—or my magic."

Before I could respond to his surprising statement, he was gone, disappearing into the darkness, his footsteps making a hollow sound in the darkness. I turned back into the front hall, holding the lamp in front of me. For the first time I had a chance to look carefully at the house again—at the large square room that was the grand entry hall, the high molded ceilings, and the light wood floors laid in an intricate parquet design. I saw the familiar arched doorways opening on each side, and on each side of the doorways, candleholders carved from white marble in the delicate shape of a woman's hand grasping at nothing. Papa had never let the hands be without candles, which he burned nightly, but apparently my brother had forgotten the practice. Directly in the back center of the entry hall and through another archway was the great staircase, wide and sweeping, the steps hewn from the same marble as the candleholders. Fine teakwood panels lined the walls of the stairway. It was all very much as I remembered, yet it looked alien somehow.

I turned to my left to enter the parlor, still holding the lamp in front of me. The light seemed lost in the cavernous room. Ghostlike mounds that I knew to be furniture hovered silently, then appeared to move as the flickering light from the lamp cast uneven shadows. It was obvious that the room had been left untended. The furniture looked worn and sagging, and the walls above the teakwood wainscoting were as dingy as the outside of the house had been.

Ah, well, I thought as I turned away, the old house was not my worry. Anton would have left it to someone else, of course, or perhaps it would have to be sold to pay his debts, since, by the looks of things, he had not been enjoying the greatest of prosperity after all. It occurred to me then, as I made my way up the stairs toward what had been my old bedroom, that I might be considered trespassing, but I brushed the thought aside. My stay would be brief, and surely whoever the benefactor was would be understanding of my circumstances.

At the top of the stairs I turned down the long hallway to my room near the landing of the back stairwell. The heat was heavy in the hallway, and I removed my jacket and unbuttoned my shirtwaist as I walked. I paused as I reached the door, noting that it was closed. Strange, I thought, since I didn't remember Felix closing it as he left. Reaching for the cloisonné doorknob, I gave it a twist and a push, but the door refused to open, remaining as firmly closed as the front and back entries had done. The house, it seemed, did not want me.

Setting the lamp and my jacket aside on the floor, I used both hands and a shoulder to push at the door. This time it opened, and immediately I saw thin white tendrils stretching themselves toward me, reaching and clawing. I felt a moment of fright until I realized the eerie shapes were nothing more than the lace curtains on the opened windows, blowing in the stiff, howling wind. The force of the wind, I now knew, was what had kept me from being able to open the door easily.

Picking up the lamp from the floor in the hallway, I set it on the rosewood dressing table in my room and ran to the window to close the shutters. I reached for them, struggling against the force of the gale and fighting with it as it tried to rob me of my breath. The wind tore my hat from my head as I grasped at one of the shutters, then it snatched the shutter from my hands. When I reached for the shutter again, leaning my upper body out into the night, I glimpsed in the moonlight a white shadow below me, near the edge of the water. Then I heard a cry, muffled and distant, competing with the sound of the wind and the sea. When I looked closer, I knew that the cry had been the neighing of the white horse I saw below as it reared on hind legs then galloped toward the house. The horse's rider was dressed in black, making him appear almost as an apparition in the moonlight.

The pale horse and its dark rider rode toward me until they were lost in the shadows of the house. Then I heard a voice, barely audible in the wind, commanding the horse to halt and calling him Sir Blanco—the name Felix had used for my brother's horse.

I stood, too frightened to move, while the wind from the opened window tore at my hair, loosening it from its pins and tossing it around my face. The lamp on the dressing table flickered, the flame rising to lick at the top of the globe in a frenzied swirl, casting grotesque shadows into the gloom of night.

In the same instant I heard the footsteps in the back stairwell, and I knew that the dark rider had entered the house.

Chapter 2

THE steps were slow and measured, and there was no evidence of stumbling, although I knew the intruder was walking in the dark. That meant it had to be someone who knew the house very well. But there was no one in my acquaintance who knew the house well enough to find his way through it in the dark. No one except Anton.

Anton? Ridiculous, I told myself. Anton was dead, and I did not believe in ghosts. My attempts to be rational were failing me, though, and I quickly ran to close the door to my room and to bolt it from the inside. I had just slammed it shut and was pushing the heavy bolt into place when I felt pressure against me. Someone or some*thing* was trying to force the door open.

I dropped my hand from the latch, leaving it unfastened, and used both my hands to hold the doorknob, pressing all the weight of my body against the door to hold it closed. The door rattled on its hinges as my opponent pushed against it. I in turn pushed even harder with all my strength, but all my strength was not enough. I felt the door being forced toward me.

"Go away!" I cried. "Go away, please, whoever—"

I was never able to finish my frantic plea. In the next second I felt myself being hurled by the force of the door as it flew open. I screamed and stumbled backward against the high poster bed that I had slept in as a child. A tall man rushed toward me, his visage taking on an eerie cast as the light from the flickering lamp made dancing shadows across his face. I screamed again and pulled myself up onto the bed. Scrambling to the middle, I brought myself to a crouching position with my feet tucked under me.

Lady of the Shadows

This was no ghost, I saw, but flesh and blood, someone who had entered the house uninvited and was now moving toward me. A combination of anger and fear surged through me, and I pulled myself up, standing unsteadily on the soft feather mattress while I flailed my arms at the stranger.

"Get out of the house. Get away from me, or I'll hurt you," I said, swinging my doubled right fist at him.

I missed, and the man laughed. Grabbing my arm, he twisted it behind me. I fell backward onto the bed, and since he still held my arm, I pulled him along with me. He lay partly on top of me, his face very close to mine. I could feel his warm breath on my cheek, and I could see his eyes, cool gray and dancing with smoldering blue lights, strangely compelling. For a moment, and for a reason I could not understand, I felt stunned, as if my heart had momentarily stopped beating then had started again all too fast. In the next second I had come to my senses and used my free hand to strike him again, hard on the shoulder.

He laughed once more, a deep, throaty sound, and he stood holding both my arms as he pulled me up with him. "You'll hurt me, will you? And with what? A kitten's paw?"

"Who are you? What are you doing here?" I asked, backing away from him, trying to conceal the tremor in my voice. I couldn't let him sense my fear. I had to keep the upper hand.

"I might ask you the same thing," the stranger said. "For all the signs that the Shadows is uninhabited, it is not a house for vagrants or just any gypsy tramp who passes."

"Vagrants!" I said, startled and angry. "Gypsy tramp! I'll have you know I am neither. This is my—" I was backing away from him as I spoke, and I stopped in midsentence when I caught a glimpse of myself in the mirror. I had forgotten that the wind had blown my hat away and loosened my hair so that it hung about my shoulders with wisps of it flying into my face. My wool gabardine skirt was damp and wrinkled, and my once-starched shirtwaist was limp from the humidity and open in the front, revealing my chemise. Quickly I gathered the front together and clutched it at the top of my breasts.

My discomfort seemed to amuse the stranger. He had a half smile on his face as he advanced toward me. "You were about to say something?" he asked in a mocking tone.

"This is my—my brother's house," I stammered. "I'm no—"

"What?" the man bellowed. "What did you say?"

"Why do you keep asking me questions, then interrupting me with another question when I try to answer you?" I said, dropping my hands to rest on my hips. "If you will just allow me to speak, I will tell you I am not some vagrant or gypsy, I am—"

He grabbed my arm, roughly jerking me closer to him. "Whose house do you claim this is?" he demanded.

"Why, it is—was—Anton's, my brother's, and I demand that you take your hands off me!"

"By God, you know his name." He dropped my arm with another rough and quick movement.

"Of course I know my own brother's name. Not that it is any of your business. Now I insist that you get out of here. If that is Sir Blanco you are riding, and I did hear you call the horse by that name, then I insist that you stable him and leave on foot. I will ask no questions as to why you were riding a horse that does not belong to you, if you will leave immediately." I was shaking as I spoke to the man, but I worked hard at concealing it. If I could make him think that I was sure of myself, perhaps he would be intimidated and leave me unharmed.

"You are Miss Laura? Anton's spinster sister from New York?" he asked, still standing in the middle of my bedroom as if he had no intention of leaving.

"I am."

His eyes swept over me before he spoke again. "You are not at all as I expected."

Once again I was embarrassed by my appearance. Of course, no one would expect Anton King's sister to be such an unkempt, soggy, and wind-tattered woman.

"What did you hope to accomplish by coming here unannounced?" he asked. His eyes had grown suddenly very cold.

"Unannounced? But I—"

"Never mind. Mr. Hienz will contact you in the morning," the man said. With that he opened the door and was gone, leaving me standing in the middle of the floor, stunned. He had not even told me his name. I felt I certainly had a right to know the name of the person who had been so insulting to me, especially since he seemed to know so much about me, including *my* name.

In a little while I heard the door downstairs slam and, within a few seconds, the sound of horse's hooves. The insolent stranger was riding away on my brother's horse.

When he was gone, I hurried downstairs to make certain all the doors were locked, and indeed they were. Did the stranger have a key to the house? Or had he worked some sort of magic to enter through a locked door, as the strange Felix LeFeu had claimed he had done? I brushed aside the latter thought, reminding myself that I was a pragmatic spinster lady with no time for such foolish notions as believing in magic. Nevertheless, it was disconcerting to know that two strangers had, by whatever means, so easily gotten into the house in which I was obliged to spend the night. But one cannot allow oneself to be consumed by fear, so I undressed and prepared myself for bed as quickly as possible. My journey had been a tiring one, and I was anxious to rest.

The wind whistling through the marsh grass and the distant, mournful voice of the sea—the very sounds that had lulled me to sleep as a child—now kept me awake. And to make me even more wakeful, I kept seeing in my mind's eye the dark stranger riding along the shore on the white horse and then bursting into my room to laugh at me, to insult me, and then to leave me feeling confused and angry.

Sometime during the night the wind stopped, and my thoughts of the stranger dimmed until eventually I fell asleep. I awoke the next morning to the sound of a loud knocking at the front door. Hurriedly I pulled my dressing gown from my trunk, put it on over my nightgown, and rushed downstairs. I opened the door to a thin middle-aged man wearing spectacles and a natty-looking linen suit. He removed his flat-brimmed straw hat as soon as I opened the door.

"Good morning, miss," he said, holding his hat in both hands and appearing somewhat embarrassed. "I'm William Hienz."

"Mr. Hienz!" I answered, not attempting to hide my anger. "I fully expected you to meet me at the docks yesterday."

"I am so sorry," he said, pronouncing each syllable in the drawn-out manner of the South, the accent common to the Texas coast. "The mails, I'm afraid, are not always reliable," he said timidly. "I received your letter informing me of your arrival date this morning. I assumed you would come here, so I rode out soon as I could to look for you."

He looked and sounded so timid that I felt my anger begin to evaporate, but not entirely. Anger and chagrin, I have found, are hard to give up when a woman feels she's been inconvenienced. I stepped aside for him to enter the house, but I kept my tone sharp. "If you will come in and wait in the parlor, I'll be down in a minute."

"At your convenience," he answered politely. Once he stepped inside, he seemed to grow quite nervous. "I—ahem—forgot that the servants had been dismissed," he said. "And since we are—ahem—alone, perhaps I ought to wait in the carriage." He was clutching his hat so desperately that I feared he would break the straw brim.

"Nonsense," I said in my best schoolmarm tone. "There is nothing improper about your waiting inside out of the damp air." With that I turned to make my way upstairs again.

"So sorry the weather couldn't have been better," he called after me, "and I'm really very sorry you had to make do last night without the servants."

Without replying, I gave him a wave of my hand. The man seemed intent upon apologizing for everything. Apologizing for the weather was ridiculous, since no man or woman can control that, and in truth, there was no need for an apology about the servants either. I was quite used to an existence without them.

Back in my room I pulled a dress of pale yellow batiste from my trunk and shook it to rid it of as many wrinkles as possible. I was well aware of the fact that I should have worn black in mourning for my brother, but I did not possess a black dress. In spite of the fact that I knew it was de rigueur for spinsters to dress in dark colors, I preferred lighter hues, although I did bend to convention to the extent of keeping my clothes simple in pattern. I pulled the dress on over my white ruffled petticoats, my only bit of secret frivolity. I brushed my hair and drew it up from my face, pinning it in a loose bun at the back before I set a wide-brimmed hat of yellow straw and white netting at the top of my head. Then, feeling anxious to get on with the business at hand, I pulled on my white gloves as I made my way down the stairs.

Mr. Hienz, I saw to my puzzlement, was not in the front hallway where I had left him, nor was he in the parlor where I had invited him to wait.

"I'm in here, Miss Laura," I heard him calling from the library. I stepped through the archway to see him standing beside a small tea table. The delicious smell of the steaming coffee he poured into cups on the table greeted me as I walked closer.

"With no servants around I knew you'd had no breakfast," he said, smiling at me as I entered. "I'm afraid I couldn't find enough for a feast, but there's coffee and half a loaf of bread with a smidgen of honey to spread on it. I'm sorry the bread's not fresh, but I cut away the mold," he said, pointing to a plate with four slices of bread on it.

For a moment I was speechless with surprise, as well as with delight. I was so hungry I could have eaten almost anything. "How thoughtful of you," I said, recovering enough to walk toward him and accept the cup he handed me. By now all the anger I'd felt earlier had disappeared completely. As I ate, I thought that no meal had ever tasted better to me, and though I knew it was unladylike to do so, I ate three of the four slices of the bread down to the last crust, while Mr. Hienz munched rather timidly on the other slice.

While we ate, he kept up a steady stream of apologies—for having awakened me when he arrived, for failing to meet me at the dock, and for the state in which I'd found the house.

"It's a pity, but young Mr. Anton let the house go, you know. He much preferred staying in his apartment in the hotel in town. He liked having people around him, not an empty house and the lonely sea, he used to say. But I do regret that you found the house so—"

"Don't apologize," I said, interrupting him with some impatience. "I don't expect to be here long."

"But you—"

"I learned long ago not to let the way my brother conducted his affairs trouble me," I said with a wave of my hand. I stood then and, brushing the crumbs from my skirt, suggested that we leave. "I'm sure you're anxious to be about your other business, Mr. Hienz," I said, "and the sooner I can take care of whatever legal details there are, the better."

"Of course," Hienz said, managing to sound apologetic even with so simple a phrase. I walked ahead of him toward the front door. "I am so sorry that you have to be subjected to such details as probate requires." He followed several paces behind me. "I understand that matters of a business nature can be taxing to females, but you must know your brother was—ah—eccentric at times. And under the circumstances, it seems the burden of the whole mysterious affair has fallen upon you."

I stopped just as my hand touched the large brass doorknob and turned my head to look at Mr. Hienz. "Mysterious affair?" I asked.

"Your brother died leaving no will. I reckon you didn't know how much it will complicate things for you, since you are the only surviving relative and therefore his heir."

"His heir? I am to inherit—?"

"The process will be complicated and drawn out, but yes, you have inherited not only the estate and the business, but the entire mess to be straightened out."

I looked at him, too stunned to speak.

"Oh, I am so sorry. I didn't mean to upset you," he said, giving me a worried look.

"What was that you said earlier?" I asked, still trying to sort things out in my mind. "Something about a mystery?"

"Oh, the mystery," Hienz said. "Well, the mystery is that Anton always claimed he *did* have a will. I regret to say that I can't substantiate that. It was my law partner, who has, I'm sorry to say, passed on, who was supposed to have helped Anton write the document, though I never saw it. I know Anton was always talking of changing little things in his will. It used to irritate my partner to no end. Anton would consider making first one charity and then another the benefactor, or he would talk of setting aside a sum for a particular friend, then change his mind and say it was to be another. But forgive me, I just don't know what changes, if any, he ever actually made. Anyway, as I said, the mystery, the real mystery, is that no will was ever found. It was not in any of Anton's papers he kept in his safe, and nothing could be found in his home. I reckon he could have destroyed it. Anton could be quite eccentric, as I said. But in any event, that makes you the benefactor, if only by default."

I was stunned. Because of Anton's carelessness I was to be his heir! I tried to remind myself that his careless nature could also mean that he had managed so poorly that there might be nothing left. Nevertheless, I was so much in shock that I hardly remembered the ride to town in Mr. Hienz's carriage.

When the carriage stopped in the front of an imposing brick building on Strand Street, Mr. Hienz offered me his hand to help me out.

"My offices are inside," he said. "We can begin with some of the documents you have to go through."

There seemed no end to the documents I read and signed, attesting to my relationship to Anton and giving the courts power to pay any debts Anton or the business might have owed, although I had not as yet seen any of his business papers. There was, however, a stack of Anton's personal papers that Mr. Hienz asked me to go through. The papers were primarily notes for personal debts to tailors and haberdashers or for the care and feeding of Sir Blanco, as well as a surprising number of bills for articles of female finery. My brother obviously had been generous to his lady friends. Some of the notes were marked "paid," but some apparently were outstanding, and I spent most of the morning trying to sort out the paid bills from the unpaid ones.

Finally Mr. Hienz suggested that we stop for a bite of lunch. I found that I was in fact hungry, even after my ample if humble breakfast, and furthermore I was glad for the excuse to get away from the seemingly endless stack of papers for a while. When we stepped out into the street, my eyes fell upon the sign above the building across from us. It read Sealy and Bradley Ltd. It must be, I thought with delight, the business of the pleasant and thoughtful Thomas Sealy I'd met on the ship.

Mr. Hienz had taken my arm and was helping me across the street, and we were walking toward the Sealy and Bradley building when I saw a tall man emerge from the door, leading a woman by the arm. I stopped, my breath catching in my throat, when I realized that the man was the same one who had invaded my house the night before. He was dressed now, not in the rough riding trousers he had worn at night, but in a dark suit of fine lightweight wool. I noticed that he was wearing Spanish-style boots, the kind worn by cowmen of western Texas, and his hat was the wide-brimmed western style. He looked like the pictures of gunfighters I'd seen on posters as a young girl. It would be easy to believe that the long-tailed frock coat he wore hid a gunbelt. Without a doubt he embodied the character of Galveston, part cosmopolitan and part frontier.

Before I could turn away, the man's eyes met mine, and our gazes locked for a moment. I sensed that he recognized me, but he said nothing. The dark smolder of his eyes reminded me of the way they had looked when he lay on top of me on the bed after he had forced his way into my bedroom.

Remembering the awkward incident, I turned my eyes away from him to cover my embarrassment. It was then that I noticed that the woman clinging to his arm was remarkably beautiful. She wore a dazzling dress of blue broadcloth trimmed in appliqués of white silk. Cascades of blond curls fell from beneath a small feathered hat that matched her dress exactly.

By now Mr. Hienz and I had crossed the street, and it was obvious that we could not avoid meeting the couple. Mr. Hienz tipped his hat to the lady and extended his hand to the man, greeting him heartily.

"Chase, I see you're back from Houston. So good to see you. Sorry the weather wasn't good for traveling."

The man shook William Hienz's hand, but his eyes never left me.

Mr. Hienz, becoming aware of it, grew flustered and began apologizing again.

"Oh, dear, forgive me for forgetting my manners," he said. "Miss Laura King, may I present Miss Rachel Blackburn and Mr. Chase Bradley."

Chase Bradley. Could he be the other half of Sealy and Bradley Ltd.? But how, I wondered, could a perfect gentleman, such as the Thomas Sealy I'd met on the ship, be associated with a man like this Chase Bradley, who, in spite of his smooth appearance today, had the manners of a boorish ruffian?

"A pleasure to see you again," Chase Bradley said with a slight bow.

Miss Blackburn turned toward her companion with a raised eyebrow, as if to ask what he meant by "again."

"I met Miss King last night in her b— at Shadow Cove," Mr. Bradley said.

He had been about to say bedroom, and I could see the amused expression in his eyes as he looked at me, sharing the secret.

I was thankful that Miss Blackburn spoke up again in time to cover the embarrassing moment.

"Shadow Cove?" she asked.

"Yes," Chase answered. "I saw a light in the house and went by to have a look. I didn't expect Miss King to be there."

"Then you are Anton's sister," Rachel said. Her voice sounded oddly cold, as if she did not approve of my being Anton's sister.

"Yes," I answered. "You knew my brother?"

"Anton was a dear friend," she said. Then she added, as if she was making an important point, "He had many friends."

"Yes, I'm sure he did," I said, wondering just how friendly she and Anton had been. Had she been one for whom he'd bought shawls or lace handkerchiefs or pendants? She clung closely to Chase Bradley now, however, leading me to believe that she had no thought for any other man.

"Will you be staying at the Shadows long?" she asked.

"I'm not certain," I said. "I hadn't planned to, actually. I have a teaching position to get back to in New York, but there is some unexpected business to attend to regarding Anton's estate."

Rachel gave me an icy smile, and I could sense that she was scrutinizing me, comparing me to herself. She needn't have bothered. Her costume and coiffure were far superior to mine. In fact, I was superior only in height. Rachel Blackburn was fashionably petite and plump. I, on the other hand, was unfashionably tall and thin.

"Well, we do hope your business will be taken care of soon so you can return to your school. I'm sure you're needed there." Rachel had put emphasis on the word *there* as if to suggest that I wasn't needed here. Her smile turned saccharine as she lifted her skirt daintily to step around me. Her arm was still hooked through Chase Bradley's, and she attempted to pull him along with her as she walked.

Chase Bradley would not be pulled, however. He stopped, allowing Rachel's arm to slip from his. "Those papers you mentioned," he said, speaking to Mr. Hienz. "I've located them, and you're welcome to inspect them at your convenience."

"Very kind of you," Mr. Hienz said. "I'll contact you soon and go through them as quickly as possible. I don't want to be a bother," he said, managing to sound apologetic again.

Mr. Bradley turned toward me. "If I can be of any help in clearing up the legal maze so you can be on your way back to New York, let me know," he said. His voice sounded remarkably civil, but his expression, especially in his eyes, was dark and cold.

Mr. Hienz murmured a thank you, apparently embarrassed that I hadn't done so, then he tipped his hat to Rachel once more before he led me toward the restaurant. Once we were inside, I couldn't help thinking as we ate our lunch how anxious both Rachel Blackburn and Chase Bradley had seemed to have me out of Galveston and returned to New York. They were no more anxious than I.

After lunch Mr. Hienz took me back to his office to review more papers. By midafternoon my vision was blurred, and my head was aching. Mr. Hienz, always unwilling to offend, noticed that I held my fingertips to my throbbing temples and quickly apologized for keeping me so long. I accepted his offer to drive me back to the Shadows as well as the offer to stop by a waterfront market so I could buy a few provisions for my meals.

He apologized for the fact that Anton's estate being tied up in probate made it impossible for me to have money even to hire a cook, but I assured him, to his apparent surprise, that I was quite capable of cooking my own meals and that I had in fact done it for years. I knew that living in the large old house in its present crumbling condition would not be entirely pleasant for me, but I assured Mr. Hienz that I would manage. I knew that even if my stay was to be longer than I'd expected, it still wouldn't be permanent. By now, judging from what I had seen of Anton's personal affairs, I had come to expect fully that he would be in such great debt that there would be nothing left. I was grateful that I still had my small but decent rented rooms in New York.

My biggest concern for the moment, however, was that Shadow Cove was such a distance from town and that I had no carriage or horse to transport me to town when the need arose. In fact, I would have been grateful for the horse without the carriage. When I was younger, I had been quite an adept rider—the one thing Papa had taught me to do. If I had a horse now, I could ride to town when I needed to and would be neither so totally isolated nor so dependent upon Mr. Hienz. I resolved then to make it a point to find out whether Sir

Blanco had been sold to Chase Bradley or if the horse was rightfully mine.

I didn't speak of any of my concerns to Mr. Hienz, however, for fear that it would provoke another series of apologies, making it just that much longer before I could have my supper, a hot bath, and bed. At least I would have no worries about transportation for the following day. Mr. Hienz was already informing me that he would be out to fetch me at eight o'clock in the morning.

As soon as Mr. Hienz left and I was alone in the house, it seemed to take on an eerie quality. My footsteps on the parquet floors and even the sound of my breathing echoed through the rooms as if the walls were angrily throwing back any sounds of the living. It was a place that seemed to want to die. In spite of the heavy, warm air inside the house, I felt myself shiver, but I tried to shake off the uncomfortable feeling. This was my home, I told myself, a place where I had felt secure as a child, if not entirely happy. There was no reason to feel uncomfortable here.

To keep from dwelling upon the disquieting feeling, I busied myself by preparing a quick and simple supper, then ate it while I heated water for my bath. By the time I had finished dragging the last heavy kettle of water to the large cast iron tub in a small room off the kitchen, I was silently cursing my brother for not having installed modern plumbing. It was becoming quite commonplace in New York.

After a long soak in the warm water, which I had scented with a few splashes of my cologne, I knew that each heavy kettle had been worth it. Even after the tedious task of removing the water from the tub, I felt calm and refreshed as I made my way upstairs. When I had dressed in a lightweight summer nightgown, I unwound my hair and sat on the sill of the opened window in my room while I brushed it. The breeze, much less stiff and fierce than the howling wind of the previous night, felt refreshing as it ruffled my hair and caressed the bare skin of my arms, my throat, and my face.

The effect was to relax me even more, and I made one last long, lazy stroke of the brush down the length of my hair to the very ends where a strand of it tumbled across my breast and down almost to my waist. Dropping my hand that held the brush to my side, I leaned against the casing of the window, my eyes half-closed, watching the waves in the distance as they licked at the shore, whispering their mournful song.

While I watched in my dreamlike state, a figure seemed to materialize out of the mists of the foaming surf and out of the dim half light of the early evening to move along the edge of the water. The form did not seem out of place at first. During all my childhood, I'd heard the legend of the ghost of the pirate Jean Laffite, who'd made Galveston Island his home. His ghost was said to roam the shores, and in my relaxed state, staring into the ethereal atmosphere of the night, the specter was not jarring. But realization slowly awakened in me, and I sat up, wondering who was on the isolated stretch of beach so far from any other dwellings.

Looking more closely, I saw that the form appeared to be a woman in a long, flowing white dress, and I could hear the sounds of her haunting cry blending in with the wail of the sea. She walked to the edge of the water, and I saw a wave dash at her feet. In the next instant I saw that she had stepped farther into the sea until the water was at her waist. I heard her cry again, and feeling alarmed, I reached for my dressing gown and slippers and hurried out of the house. I dashed through what had been the back lawn, passed the gate, and stepped onto the stretch of rocky soil that eventually gave way to the beach.

Trees that Papa had planted at the back of the house had obscured my view of the woman before I reached the beach, and now that I was clear of them, a slight sloping of the land combined with the growing darkness to hide her from me still. But I knew the area where I'd seen her, and I ran toward it. I felt compelled to go to her, believing that she was in some sort of stress and that she was in danger of drowning. I stumbled once in the thick, sticky sand and fell to my knees. Picking myself up, I ran on until I reached the spot on which I'd seen her from my bedroom window. She was not there.

I looked around frantically for footprints, but there were none. There was only the frenzied crescendo of the sea building itself to high tide. Either she had drowned, or she had vanished into the mists.

Chapter 3

I SPENT a restless night, finally falling asleep just before dawn, and was awakened all too soon by a ribbon of light shining through the shutters of my window and falling across my face. When I walked to the window and opened the shutters, brilliant sunlight flooded the room, almost blinding me. I squinted into the light, searching the length of the beach for any signs of the wraithlike figure I'd seen the night before, but the stretch of sand along the water's edge looked empty and benign. I could almost believe, in this stark light of morning, that the entire experience had been nothing more than a dream. The strange figure on the lonely beach and the odd manner in which she had disappeared had been real, though, and it was one more thing to add to the growing uneasiness I'd felt since my homecoming.

I couldn't dwell on the strange events, however. I had more mundane things to deal with now, such as getting dressed and preparing myself a breakfast in the short time I had before William Hienz would arrive to take me to town for more of the drudgery of settling Anton's estate.

Mr. Hienz arrived exactly on time, and I was ready and waiting for him. During the drive to town, I thought I did very well with concealing my unsettled feelings about the events of the night. I also managed to remain composed while he apologized for everything from the early hour to the morning humidity and the amount of "mental fatigue" I was being subjected to, for which, he said, women were by nature unsuited. His suggestion that I might be suffering such mental distress confirmed my decision not to mention the figure I'd seen on the beach. He would probably lay it all to my overtaxed "feminine" brain. I did manage to ask in a casual manner, however, whether any houses had been built along the beach near Shadow Cove during the five years I had been gone.

"Oh, I'm sorry to say that there haven't been," Mr. Hienz said. "Not many families like the remoteness. I'm afraid it's a great inconvenience to a woman living alone, as you do, not to have any neighbors nearby, isn't it?"

"It's no great concern," I answered. "My stay here will be short."

"Of course, and I highly recommend that you return to your accustomed life in the East," Mr. Hienz said, his southern accent making the words flow like a warm, sticky liquid. "Running the business would be asking too much of you. I advise you to sell it, and I believe that can be arranged. In spite of the fact that Anton's business practices were somewhat, shall we say, lackadaisical, the business does hold a great deal of potential if it could be managed properly."

I had no idea whether Mr. Hienz was right or not about the fact that running the business would be out of the realm of my ability. I knew nothing about it since my father had kept me well protected from anything remotely connected to King Enterprises. Still, if it had all been left in my hands now by whatever accident, I felt I at least owed it to myself as the sole survivor of what was once the King empire to try to understand as much as I could about the business. If nothing else, I needed to know enough that I could be as certain as possible of getting a fair price when I sold it.

"Mr. Hienz," I said, keeping my voice strong and even, "I feel that before I make any decision about selling King Enterprises, I need to know more about it, so instead of going to your office today to go over Anton's small personal bills, I'd prefer to go to the company office at the wharves. I'd like to have a look at the ledgers."

"But, Miss Laura, I would be loath to subject you to more mental drudgery. I—"

"You're very kind, Mr. Hienz, but there's no need to be overly protective. I want to have a look at the books now. This morning," I said, using the tone I used when my students balked at an assignment.

"Miss Laura, it would be so difficult—so taxing and—" Mr. Hienz sputtered a few minutes longer before he succumbed to my silent, steady gaze. "Very well," he said at last. Reluctantly he turned the carriage in the direction of the wharves.

The waterfront area where the family business was located had always seemed enchanting to me as a child, and it was no less so now with the view of ships under full sail just offshore and other vessels, their sails reefed, sitting like skeletons along the pier. The piers were lined with cargo from countries I had only read about, but that I imagined to be exotic. Perhaps there was, after all, this one part of Galveston that still did appeal to me and that was capable of infusing me with the magic that other residents talked about. In truth, I really had never been a part of it, but had been allowed only to linger at the edges of the enchantment.

The inside of the building housing King Enterprises was still very much as I remembered it from the few times I'd visited it when I was growing up. There was a large warehouselike area for the storage of cargo, some bound for those exotic places I'd heard of, and some only recently arrived from there. On one side of the warehouse and separated from the open area by a glass partition were the rooms that served as offices for the family business. Through the glass I could see the large oak desk that I remembered my father sitting behind when he wasn't out on the wharves or aboard ship, and above the desk was his portrait. The thick dark hair, fine aquiline nose, and firm jaw gave him the look of royalty, and the artist had captured the steely glint of his sea-blue eyes as well.

Seated behind a desk in the corner was a man in a well-tailored suit. His head was bent over a ledger, a shock of thick, sandy-colored hair falling over his forehead. His hands, one of which held a pen while the other rested on the open ledger, were long, slender, and delicate in appearance, almost like those of a woman. The man looked up, staring at us with hazel eyes through the glass partition. The surprised expression on his face and the unruly shock of hair falling on his forehead gave him a boyish look, softening the angular shape of his face. Mr. Hienz opened the door, and we both entered the office.

"Miss King, may I present Robert Thorn, your brother's accountant and business manager," Mr. Hienz said when we were inside.

Robert Thorn rose to his feet and moved toward me. Giving me a slow and charming smile, he bowed slightly, picked up my hand, and raised it to brush against his lips. His eyes never left my face, and the smoky, muted shade of them reminded me of the waters of the gulf before a storm.

"I'm so happy to meet you at last." His voice was a slow, easy drawl. "But I regret it had to be under such unfortunate circumstances," he added, lowering his long lashes over his eyes, giving him once again a decidedly charming and boyish look. He did not at all fit the stereotype of a hunch-shouldered, squinting bookkeeper.

"Thank you," I answered uneasily. In spite of Robert Thorn's charm, I still was uncomfortable in what had always been territory in which I had been unwelcome in the past.

William Hienz cleared his throat nervously. "I'm sorry to trouble you, since you are obviously very busy, but Miss Laura would like to have a look at the ledgers," he said.

Robert Thorn glanced at me, his brows raised slightly. "Quite a surprise," he said.

"A surprise? What do you mean?"

"Anton seldom bothered."

Mr. Hienz spoke up, as if in defense of Anton. "Anton's talents lay in his ability to meet people easily. To make friends, you see, to attract customers. He left the details of the accounting to Robert. Anton had the utmost trust in him."

"Which, I assume, was well deserved," I said, reaching for the ledger Robert Thorn had thrust in front of me.

Mr. Hienz reached across me, intercepting and taking the account book before I could grasp it. At the same time he coughed nervously and was compelled to defend Mr. Thorn. "Of course," he said, "most certainly well deserved."

With the book in his hands, he led me aside to a desk in the corner. When we were both seated, he began explaining the bookkeeping system used in the ledger. He needn't have been so patronizing. Even though I'd had no formal training in the weightier matters of business, I'd learned bookkeeping methods and procedures from the owner of the private school that employed me. Seeing to the books had become part of my duties in exchange for rent on my apartment. I'd learned enough from that experience to determine very quickly that Anton was not the sharp businessman that my father apparently had been. In spite of the fact that the column for income showed evidence of an active business, the column showing money for payment of loans and other expenditures far outweighed it. My brother had obviously overextended his credit.

As I studied the ledger, I was aware of Robert watching me from his corner of the room. When I happened to look up and my eyes caught his, he was not embarrassed. He merely smiled and laid his pen aside, settling back in his chair to watch me even more closely, as if I were a circus act come to amuse him. I did my best to concentrate on the ledgers, going over each line painstakingly. Mr. Hienz grew tired of the drudgery and soon stopped his attempts at explaining the details to me when it became apparent that I frequently had to correct him on some points. In a little while he became as fidgety as some of my students do when recess is overdue.

"Mr. Hienz, I'm afraid I'm keeping you from other business," I said.

He coughed his nervous cough again and tugged at his tie. "Of course not," he answered.

"You're too kind to admit otherwise," I said. Then, hoping to give him further incentive to leave, I added, "I'm afraid I'm going to be at this a while longer. Why don't you go back to your office, and I'll send for a carriage when I'm finished."

"Oh, no, I couldn't. I'm quite all right, really," he said, giving me an obligatory protest.

In the end, and in a very short time, actually, he conceded that there was no need to stay. Robert Thorn eased his conscience even more by assuring him that he would see to my safety and comfort.

Soon after Mr. Hienz left, I asked to see more information on the loans Anton had made.

"Of course," Robert answered. "Those papers are locked in the safe. I'll get them for you."

"And the ledgers from last year."

Robert, who was walking toward the elaborate steel safe in the corner of the room, stopped and turned around slowly to stare at me, his eyes open wide in surprise.

"Make that for the last five years, if you will, please," I added.

"Miss King," Robert said, taking a step toward me. "I will be happy to go to the storage lockers to get those for you if you wish, but are you certain . . . ?"

"Am I certain of what, Mr. Thorn?"

"Well, what I mean is, it would be a great deal of trouble—not for me, please understand," he said, holding his hands up, palms outward. "Not for me, but for you. Are you certain you want to trouble yourself with such a tedious task? I could easily summarize for you the—"

"That won't be necessary, Mr. Thorn, and I can assure you I'm quite used to tedious tasks."

He smiled in his charming boyish manner. "And quite headstrong, too, aren't you?" he asked.

I wasn't sure why he mistook what I considered doing my duty for being headstrong, but before I could either protest or question him, he spoke again. "I'll have everything you want sent up," he said. With that he left the room through the door leading to the warehouse area. He was headed, I presumed, for the storage lockers.

I went back to studying the ledger, and I was busy matching figures in the credit column with invoices when I became aware of someone watching me. When I raised my eyes, the dark eyes of Felix LeFeu looked back at me. He was standing exactly in front of the desk at which I was working, yet I'd never known when he entered the room. Startled, I drew in my breath.

"Miss King," he said. "Chase Bradley sends me to ask if he kin see you."

"See me? For—for what reason?" I stammered, still trying to regain my composure.

"Maybe you ought to ask Chase for what reason. He stands over yonder, at the end of the warehouse." He had not used the formal "Mr." with Chase's name, as most men of color were obliged to do, but had spoken as if they were friends on equal footing.

"Tell him that if he wishes to see me, he can come into my—" Before I could finish speaking, Felix had disappeared through the doorway. I sat at my desk for several minutes and considered staying there until Chase Bradley came to find me, but I changed my mind, deciding I needed a break away from the task that was beginning to cause my eyes to burn and my shoulders to ache. Pushing the ledger aside, I stood and walked toward the door.

I made my way through the warehouse area, weaving a meandering path around bales of cotton and packing crates.

Men were moving them with large metal hooks joined to ropes that were threaded around pulleys attached to the high ceiling of the warehouse. I was trying to stay clear of the ropes and hooks and all the activity as I neared the front of the building where it opened onto the loading docks. As soon as I saw the opening, I spotted Chase just outside. He seemed to be arguing with someone.

"Damn it, she's not to know," he said angrily. "Make sure there's no chance to make her suspect." The person he was speaking to was hidden from my view by one of the large crates still sitting on the dock, waiting to be moved either aboard a ship or into the warehouse. Someone responded, I couldn't tell who, or what he said, but I could easily hear Chase's reply. "Laura King will go to her grave ignorant of all of it if I have my way."

My first reaction was shock that he would be talking to anyone about me, but I was also curious. What was he talking about? What was it that he didn't want me to know? Fueled with indignation, I started toward him, ready to demand an explanation.

As I took the first step, something stopped me—a tug at my skirt, it seemed at first—then I realized my feet were tangled. I tried to move away, but I stumbled and I looked down to see the heavy rope at my feet. I had tripped over it somehow, but it wasn't just my carelessness that had ensnared me; the rope was moving, being pulled by some unseen force. I felt myself falling forward, and in that same instant I saw in front of me one of the large metal hooks being lowered from the ceiling and swinging in a wide arc toward me. Then suddenly Felix LeFeu was standing in front of me again. I heard my own scream and a loud commotion just before I was aware of being struck by something heavy, and then there was darkness.

Slowly the darkness turned to a spiderwebbed gray, accompanied by a tremendous aching and throbbing in my head. No, it wasn't just my head that was throbbing; it was my entire body. It felt stiff and heavy, as if each of my muscles had been bound to weights of lead. Even my eyelids seemed too heavy to open. I felt that I must open them, though, to see where the singing was coming from.

It was a distant singing, but growing closer, while remaining soft, very soft. The song seemed to be intermittent, or was it my consciousness that was intermittent? I heard it again, louder now and very clear, angelic almost, except that it was slightly offkey.

"Amaazin' grace, how sweet the sound, that saaved a wretch like meee...."

I opened my eyes and saw the bow-shaped mouth from which the notes came and a cherubic face, surrounded in light like a halo. It was an angel. Maybe I was in heaven. I closed my eyes again, too groggy to ponder it.

"You're the first one I've ever seen, and you don't look so wicked to me."

The words startled me, and I opened my eyes again. This time they focused more steadily on the face. It could not be an angel, I thought, unless angels have freckles. It was a little boy about six years old who stood beside my bed. The halo I'd seen now appeared as a shaft of late-afternoon sunlight flooding the window and playing across his very blond head.

"I'm the first what you've ever seen?" I asked groggily.

"The first fallen woman."

"The first what?" I tried to sit up, but the pain shooting across my shoulder and down my arm stopped me.

"Aunty said you fell on the loading docks and had to be brought here to get better. I've heard her talk about fallen women down by the waterfront. Are there a lot of you? And why aren't you all more careful so you won't fall so much?"

"I—I'm not sure. I mean, I don't think your aunt means—"

"If you'd be more careful and watch where you're going, you wouldn't fall. That's what Aunty tells me."

"I'm sure she's right," I said and managed a smile.

He didn't return my smile but looked at me silently for a moment with a very serious expression as if he wanted to make sure I understood that Aunty, whoever she was, was always right. "I'm glad you're awake," he said at length.

"Thank you," I answered. I managed to ease myself into a sitting position. "Would you tell me your name?"

"Johnny," he said, then added as an afterthought, "John."

"How do you do, Johnny John."

He giggled and asked for my name.

"Laura King," I answered.

"Do I have to call you Miss King or may I call you Miss Laura? Aunty says that's proper if we are very good friends."

"Miss Laura will do fine, since I would like to be very good friends," I answered.

"Do you know any games, Miss Laura?" he asked.

"I know a lot of games," I said. "Everything from tic-tac-toe to baseball."

"Baseball?" Johnny asked, excited. "Will you teach me that?"

I laughed. "Not until I've limbered up a bit. I seem to have a few sore muscles," I said, shifting my body gingerly. When I raised my hand to my head, I felt a small bandage near my right temple. "And if we are to be friends," I added, "maybe you can tell me how I got here."

"I don't know," Johnny said, his eyes growing wide with the wonder of it. "I was out playing with Billy Johnson, and when I came back, Aunty told me you were here. She told me you fell and hurt yourself."

I nodded, remembering the warehouse and Chase Bradley, then the rope and the swinging hook, and the face of Felix LeFeu appearing suddenly, and I shuddered at the memory of all of it. Then I looked down at my arms and saw them covered with the long sleeves of a white lace-trimmed cotton nightgown. Who had dressed me in it? I wondered.

"Did your aunty tell you anything else?" I asked.

"Yes. She said I was not to bother you." He paused, staring at me silently for several seconds before he spoke again, very quietly. "I wasn't bothering you. I was only singing to you to make you feel better."

"And I loved your singing," I told him.

"Did you really?" Johnny asked, sounding pleased. "I can sing for you again." With that he began in his offkey little-boy voice to sing "Sweet Betsy from Pike." When I laughed at the slightly bawdy words, he sang even louder. I was holding my side as I laughed, trying to keep my bruised ribs from hurting, when I looked up and saw Chase Bradley standing in the doorway.

My laughter stopped suddenly, and Johnny, noticing it, stopped his singing and turned to stare guiltily at Chase.

"What are you doing, Johnny?" Chase asked.

"I'm singing, Papa," the boy answered.

The word *Papa* resounded in my head. Could this delightful child belong to the boorish man who had forced his way into my house and into my bedroom two days before—and whom I had only recently overheard suggesting he wanted to get rid of me?

"And such singing it is," Chase said. "Didn't Aunty forbid you to sing that song? And I believe she also told you not to disturb the lady," Chase said, taking a step into the room. As he moved closer, I saw his mouth twitch as he tried to keep from smiling. I realized, to my surprise, that he was having a hard time scolding the boy.

"Miss Laura loves my singing. Yes, she does. She says so," Johnny said. He impulsively rushed toward Chase, and Chase stooped until their eyes were level. Johnny threw his arms around his father's neck. "Miss Laura is going to teach me to play baseball, too," he said, giggling as Chase lifted him up into his arms. "As soon as she's well enough. Aunty will help her get well, won't she? Like she does me. Can we keep her after she's well? She could share my room with me. If you let her stay, she would teach you baseball, too."

Johnny had spoken so rapidly he was breathless when he finished, and Chase could no longer hide his smile. He put Johnny on the floor and tousled his mop of blond hair. "Miss Laura is not a lost puppy that we decide whether to keep or not," he said. "Now, run along and find Aunty to bring her some tea." He gave Johnny a gentle shove.

Johnny ran toward the door, but he turned around just after he reached it. "I know she's not a puppy," he called back. "She's a fallen woman." With that he was gone, slamming the door behind him.

A startled look swept across Chase's face, and I felt my own face flush. I had an overwhelming urge to pull the covers over my head, but I restrained myself, forcing myself to keep my head high and my eyes unaverted. In short order Chase's startled look was replaced with an amused grin, and in the next second he had thrown his head back roaring with laughter just as he had done the night he invaded my room. Johnny's innocent conclusion was amusing, I had to admit, but when Chase kept laughing, I began to feel a bit chagrined.

"Really," I said, "it's not that funny."

My protest only made Chase laugh harder. "You were a fallen woman, all right," he said. "Flat on the warehouse floor."

"And I must have hit my head," I said, my mild anger still smoldering because he found my accident so amusing. "I don't remember what—"

"The hook only grazed the side of your head. Felix pushed you out of the way," Chase said. "He sends his apologies that he knocked you out cold."

I stared at him, remembering the words I'd overheard—that there was something he didn't want me to know, remembering, too, that he'd made it clear he wanted me out of Galveston. I couldn't help but feel that my "accident" fit into that some way. Had he somehow arranged for the hook to swing and the rope to tangle at my feet? Was that why he had summoned me to meet him? As he stood looking down at me, I became suddenly very aware that I was sitting propped in bed without a bed jacket to cover the nightgown I wore. Feeling very exposed, I pulled the covers to my chin. "You were very kind to bring me here," I said, "but if you will ask your wife to bring me my clothes, I'll be on my way."

"I have no wife," he said. "I'll send Aunt Stella in if you wish." He turned to walk away, but turned back again to glare at me. "And you can relax your grip on those covers. I have no interest in attacking you."

With that he was gone, leaving me to wonder whether or not he had just insulted me.

Chapter 4

I STARED at the closed door for several seconds while I wrestled with my emotions. I couldn't shake the feeling that Mr. Bradley had something to do with my "accident" in the warehouse and that it was somehow connected with his appearance a few nights earlier riding Anton's horse and then invading my house. I couldn't quite put together why the man would want me harmed, though, and I was more than a little curious about what it was he'd told some unknown person I was "not to know."

To add to my confusion was the fact that, in spite of the sense of danger and excitement that surrounded him, his son, Johnny, was a darling child I knew I could become quickly attached to. And then there was that bit of information he dropped—that he had no wife. That undoubtedly meant he was widowed, and in spite of myself, I found that intriguing.

But why should I? I asked myself, feeling vaguely uncomfortable. I'd known plenty of men who were widowed with young children, and that certainly didn't make them particularly intriguing. They were always looking for someone to marry as a permanent, built-in nursemaid, and I had no time for that. I had my career to think of. Not that Chase Bradley was looking for a nursemaid. He had someone he called Aunt Stella, who apparently saw after household duties for him. Besides, he'd made it perfectly clear he had no interest in me.

Well, I had no interest in him either, I told myself as I threw the covers back and swung my legs over the edge of the bed, and the sooner I got out of Chase Bradley's house the better. I'd just have a look in the wardrobe closet on the wall opposite the bed, and I'd see if perhaps my clothes had been stored there. I tried to stand, but a tide of dizziness swept over me, making me feel as if I were floating. I tried to steady myself against the nightstand next to the bed, but I stumbled and lurched against it, sending the water glass that had been sitting near the edge crashing to the hardwood floor, where it broke into hundreds of pieces.

The "Oh!" that I cried out was involuntary and, I thought, not too loud, but it, along with the sound of the glass falling, was enough to bring a plump, middle-aged woman bustling into my room.

"Lord a mercy, what's going on in—miss! Get back in that bed!" She hurried toward me, her arms outstretched as if I were about to fall and she was going to catch me. "We can't have you up like this, you know. You've just had a nasty blow on your head, and I'll bet you would have been resting if it hadn't been for Johnny, the dear little mischief. He was back in here, I'd guess, and waking you up." She had her hands on my arms, pushing me gently but firmly onto the bed. "I'll see to it that he's disciplined, miss, don't you worry about that. Now, you just get back in that bed and rest. That's what the doctor said you were to do."

"The doctor?"

"That's right. He was here. Gave you a going-over, but said you'd be fine if you take it easy. How's the head, dear?" She squinted her bright blue eyes at my head, inspecting it, and touched it gently with a plump finger. "A bit sore, I'd venture. Dizzy, too, aren't you? Mercy, lamb, no more of this getting out of bed. See that you rest, and I'll see to Master Johnny, the little mischief. I'll see that he gets his discipline."

"Oh, it wasn't Johnny," I said when I could finally get a word in. I couldn't bear to have the little boy disciplined in any way for his sweet and caring act. "He didn't disturb me at all. He was just singing to me. And I found it pleasant," I added quickly, lest I get Johnny into more trouble. "Really, I would have invited him to stay, but his father came in and made him—"

"His father?" The woman looked alarmed.

"Why, yes, Mr. Bradley—"

"Chase was in here?"

"Yes, as I said, he—"

"Now, he knows that's not proper, coming into a lady's room like that without another lady present. The two of them!"

She threw up her hands and raised her eyes to heaven. "The two of them will be the death of me. Well," she said, changing her mood quickly, "back to bed with you." She fluffed my pillows and straightened the covers, her head bobbing as she bustled about me. "I'll clean up the broken glass, and then later I'll have a talk with the two of them and see that they conduct themselves properly around a lady."

"But, ma'am," I said, trying to protest the fact that she had gotten me back in bed, "I really must be getting back to my house. You see, I—"

"I won't hear of it, my dear. And Mr. Bradley wouldn't either." I could see wisps of reddish hair, a bit faded and streaked with gray, around the edges of the old-fashioned lace cap she wore, and I saw that her eyes crackled with good humor when she smiled. "In spite of the fact that he forgets his manners once in a while and is a bit of a grouch at times, he has his good side, and he wouldn't want you up and about until he was sure you were well enough. Oh, and speaking of manners, I'd do well to mend my own. Me, forgetting to introduce myself! I'm Miss Stella Beaufort at your service. Aunt Stella to most. Mr. Bradley's cousin, twice removed on his mother's side."

"I'm Laura King, and I—"

"I know who you are, miss. Anton King's sister. Mr. Bradley told me."

"I see. Well, I'm happy to meet you, Aunt Stella, and you've been most kind, but really—"

"I've been with Chase six years now. Ever since he took on the young master as his ward, and I must say that of all the people he's taken in over the years, you're the prettiest. I *do* hope you're not offended by his brusqueness. There's a dark side to him, you know, but all in all . . ."

She trailed off, seeming to have forgotten whatever it was she wanted to say about Chase Bradley's dark side as she inspected the broken glass all over the floor.

"And you with your bare feet," she said, shaking her head.

"Excuse me," I said, seizing another rare opportunity to speak, "but did you say Johnny is Mr. Bradley's ward? Not his son?"

"That's right. The boy's a distant relative on Chase's father's side. An orphan. Chase doesn't like to speak of the details of the demise of the poor child's parents. Keeps things bottled up inside him, that one does. But I never pry. No time for it, to tell you the truth. The two of them keep me busy just caring for them. Have you ever seen anything any more helpless than a man creature? Poor dears! At least God created women to keep them from killing themselves."

With that she was out the door. I tried once again to slip out of bed, but she popped her head back in and admonished me with a wag of her finger that I wasn't to try it. In a little while she returned with my lunch on a tray. As usual, my appetite was ravenous, and I couldn't resist. While I ate the wonderful concoction of fresh gulf shrimp and vegetables, she apologized that someone she called Babette, who apparently was a housemaid, had taken the morning off, and she kept up a constant stream of pleasant chatter about her flower garden, Johnny's new accomplishments with his lessons, and the roast beef she and the cook had managed to buy from the butcher. When I finished eating, she helped me with my toilette, brushing and arranging my hair. She gave in reluctantly to my insistence that I was well enough to get dressed and that the dizziness was short-lived, but she wouldn't hear of me calling a carriage to take me home to the Shadows.

"You can't go just yet," she insisted. "You'll bear watching for a while. You're staying out there all alone in that old house, are you?"

"Why, yes. It's my childhood home, you know."

"But you haven't lived in the house in some time." She looked at me with a worried frown.

"That's right," I said. "I've been living in New York, where I have a teaching position."

"It's not safe out there. There are strange goings-on." Her normally sparkling eyes had darkened like storm clouds.

I felt suddenly uneasy and wondered how much I should tell her about the strange figure I'd seen walking along the shoreline. "What do you mean, strange goings-on?" I asked, deciding to be cautious.

"I hear people talk," she said. "They say—"

"They say what?"

"They say there's spirits," she said, as if she were reluctant to utter the words. "Evil spirits," she whispered. Giving me a worried look, she picked up my breakfast tray and hurried to the door. "I don't believe in them myself, mind you," she said, turning back. "But still, people say they've seen things." She left, shaking her head.

I felt an eerie chill run the length of my spine and an odd coldness to my flesh. What did she mean by evil spirits? It was just superstitious talk, of course. Whomever or whatever I had seen was no ghostly evil spirit. It had to be an ordinary human being. But why, I wondered, had she disappeared into the sea?

I had to give up trying to leave, for the moment at least, because of Aunt Stella's steadfast insistence. I decided, then, that if I had to stay, I'd make the best of it. I'd wait for Chase Bradley to return, and this time I'd make sure he didn't catch me unprepared. I'd ask him what he'd been doing in the warehouse of King Enterprises. He'd had me at a definite disadvantage during the morning when he came into my room. Since I was just awakening and since I was quite unused to having a gentleman in my bedroom, I was too rattled to discuss anything with him.

I passed the rest of the day in relative quiet, looking over some of the papers I still had in my valise. William Hienz came calling in the early afternoon, and he seemed to want to take the entire blame for my accident because he had left me alone in the warehouse. I accepted his apology and tried to insist that I would have tried to make my way through the tangled maze of the warehouse whether he had been there or not and therefore would have had the accident anyway.

"I do most deeply regret this," he was saying for the hundredth time. "The gentle sex is so fragile! I do hope you've not done some dreadful internal damage. Why, I could never forgive myself if—"

"Mr. Hienz," I said in a voice strong enough to let him know I had suffered no dreadful internal damage. It was also strong enough to cause him to jump and to stare at me with wide, startled eyes. "There is something you can do for me, if you please."

"Oh, anything, miss, anything. Call a doctor perhaps, or—"

"A doctor has seen me, and another visit won't be necessary, but if you would be so kind as to return later with your carriage to drive me home, I would be most appreciative."

"Why, of course I want to help, but are you sure you ought to be out there?"

"I'm sure, Mr. Hienz. About six o'clock, shall we say? I want to have time to speak with Mr. Bradley again when he returns."

"Well, of course, Miss King, if you're sure you'll be all right."

"I will be fine."

His uneasy smile crept to his lips. "I do appreciate you letting me do some small thing to make amends."

"Of course, Mr. Hienz," I said, doing my best to steer him toward the door. His insistence on apologizing no matter what I said left me with a headache, and I found I needed to rest with a cool cloth on my head after he left.

To my surprise, I fell asleep. Apparently the fall and the blow on the head had taken more out of me than I realized. When I awoke, it was with the distinct feeling that someone was watching me. I was right. Johnny was peering at me with wide round eyes from around the edge of the bedroom door. Sitting with my back against the headboard, I beckoned for him to enter. His slightly guilty expression was overtaken by a wide smile.

"I can't come in," he said in a loud whisper. "Aunty says I can't."

"Not even if I invite you?"

He shook his head, then looked around to see if he was about to get caught. "But you could come out," he said.

I laughed and stood up to smooth my skirts and picked up my shoes. This time I was completely steady on my feet. "Just give me time to get these shoes laced and buttoned, and I'll be right out," I said. "We can start on that baseball lesson."

"But you have to have a bat," he said, "and a baseball. I don't have either."

"Never mind that. We'll use any other ball you have. And Aunt Stella can help us find a rolling pin to use for a bat."

Johnny burst into laughter and ran down the hall. He was back a few seconds later. "I'll get the ball," he said, then pointed a commanding finger at me. *"You* get the rolling pin."

Aunt Stella's protests over using the cook's rolling pin weren't easily overcome. I promised to replace it if it suffered the slightest damage, but that wasn't enough.

"It would be such a nice thing for the young master to have a *real* teacher hear his lessons tonight," she said. "Arithmetic and reading both. He's quick with his sums, but he could use the practice with his subtraction. A good three quarters of an hour wouldn't hurt."

"Of course," I said, "I'll be glad to, but perhaps I could come back another day. I promised Johnny this one game, and I plan to stay long enough to speak to Mr. Bradley, and then I really *must* be getting home."

"You'll be back?" she asked.

"I'll come to visit Johnny," I said, "at least once before I return home."

"Run along with you, then," she said, handing me the rolling pin with a quickness that surprised me.

Johnny greeted me with enthusiasm, and he already had the playing field laid out with lawn cushions when I got to the grassy backyard.

"Why, Johnny, I thought you didn't know how to play baseball," I said.

"I've seen the other boys playing," he said, "but they won't let me hit the ball. They say I'm too little. They say I don't know how."

"And Mr. Bradley—your papa—doesn't teach you?"

"Papa doesn't know how either. He never plays games."

"Oh, that's too bad." I found myself wondering what it would be like to teach Chase Bradley how to play games as I picked the ball up off of home plate.

The time passed swiftly as I taught Johnny how to hold and swing the bat, and then how to pitch the ball. I was familiar with the game because a gentleman I'd once met had taken me to several of the events at the new Yankee Stadium. Our relationship was short-lived, however, since, aside from his interest in baseball, I'd found him quite the uninteresting companion.

"All right, it's your turn to pitch," I said to Johnny after he'd had a long session at bat. "And remember, the point is to try to make me swing at the ball but not hit it."

"I know!" he shouted, excited.

He hurled the ball at me, and I hit it. It felt as if the ball glanced off the edge of the rolling pin, but instinct made me drop the makeshift bat and pull up my skirts to run to first base. I was halfway there when I heard the pop and turned around to see the ball, which had merely flown up in the air as a foul, coming down precisely on the head of Chase Bradley, who was just walking down the garden path. I stood there looking at him, my skirts raised, my chest heaving, and my hair falling about my face in sweaty tendrils.

For a moment there was dead silence while Chase rubbed his head and looked first at me and then at Johnny and then at me again.

"Papa!" Johnny shouted finally, breaking the silence. He ran to him, and Chase squatted to be on a level with the boy and put his arms out for an embrace. "Papa, did we hurt you?" Johnny asked.

"I'm fine," he said, "and how are you, my boy?"

"I'm fine, too, Papa, and I know how to hit a baseball."

"Do you now? Better than your teacher, I hope."

"Oh, she's a wonderful teacher," Johnny said. "She could teach you some things, too."

"I have no doubt of that," Chase said with a glance in my direction.

I felt myself blush. I let go of the grip I had on my skirts, which, I hadn't realized until that moment, was allowing daring exposure of my ankles. The thought of that embarrassed me even more, but I managed to square my shoulders and walk toward Chase Bradley with as much pride and dignity as I could recover.

"I would like a moment of your time, Mr. Bradley," I said. "And then I'll be returning to Shadow Cove. My driver will be here soon." I noticed as I approached him that a very large red bump had formed on his forehead where the ball had hit him. It was really rather odd-looking, and I bit my lip to keep from laughing.

"You'll be staying here for dinner," he said. It wasn't an invitation, but rather a command. Immediately I lost my sense of humor and felt irritated that he was ordering me around.

"Very kind of you," I said coolly, "but I've asked Mr.—"

"Mr. Hienz won't be coming by for you."

"I beg your pardon?"

"I told him not to bother."

"You told him what? Mr. Bradley, I see no reason for you to take charge of my life in such a—"

"I've arranged for a carriage. You'll be going home after dinner, but I believe we have some things to discuss first."

I looked at him, and several seconds passed while I tried to think what to say, but all I could manage was "I see."

I started for the door again when he said, "And I've arranged for a change of clothes for you. Aunt Stella insists that we dress for dinner."

I turned around and gave him an alarmed look, but I was still at a loss for words. The only way I could keep my dignity was to say nothing, so I left him with my head held high, pretending a self-confidence I didn't feel as I marched into the house.

The man was used to riding roughshod over everyone. That was obvious, since he had taken Anton's horse without permission, barged his way into my house uninvited, brought me here to *this* house with instructions not to leave, canceled my carriage request, insisted that I stay for dinner, and then had even gone so far as to decide how I would dress! Well, we would see about that. I would stay for dinner, since I saw no way of getting out of it now without an embarrassing scene, but I would wear my own gray gabardine frock.

As I stepped in through the back entrance and into the kitchen, I saw Aunt Stella standing there instructing a small staff of two maids and a cook who had appeared from somewhere. The kitchen was not in use. Obviously Mr. Bradley's household followed the southern tradition we had followed at the Shadows, using the kitchen only in the winter and making use of the "summer" kitchen during warm weather so as not to heat up the house. It would be a small building detached from the house and accessible, I assumed, through the walled walkway at the side of the backyard.

"I've laid out your toilette, miss," Aunt Stella said, pausing in her instructions long enough to speak to me. "Babette will help you."

"Oh, that won't be necessary," I said. "I'm only going to brush my hair and wash my face, and—"

Aunt Stella had gone back to instructing the servants and seemed to have forgotten me. A young girl wearing black broadcloth and a starched white apron had moved to my side and was giving me a shy smile. She bobbed a curtsy and spoke in a high-pitched little-girl voice with the hint of a Cajun accent. "Babette at your service, miss."

She looked as if she could easily burst into tears if I said anything, so I breathed a sigh of resignation, gave her a polite smile, and turned toward the downstairs bedroom I'd been in earlier. Babette followed me and closed the door softly once we were inside the bedroom. I saw out of the corner of my eye a soft, rippling sea of black satin and frothy black tulle on the bed, but I refused to look at it directly, since I wasn't going to be wearing it anyway. Instead I went directly to the bureau, where a pitcher of water sat. I poured some in the basin and splashed it at my face. While I was doing that, Babette began unfastening the buttons at the back of my dress. I stood up quickly and turned to her.

"That won't be necessary," I said, grabbing a towel. "I'll be wearing this dress for dinner tonight."

"But, mamselle—" Babette's eyes went to the front of my dress. I followed her gaze and looked down to see a circular perspiration stain down the middle and under each arm.

"Oh, dear!" I said, looking at her with consternation and a little embarrassment. My eyes went to the dark whisper of tulle and chiffon on the bed. Babette's gaze followed mine, then she glanced back at me again and smiled shyly. "Very well," I said. "It seems I have no choice. Help me out of this. I'll need more water if I'm to be presentable." She curtsied again and buzzed about to do my bidding.

After I'd had a very thorough sponge bath, Babette dressed my hair. She proved to be an absolute master, and in a moment's time she had done it up into cascades of curls with wisps about my face and neck that provided a softer, more feminine look than I had ever been able to manage with my schoolteacher's bun at the back of my head.

Then she helped me into the dress. It had a fitted bodice that followed the curve of my breasts at the top and tiny cap sleeves made of chiffon that left my shoulders bare. I'd never worn such a daring dress before, and I felt a moment of insecurity and discomfort, but Babette's oohs and aahs shored up my courage. She turned me around so I could see myself in the mirror, and I was stunned at what I saw. I didn't know the woman who stared back at me. The sheer black of the dress made my skin look ivory pale, and the perfect fit emphasized my waistline and high breasts, which had always been smaller than the ample bosoms that were so fashionable. Yet the cut of this dress allowed just a hint of décolletage I'd never dared before.

In the mirror I saw Babette pick up the cameo pin I always wore and study it, then she looked at me. "Une 'tee moment!" she said in the fractured French of her Cajun ancestry. Before I could respond, she ran out of the room and returned in a little while with a silver chain. It was obviously one from her own collection, but she clipped the pin onto it and fastened it around my neck. The cameo nestled at the top of the daring cleavage.

"Oh, I couldn't possibly—"

"*S'il vous plaît,* mamselle. 'twould be *ma plaisir*. Mamselle is *très jolie*, and for my humble silver chain to be on so fair a neck would be my honor."

She looked so genuinely sincere, and truthfully I did like the look of it, so I gave her a smile and squeezed her hand. I felt as if I were Cinderella being dressed up by a fairy godmother.

"Oh! mamselle, you must hurry," said Babette, becoming suddenly frustrated. "M'sieur Bradley and Johnny and the old mamselle are already in the dining room. They wait for you."

Suddenly I felt very nervous and unsure of myself again. Perhaps I felt a little foolish, too, as if I were playing make-believe, dressed up in someone else's clothes. But I took a deep breath, trying to maintain my composure, and I forced myself to walk unhurriedly out into the hall and toward the dining room.

The dining room was at the end of the long hall, and I could see Mr. Bradley, Aunt Stella, and Johnny already at the table. Johnny was telling his papa something in a very animated manner, and the swing of his arms led me to believe he was recounting our baseball game of the afternoon. Mr. Bradley listened intently, his chin in his hand. He made murmured comments and joined Johnny in laughter from time to time. He glanced up just as I got to the arched entryway into the dining room, and his laughter stopped as his eyes held mine.

It seemed as if the moment had frozen in time. Neither of us moved or spoke for that brief moment, but I sensed his approval, his admiration even, and something, some unspoken message, passed between us.

The moment passed when Johnny called out, "Miss Laura!" I felt a little uncomfortable with the unfamiliar feeling of having a man look at me that way, especially Chase Bradley, so I dropped my eyes and moved toward the place at the table that had been set for me, opposite Johnny and next to Aunt Stella. Mr. Bradley was at the head. As I approached, Mr. Bradley and Johnny stood, and Mr. Bradley held my chair for me while I sat.

"You look different," Johnny said, giving me a big smile. I returned his smile, but before I could speak, he added, "But you would get a terrible sunburn if you wore that dress outdoors. When you come to see me again, please wear your other dress so we can play baseball?"

"The lady looks lovely tonight, Johnny," Mr. Bradley said. "You should compliment her."

"Indeed," Aunt Stella added. "Watch your manners, child."

Johnny beamed at me. "You look beautiful!"

"And I don't think she likes being told what to wear," Mr. Bradley added. He looked at me and gave me a wink, and I felt my face flush. I flushed even deeper when I noted that the bump on his head was still prominent.

"I told Papa about baseball," Johnny said, "and he says he'll buy me a real bat."

"But you must learn a few more secrets of the game," Mr. Bradley said. "For example, I believe your teacher could show you the proper way to hit the ball."

He touched the bump on his head ever so briefly, as if he was brushing away an imaginary wisp of his thick dark hair. Obviously he was having great fun at my expense, but I was determined not to let him think it bothered me.

"I'm afraid it's up to Johnny just to practice now," I said brightly. "I'm afraid I have no more secrets to reveal." As I spoke, I moved toward him slightly to allow the maid to fill my wineglass.

"Oh, I wouldn't say that," Mr. Bradley said, letting his glance fall ever so briefly to my décolletage.

I straightened and glanced at Aunt Stella, but she was busy instructing the maid. "I am very careful about the people to whom I reveal my secrets, Mr. Bradley," I said.

"I have no doubt." He picked up his wineglass and raised it in a toast. "To the joy of secrets revealed," he said, touching first Johnny's glass of lemonade and then Aunt Stella's wineglass and finally mine.

"Secrets?" Aunt Stella said, joining the conversation late. "It's no secret the boy loved the game. So patient you are to teach him, my dear."

I tasted the wine, then cleared my throat uneasily. "I trust your head wound is not too serious, Mr. Bradley."

"It's quite serious, Miss King. Aunt Stella seems to think I'm to be disfigured for life."

"Ridiculous! You're fit as a fiddle!" Aunt Stella said as she gave a hand signal to one of the staff entering from the back kitchen.

The insufferable man was still teasing me, and I was glad to be able to retreat into the first course now being served to us.

"You bopped him good, Miss Laura, and I never seen *anybody* bop Papa before," Johnny said, then, turning to his father, added, "You have to forgive her, Papa, because she didn't mean to. Did you, Miss Laura?" he asked, glancing at me. "Please say you didn't mean to so Papa will let you come back."

"Of course I didn't mean to, Johnny," I said. "It was an accident. Just as my fall at the warehouse was an accident. You do understand, don't you, Mr. Bradley?" I glanced at him to see if he would react to my suggestion that it was possible neither of the incidents had been true accidents, but he merely nodded and picked up his fork.

Since Aunt Stella and Johnny seemed ready to enjoy the meal, I decided not to allow my suspicion of Mr. Bradley to ruin it for them, and before long I began to relax somewhat myself. In fact, I actually enjoyed myself with Johnny and Aunt Stella, and Mr. Bradley, I noticed, was quite at ease with the boy and seemed to be enjoying himself as well. It was obvious they felt a great affection for each other, and it showed me a side of Chase Bradley I had never suspected.

Soon after dessert, however, Johnny was told it was his bedtime.

"Please, not so early this time, Papa," he pleaded. "I want to stay with Miss Laura. I could teach her to play my new card game in the library."

"Absolutely not," Aunt Stella said, standing and offering him her hand.

"Aunt Stella is right, absolutely not," Mr. Bradley said, giving the boy's head a loving ruffle. "You have school tomorrow, and besides, you've had Miss Laura to yourself all day long. Now be a good boy and bid us good night."

"Aw, Papa—"

"Young man!" In spite of his stern voice Mr. Bradley had his arms outstretched, and Johnny fell into them, giving his papa a hearty hug and a kiss on the cheek. Then he walked around the table and picked up my hand to kiss it in a most gallant manner.

"Good night, Miss Laura. I hope you'll come again," he said, then walked away with Aunt Stella, leaving me completely charmed.

Mr. Bradley stood and held my chair for me. "We'll have coffee on the veranda," he said. Once again he spoke in a commanding voice, and I found myself rising to his command. He offered his arm and led me out the wide front door. The night air wrapped itself around us like a damp sheet, but the magnificent view of the twinkling lights of the city and of the ships in the harbor was enough to make anyone forget a slight discomfort. Coffee was already waiting for us, and Mr. Bradley picked up a cup and handed it to me, then joined me at the rail.

"Beautiful, isn't it?"

"Mr. Bradley," I said quickly—it was as if I was trying to avoid being caught in a spell—"I have hoped all day to have an opportunity to speak with you, and now that Johnny has left us, perhaps I can speak candidly."

"You want to know what I was doing at King Enterprises today and you want to know what business I have with Anton's horse and why I was in his house." The cold hard quality had returned to his voice now, putting him in direct contrast to the mellow, joking man he had been in Johnny's presence. "The reason I came to the King warehouse today was precisely to talk to you about those things," he said without giving me an opportunity to say a word. "Unfortunately you met with the accident before I got the chance." I watched him closely to see if he would give away any hint that he'd had something to do with the accident, as I'd suspected. He revealed nothing, and my confused feeling about him seemed to be compounding by the second.

"I only wanted you to know that I became more or less the unofficial caretaker of your brother's personal property after his death. That was a natural thing for me to do, since we were good friends, but now that you're here, of course, I—"

"You and Anton were friends?"

"Very close friends actually. Does that surprise you?"

"I learned long ago not to be surprised at anyone Anton chose to associate with."

"Don't judge your brother too harshly, Laura. He may have made some unwise choices in his life, but he was at heart a good man."

"How kind of you to say so, Mr. Bradley," I said coolly. "Actually I hardly knew my brother, so I have no intention of judging him." I was acutely aware of the fact that Mr. Bradley had just called me Laura rather than Miss King, as would have been proper, considering our brief acquaintance. His familiarity made me all the more wary of him. "And speaking of my accident in the warehouse," I said with as much coldness in my voice as I could manage, "I overheard a bit of your conversation as I walked toward you, and I'm quite curious as to what it is you say I'm not to know."

"I beg your pardon?"

"I overheard you, Mr. Bradley, just before my accident, talking to someone. 'Laura King will go to her grave ignorant of all of it,' I believe were your exact words. You seemed quite emphatic."

"I'm afraid I don't know what you're talking about."

"Of course you do—"

"You misunderstood some bit of conversation." Again he managed to make a simple statement sound like a command. It was obvious, though, that I was not going to get all the information I wanted from him.

"Very well, Mr. Bradley." Seeing that I was getting nowhere, I decided to try another tactic. "Did I also imagine that you were trespassing in my brother's house the night I arrived?"

"I didn't consider it trespassing at the time."

"Indeed."

"After Anton's death I took the liberty of taking the key to his house so I could see after his property until the estate was settled. That's how I was able to get inside the night you were there." He turned his gaze back to me. "I thought vagrants had broken in."

"Why didn't you tell me all this the night you were there? I told you I was Anton's sister," I said, meeting his gaze.

"My dear, I had to make certain you *were* Anton's sister. You could have been a wild gypsy tramp for all I knew." I felt myself blush again, remembering how I'd looked that night with my bodice opened and my hair blown about by the wind. "I waited until I had the opportunity to check with Bill Hienz. He, of course, apologized for not letting me know sooner that you were there, although I don't know how the devil he could have, since he didn't even know you'd arrived until the next morning. And anyway, after I saw you with him the other day, I was convinced you were no vagrant."

"Thank you, Mr. Bradley." I saw his enigmatic smile in the dim light of the veranda, but I pretended that I hadn't. "I suppose there is also some explanation as to why you were riding Anton's horse?"

"Of course," he said. He turned away from me again and stared out across the gulf, resting his hands on the railing. "Anton promised the horse to Johnny." His voice seemed oddly strained. "I don't allow Johnny to ride Sir Blanco, though, because it's too dangerous. Sir Blanco is too much the horse for him." He turned back to me, and even in the semidarkness I could see that his smile was gone and his expression serious, almost grave. "There are no official papers saying the horse belongs to Johnny, so of course I will return the animal to you."

"But if Anton really meant for Johnny to have him—" I had no way of knowing whether or not Mr. Bradley was manipulating me and using my obvious affection for Johnny as a means of acquiring himself a fine horse, but he must have known I couldn't take anything away from the darling little boy.

"I assume he did. Anton was fond of Johnny and Johnny of him, but that makes no difference, of course."

"Certainly it does," I said, deciding exactly what I would do. "Johnny will have the horse. I'll even have Mr. Hienz draw up an official paper saying the horse belongs to him, but since Johnny can't ride Sir Blanco yet, I should like to keep him for a while at the Shadows. Until I return to New York, at least, since I have no other means of transportation into town while I'm here."

He studied my face a moment. "Are you sure you can handle Sir Blanco? He's quite a challenge."

"I'm used to a challenge, Mr. Bradley, and anyway, the one thing my father taught me to do was to ride a horse."

I saw his smile return for just a moment, then he settled himself against the rail, his back to it this time as he leisurely pulled a cheroot from his breast pocket. "Tell me, Miss King, what are your plans for the Shadows?" He struck a match on the rail to light his smoke, and I could see for just a moment the outline of his strong jaw and the icy blue of his eyes. I felt oddly disturbed again and filled with distrust. What business did he have asking my plans for the Shadows?

"I'm not certain. Perhaps I'll even change my mind about returning to New York," I said to test his reaction. In reality, I had no intention of staying in Galveston.

He blew out a plume of smoke, and it hung there in the heavy air like a spectrum dancing around us. "It's best you don't," he said.

"I don't see why not," I said, becoming annoyed at his presumptuousness.

"Take my word for it. Go back to New York. Leave Shadow Cove to its shadows."

I laughed—a sound more nervous than I intended. "You sound so melodramatic, Mr. Bradley."

"I'm not being melodramatic, Laura. I'm being quite practical. Go back to New York."

I felt uneasy again, not only because he'd used my first name once more, but because of the tone his words had taken on—almost threatening, I thought.

"We shall see, Mr. Bradley," I said, sounding as crisp as I could manage. "But in the meantime, I believe you promised me a carriage to drive me home."

"Of course." He moved toward me and took my arm. "The carriage is in the front. Felix is waiting for you in the drawing room." He ushered me inside, and I saw the mysterious Felix LeFeu seated in the drawing room. He stood as I entered, and he and Chase nodded to each other. It seemed to me that nod conveyed some secret message between them because they spoke not another word to each other. Mr. Bradley bowed to me slightly and bade me good night, then disappeared through the doorway to the hall.

LeFeu helped me into the carriage, and we began the drive home. It was an uneventful drive except for the haunting tune LeFeu sang on the way. The strange melody and even stranger words of a language I'd never heard drifted out into the mist and fog that had begun to materialize along the gulf like disembodied spirits.

When we arrived, LeFeu helped me from the carriage and to my door. "Good night, miss," he said with a formal bow. I closed the door, quickly lighted a lamp, then hurried toward the stairs. The house was damp and cold, and I was anxious for the warmth of my room. I set the lamp on the bureau, and as I did, an eerie sensation crept over me, and I began to feel quite uncomfortable being alone in the house.

Taking my lamp with me, I hurried up the hall toward the window, listening to my footsteps echoing through the darkness. The window was smudged with an accumulation of dirt and greasy moisture, which I rubbed away with my fingertips. When I looked down, I saw the carriage making its way up the road in the moonlit darkness, shrouded by fog and mist. I was about to turn away and return to my room when I saw the wraithlike figure in white running through the fog. It was several yards away from the carriage, closer to the beach, and it was moving toward the house, arms outstretched.

Chapter 5

I TURNED away from the window, my heart racing, and when I finally dared to look back, the apparition was gone. Feeling an uncomfortable chill, I hurried to my room and locked the door. I tried to force myself to be calm, to act rationally.

As I undressed to get ready for bed, I glanced out my window from time to time at the wispy fog. That was all I had seen, I told myself, wisps of fog. There was no woman in white, of course. It was only the fog and my overactive imagination.

I got into bed, aware of the night—how eerily peaceful it was, with the sound of the dark wind whispering through the trees and the steady, distant sound of the sea. I was still awake when the whispering became a roar intermingled with screeches as the wind tore at hinges somewhere on the outbuildings and moans as it buffeted turrets and corners of the house.

I don't know how long I lay there listening to the wind, nor when I fell asleep, but I awoke the next morning when a stream of orange light poured itself at an odd angle into my room as the sun came up over the gulf. I sat up quickly, feeling disoriented for a moment, not knowing quite why I was not in my rented room in New York. But when I saw the familiar dark rosewood of my childhood dressing table and smelled the deep aroma of the gulf waters, I relaxed against the headboard, letting my mind clear. I was suddenly sitting bold upright again, though, when I realized how late it must be. With the sun so high above the horizon, William Hienz must be waiting for me downstairs, ready to apologize for not knowing I would sleep late.

Picking up the tiny watch I always wore on a chain around my neck, I was shocked to see that it was already eight o'clock. I threw on a dressing gown and tried to do up my hair with a few pins and combs, but it wouldn't behave, so I left it down and raced down the hall to the stairs. As I reached the top of the stairs, I could almost hear my nursemaid's voice telling me that ladies never hurry and they most certainly never run. Strange, I thought, as I forced myself to slow down to descend the stairs, how being in one's childhood home can affect one.

My show of propriety was all for nothing, though, because there was no one waiting for me in the great hall and no one in the lounge or library.

I felt puzzled and a little uneasy. The punctual William Hienz was always here by seven-thirty to drive me in his carriage to his offices or to the offices of King Enterprises. I knew he was as anxious to finish the business of settling Anton's estate as I was. I suddenly felt very uncomfortable, thinking perhaps this meant I was stranded at the Shadows. It would be a long, hard walk into town even in my sensible schoolmarm shoes.

That was perhaps my only choice, I thought as I made my way to the stairs again. I would go back to my room and get dressed, preparing to walk in if I had to, and maybe in the meantime Mr. Hienz would show up full of apologies for oversleeping. As I passed through the great hall, my gaze fell upon something resting on the Queen Anne table that had been placed there to collect the calling cards of guests who used to come to the Shadows in a steady stream when my father's power was at its pinnacle. What I saw on the table now, though, was no calling card, but a riding crop. One that had not been there the night before when I returned from town.

My blood crept cold through my veins at the thought of someone being in my house while I slept. I walked slowly toward the table and touched the riding crop tentatively, as if to assure myself that it was real and not a ghostly apparition as I had imagined I had seen the night before. The riding crop was real enough. It felt hard and solid in my hand as I picked it up from the table. I had to believe that someone real had been in my house. The question remained, who was it, and was he or she still here?

A cry coming from somewhere outside startled me, and I swung around toward the back of the house, the direction from which the sound had come. Instantaneously I realized that the sound was no human cry, but the neigh of a horse, and it seemed as if the sound had come from the stables. I hurried the considerable distance to the back and pushed open the door, looking northward toward the stables. And I saw him—Sir Blanco, his fine coat white and gleaming against the blue of the sky and the gray of the gulf as he stood looking at me from the stable yard. It was as if he had called me to come see him because as soon as he caught sight of me, he pranced away, stepping high, his fine mane flying in the breeze.

Chase Bradley had sent someone out with him. I ran to the stables to see if anyone was still there, but there was no one. I could see, though, that Sir Blanco had hay in his stall and water in his trough, and sitting on the rail of his stall was a lady's sidesaddle, complete with all the tack needed for riding. I looked down at the crop I still held in my hand and realized that Chase Bradley hadn't sent anyone out with the horse. He had delivered Sir Blanco himself, and he'd left the riding crop for me to read as clearly as if it had been a gold-embossed card. He was the only one who could have left it. He still had keys to my house, and he had been inside while I slept.

That thought left me feeling both disconcerted and angry, and I turned and hurried back to the house. I would dress for the ride to town, and along with the ongoing business of the King estate, I also had some business with Chase Bradley.

It had been awhile since I had ridden, and I did have some trouble mounting Sir Blanco myself, but I found, once I got myself in the sidesaddle and my left leg hooked over the pommel, my riding skirt spread so I could sit the ride properly, I felt as if I had ridden only yesterday. Sir Blanco did indeed prove to be a challenge, but Papa had taught me well how to handle this kind of horse. I could still hear his voice coaching me.

"Sit tall, Laura! You are a King! Don't let the animal sense your fear. Don't slouch like a peasant! Loosen up on those reins! You want to ruin the poor beast's mouth? Control with your knees, girl!"

I had the benefit of those riding lessons as long as I was allowed to tag along while Anton was being taught to ride,

Lady of the Shadows

but as soon as I was forced to abandon the conventional saddle and resort to the sidesaddle that was proper for ladies, Papa would have nothing to do with my lessons. He spent all of his time with Anton, teaching him about being in control, about being a King. It didn't matter that Anton's interest was less and his attention span shorter than mine; he was John King's son and heir to the throne of his enterprises. Papa did at least hire someone to teach me to ride sidesaddle, and, since one's knees are less useful in that position, I learned that control must come with one's will.

Sir Blanco did succumb to my will at least enough to get me into Galveston still sitting upright and in one piece. I rode into town on Market Street and was acutely aware of eyes following me. I would have attracted far less attention had I been riding a bicycle since that sport was becoming quite common among ladies. I held my back straight and my head high and pretended not to notice anyone's stares.

The palm-shaded street was lined with fine mansions that had been built during the past twenty to thirty years. Each house reflected different tastes and personalities. There were the pointed Gothic arches of the Lovenberg House, and across the street was the asymmetrical new Queen Anne-style mansion of John Hanna. Mr. Hanna, I remembered, was a real estate agent with whom my father had done business. A little farther down the street was the old Grover House with its very plain Greek Revival lines built by the no-nonsense merchant George Grover, one of my father's chief rivals. Papa was determined to outshine him, and that, I long ago concluded, was one of the reasons he built the showy mansion at Shadow Cove.

Many of the mansions, like the Shadows, were built more than twenty years ago, but there were still fine homes being built on the teeming, cosmopolitan island city. In the distance, across several blocks, I could see the rising turrets of the dwelling that had outdone them all. It was the lawyer Walter Gresham's house, looking like a French castle made of pink and blue Texas granite and white limestone. Through the haze of the morning it looked like something from a fairy tale. It was in that new section, on Broadway, that Chase Bradley's new house was built with its balustrades and verandas, near the Sacred Heart School and church. Was it built near the school for Johnny's benefit? The possibility of that reminded me of how enigmatic Chase Bradley was—a man I wasn't quite sure I could trust or believe, yet someone who obviously loved his adopted son deeply.

My business would take me away from the newer section near Broadway, where new homes like Gresham Mansion and the more modest Bradley House were located, however. I would have to go to the Strand first to see Mr. Hienz.

The Strand was, as always, buzzing with activity, and as I rode my horse up to the hitching post in front of the offices of Hienz and Stratton Ltd., several people stopped to stare at me, and several gentlemen tipped their hats. I knew I was back in the South when a young man hurried up to me and offered his hands, held together as a platform, for me to step on as I dismounted. I was unspeakably grateful to him, since I had no idea how I was going to accomplish the feat otherwise with any modicum of grace. The young man could not have been more than nineteen, but he was dressed as a gentleman, so I knew it would be an insult to offer him payment for his kindness, as one might do a servant. I gave him my most gracious smile and thanked him, and I actually believe my southern accent had returned. It was amazing to me how easily I could find myself submerged in the culture of my childhood.

As I wound the reins around the post, I felt the subtle warmth of someone's gaze on me, and instinct made me turn my eyes upward. I saw a figure standing in the window of the office building across the street. It was unmistakably Chase Bradley staring down at me and whose eyes I had sensed watching me. He made no attempt to move from the window, not even when I was certain he knew I had seen him. The decisive flick of the riding crop against my thigh as I whirled around to enter William Hienz's office was all show. With Chase Bradley watching me like that, I felt anything but decisive and confident.

Mr. Hienz was sitting at his desk, bent over his work as I walked into his office, and he looked up the instant I entered. His eyes widened in a startled-animal expression, and he rose from his chair, knocking his stand-up telephone on its side. The pen he'd been holding in his hand dropped to the floor and rolled toward me, leaving an inky wake; then in an awkward flurry of striped pants and flying wispy hair, he came around his desk to greet me.

"Miss King!" He sounded as surprised as he would if I had been Anton himself standing before him. "Miss King, I'm so surprised to see you here. How did you—? I mean—"

"Surprised?"

"Why, yes. The fall you had. I thought—I mean—"

"What *did* you think, Mr. Hienz?"

"Why, that you wouldn't be up to coming in today. Mr. Bradley got word to me that you wouldn't. He said you needed the time to recuperate. He said I shouldn't bother to go out to—"

"Never mind what Mr. Bradley said, Mr. Hienz." I walked toward him, and he took a step backward and then another and another until he bumped against his desk. "I am perfectly well, and I am quite capable of deciding when I am up to coming to town and when I'm not."

"Yes, of course, Miss King. I'm terribly sorry that I—"

I staved off another of his apologies with a wave of my hand. "No need to worry, Mr. Hienz. No harm done in the final analysis, since I managed to get here anyway. And I won't be needing your services as a driver in the future, since I now have the use of my brother's horse."

"Of course, Miss King."

"If you please, I'd like to start to work immediately on the estate papers. I'm anxious to finish them."

"Of course, Miss King."

He scurried about the office to do my bidding.

"Oh, there's one more thing, Mr. Hienz."

"Yes, Miss King."

"I would appreciate it if you could arrange to have Sir Blanco stabled for me since I expect to be here most of the day."

"But, miss, all day? Forgive me, but a lady shouldn't—"

"I am quite used to working long hours in my profession, Mr. Hienz. Now, if you will just do as I asked."

"Yes, Miss King."

He hurried off to call an office boy to take care of Sir Blanco and another to bring out the papers I needed. I was soon settled at a table with more of Anton's papers to go through. It was no more than the mundane sorting of the evidence of Anton's excesses as I'd done before. It certainly wasn't enough to keep my mind occupied or to keep me from wondering why Chase

Bradley had told Mr. Hienz I wouldn't be coming in today. Was he trying to keep me away? In spite of his denial, I knew there was something he didn't want me to find out. Whatever it was, it still seemed highly possible to me that he wanted to keep it from my knowledge badly enough to have staged that accident. If he *had* been responsible for it, then his taking me to his house to care for me was no more than an elaborate cover-up.

That possibility disturbed me and left me feeling too edgy to concentrate on the uninteresting task I'd laid out for myself. Certainly whatever it was Chase Bradley was trying to keep me from learning had nothing to do with the amount of whisky Anton had bought or the bills for finery for his lady friends, not to mention all manner of toys and nonsense for Johnny Bradley. Whatever Anton was, he obviously had a soft spot in his heart for that child. But then, I asked myself, who wouldn't? Also, it was clear to me that whatever it was Chase Bradley didn't want me to see was not likely to be in this stack of papers. Rather, it was far more likely to be in the accounting books I'd been examining when the so-called accident occurred.

I pushed the papers aside and stood up, feeling a compulsion to have another look at those accounts. Mr. Hienz, seeing me rise, stood also.

"Is there something I can get for you, Miss King? Perhaps a cup of tea? A more comfortable chair? Oh, then it's the light. Hard on the eyes in that corner there. Forgive me for not thinking of that. Just allow me to—"

"There's nothing wrong with the light, Mr. Hienz, and please, keep your seat. It's just that I've tired of this task, and I think I'll take a little walk."

"Well, of course! I'll just get my hat, and—"

"Thank you, but that won't be necessary. I prefer to walk alone."

"But, miss, a lady shouldn't be out on the streets unaccompanied, it's just not—"

"I'll be fine, Mr. Hienz, thank you." I headed for the door. "Oh, and Mr. Hienz—"

"Yes, miss?"

"If it should be a while before I return, please don't worry. After my walk, I may call a carriage to take me over to Mr.

Bradley's house. He and his cousin have invited me to rest there when I need it. I do hope you understand, Mr. Hienz. A lady's delicate condition, you know."

"Of course, miss. Of course," he said, turning beet-red and leaving me to wonder what he had read into that remark about a lady's delicate condition. Not that it mattered, because it would serve my purpose anyway. He seemed convinced that the female sex was incapable of anything more mentally arduous than reading a menu or a theater program, and I was more than willing to use that prejudice to my advantage by making him think I was resting somewhere rather than going over the account books of King Enterprises. It was obvious to me that the fewer people who knew what I did, the better off I was.

It was a good ten-block walk to the waterfront warehouse, but, as I remembered from my childhood, a walk down the Strand was never boring. There was always a circuslike atmosphere. I passed a patent medicine man who had gathered a crowd about him to sell his cure for baldness and all manner of feminine ills. Oddly enough, the same medicine did both, he claimed. There was even a trained bear on one corner and two minstrels doing a dance in front of a theater to advertise the type of show inside.

I stopped once, ducking into a restaurant to have a glass of sarsaparilla and a watercress tea sandwich. It was a skimpy lunch, but that was all I could afford. I resumed my walk, thinking the exercise was good for me after the long period of time seated at a desk.

The waterfront area where the docks and wharves were was, in its own way, always as interesting as the business section of the Strand. There were the ships with their exotic cargo being loaded and unloaded by stevedores of a variety of races, their bare, muscular chests glistening with sweat. Some of them sang as they worked, and some of them stopped to stare at me as I walked alone. I pretended not to notice their stares and kept walking.

"Lady of the Shadows," I heard one of them say. I turned to see who it was. A rough-looking longshoreman met my gaze. "You old man King's gal. You be careful out there."

Once again the training of my childhood and the admonishment not to talk to men along the waterfront took over, and I started to walk away without comment.

"Heed my words!" he called out. "There's spirits to watch out for. Ghosts. Old Laffite hisself. And others. I seen 'em!"

There it was, the old superstitions about ghosts along the cove, but I kept walking, ignoring the man and ignoring the chill that crept along my spine, defying the warm, close air.

The air was heavy with smells. Mixed with the aroma of rotting fish and salt was the smell of beer and spirits wafting from the inside. It was early yet for the taverns to be crowded, but there was nevertheless the occasional shout and sounds of laughter—male and female—coming from the taverns.

I saw two of the women standing on the boardwalks, wearing dresses at a startling mid-calf length and smoking cigarettes, shockingly, as if they were men, while they watched two men in a fistfight. The women cheered the fighters on in loud, raucous voices and laughed uproariously when one of the men brought his knee up to the other's groin. When the victim of the unkind blow doubled over and fell to his knees, one of the women kicked him. I hurried away from the scene and made my way as quickly as I could to the King warehouse.

I was cautious as I entered the warehouse, remembering the accident of the day before, but nothing happened, and I went all but unnoticed except by a few workmen as I made my way to the back where the office was located.

I spotted Robert Thorn before I got to the office, though. He was standing near a group of workmen, giving them instructions. He looked undeniably handsome in tight woolen trousers and a white shirt, open at the collar and rolled at the sleeves to reveal muscular arms. He must have sensed my gaze because he turned as if I'd called him. He seemed just as surprised to see me as Mr. Hienz had been, but he was much more refined in the way he received me.

"Miss King, I didn't expect you back so soon!" he said, walking toward me. "I called at the Bradley house yesterday, but the maid said you'd already returned to the Shadows to recuperate further."

"I'm quite all right. It was no more than an embarrassing accident. Quite awkward of me, I'm sure, to get in the way of a swinging hook."

"You're not used to the warehouse. It's a busy, confusing place. I should have warned you at the least, but if I'd been any kind of a gentleman at all, I would have escorted you through

Lady of the Shadows

the place. Please accept my apology for—"

"Please!" I said, holding a hand up to ward off his words. "I've had quite enough apologies to serve me a lifetime. Do you have any idea how often—"

"How often Bill Hienz offers an apology?" He laughed as he finished the sentence for me. "The poor man even apologizes for the weather. If I start sounding like him, push *me* in front of a swinging hook." We laughed together, and he took my arm, leading me away from the work area. "However, if I'm not allowed to apologize," he continued, "then you must at least allow me to treat you to lunch."

"Oh, really, Mr. Thorn—"

"Robert, please. And may I call you Laura?"

"Of course—Robert," I said hesitantly. I was quite unused to the new familiarity. "I'm not hungry, really," I continued. I was lying, of course. As usual, I felt I could have eaten a horse. The watercress sandwich and sarsaparilla had only served to whet my appetite.

"But you'll disappoint me if you don't allow me to show you the view from a wonderful waterfront restaurant that's just been opened by a Cajun gentleman. His specialty is crawfish in a wonderful sauce and pecan pie flavored with brandy. The food's quite spicy, of course, and if you're not used to it, maybe you'd prefer—"

"Oh, I love Cajun spices," I said a little too quickly, but I was remembering a cook my father once employed whose black bean soup and spiced shrimp were in danger of being condemned by the Baptists because they were so sinfully good. Robert took my arm and smiled as he led me away again. "And pecan pie?" I asked, also remembering a thick, syrupy filling full of the tender nuts that grew so profusely on the mainland.

"And pecan pie," he said with a wink. "Just give me time to get my coat."

The meal was every bit as good as Robert had promised, and the view of the gulf was as beautiful and mysterious as it had ever been. I found myself relaxing for the first time since I'd returned to Galveston. Robert charmed me completely with his stories about the colorful characters in the city, including the sausagemaker who rode to work down the Strand every day on the back of a bull, and the ladies club that insisted on burning incense at the opera house after the cancan was performed there.

I laughed until my side hurt. "It's a strange city," I said. "Almost magical."

"Have you missed it?"

"I didn't think so until I returned. But I guess I did, a little."

"It's nothing like New York, of course. You'd miss the theater, the art galleries, all the sophistication if you should find yourself stuck here."

The truth was that I seldom had the money to attend the theater or the time for the art galleries. All the sophistication passed me by while I earned my living. But I said nothing of that to him. I merely gave him an agreeable smile and took another taste of the brandy-laced pie.

"Anyway," he continued, "I would think an attractive woman such as yourself wouldn't want to find herself stuck in such a remote old house as the Shadows."

"The remoteness doesn't bother me, really. I grew up there, remember?"

"Of course, but you weren't a woman alone then. Aren't you a little frightened sometimes?"

"Of course not. Except—"

"Except what?"

"Oh, it's nothing, really," I said, not sure how much I should tell him.

He glanced at me, a look of concern in his eyes. "Is there something wrong?"

"Well," I said with a little laugh, "I suppose I'm not used to living near the sea anymore. I keep imagining I see—"

"See what?"

"Well, apparitions." I laughed, embarrassed that I'd said it.

"Apparitions? What sort of apparitions?"

"A woman, I think. And she seems to be crying."

"Laura, my dear, are you sure you—"

"Please forget I said that," I said with a wave of my hand. I was feeling quite embarrassed now. "You're going to ask if I'm sure I didn't suffer a more serious blow to the head than I thought. But I assure you I didn't. Actually I saw the woman even before—never mind. I'm being silly."

"Laura, I think you should leave."

"What?" I looked up from my pie, startled at his sudden announcement.

"Go back to New York. Leave all this estate business to Bill Hienz."

"But—"

"It's not safe for you at Shadow Cove."

"What do you mean?" I felt suddenly very uneasy.

"There's something out there."

"What!"

"I don't know what it is. Maybe just vagrants. Probably is. I don't believe all that silly superstitious talk about ghosts, of course."

"Ghosts? Oh, of course. Jean Laffite and other spirits." I forced a laugh. "But that's ridiculous."

"Of course it is. But the fact remains that it's not safe for you to be out there alone. At least take a room in town until you can arrange for passage—"

"Robert, I won't be taking a room in town. I'll stay at the Shadows. That's my home."

He looked at me a moment, then a smile spread slowly across his handsome face. "You're a stubborn woman, aren't you?"

"Well, I—"

"Look, if you won't take my advice, at least allow me to give you the opportunity for a diversion. Come with me to the opera tonight."

I had been to the opera with my father as a child, and I'd grown to love it. Unfortunately, however, I could seldom afford it in New York. I was sorely tempted to accept Robert Thorn's invitation.

"Sarah Bernhardt is here. She's starring in *La Tosca*."

Sarah Bernhardt! I'd seen her picture and read of her fame and talent, and *La Tosca* was one of my favorite operas. "I love the opera, Robert," I said, giving up on showing restraint. "I'd love to accompany you."

"Wonderful!" He leaned across and touched my hand. "I'll come with a carriage for you at eight."

By the time we got back to the office, there was little time left to work, and I found it difficult anyway, being in the same office with Robert. He kept interrupting me with little bits of conversation—to ask me about my work, to discuss the libretto for the opera, to compare Miss Bernhardt to Emma Calvé. It was delightful to have someone to talk to who understood and appreciated the same things I was interested in, but, unfortunately, it was not at all conducive to work. To make matters worse, at precisely five o'clock, a scarce two and a half hours after our long lunch ended, Robert insisted that we leave for the day.

"But it's so early!" I protested. "And I've barely gotten started going over these accounts."

Robert laughed. "You're not at all like your brother, are you? He hated working with the accounts. He was always looking for an excuse to leave early."

"You knew Anton well, obviously."

"Well enough to miss him. And I'm sure you do, too. It must be difficult for you to have to do this when you're still grieving."

"Actually, I didn't know my brother very well at all. We hadn't been close for years." Just saying those words, though, gave me a twisted knot of grief inside me. I would have liked to have known my brother better, to have meant something more to him than a troublesome spinster sister he felt obliged to see after. My grieving was for what never was, more than for Anton's passing.

Robert came to me and took both my arms, forcing me to stand and look at him. "I see that look of sadness in your eyes," he said. "You've had enough for today."

"No, really, I—"

"Come now. It's time you went home for a rest. And anyway, I never knew a beautiful woman who didn't need hours to get herself ready for an evening out."

I looked at him, speechless for a moment. I was so unaccustomed to being called beautiful, I hardly knew what to say in response.

"I'm so looking forward to the evening," Robert said, sparing me the necessity of saying anything. "I want it to be the best you've ever had. I want to make arrangements for dinner after the show. I want to have time to have my carriage cleaned and washed." He turned away to get his hat from the rack and gave me a flirtatious wink. "At least give *me* time to get all that done."

"Well, of course," I managed to say. "If you wish, go ahead. I'm sure I'll be perfectly—"

He took a step toward me, an expression of alarm on his face. "You're not thinking of staying here alone?"

"I don't see why not. There's plenty of time."

"Laura, my dear, it's not safe for you to be here alone."

It seemed that people were always telling me I wasn't safe, one place or another, but I didn't have an opportunity to protest.

"There's a certain . . . element down here at the waterfront. I'm sure you couldn't have helped but notice that. It's questionable enough for you to be here anyway, and certainly no lady should be here without the company of a gentleman. It's completely out of the question as the evening grows later."

"Well, I—" He was right, of course. The only women who were usually along the waterfront at any time were those of the caliber I'd seen earlier—women of the demimonde who plied their trade here, and even they were wise enough to stay inside after dark, I'd heard.

"Did you take the streetcar from Hienz's office? If you'll allow me to accompany you . . ."

I'd never felt so watched over and protected in my life. Robert refused to allow me to walk the ten blocks back to Mr. Hienz's office. Instead, he accompanied me on the streetcar to the stables and waited for me while Sir Blanco was brought out. He even wanted to hire a horse to ride out with me, but I was finally able to convince him I would be perfectly safe.

Once I was home I was glad Robert had insisted I leave when I did, since I found I did need the time to get ready for the evening. I heated some bathwater and scented it with some cologne, then I slipped into the tub. Not only was I a bit stiff from the unaccustomed ride on Sir Blanco, but my mind was tumbling with thoughts of my accident at the wharf, of Chase Bradley warning me to go back to New York, of him watching me from his office window, of Aunt Stella and Robert Thorn and the man on the waterfront warning me of Shadow Cove, of the strange specter of a woman walking into the gulf, of Chase being in my house without my knowing it.

I tried to force all those thoughts from my mind and let the warm caress of the water relax me. Finally it seemed to work, and I felt my tense muscles lengthen and unknot, and my thoughts found easier paths to follow. When a vision of Chase Bradley lying on top of me on my bed upstairs crept into my thoughts, I stood up quickly and dried myself off. It was time I got dressed!

Upstairs, wrapped in my dressing gown, I found another reason to be disturbed, however. I had nothing suitable to wear. I had my traveling suit, which I'd worn all day because it was the only thing suitable for riding a horse. I had two blue serge dresses with high necks, one with a white shawl collar and one without, which I wore for teaching; and I had two moderately dressy day dresses, one of which I'd worn the first day Mr. Hienz took me to town. There was absolutely nothing suitable for the theater. Nothing, that is, except the daring black tulle and taffeta gown Chase Bradley had given me to wear for dinner in his home.

But I couldn't wear that! In fact, I should consider it only a loan and return it to him as quickly as possible. I thought of wearing the yellow batiste I'd worn the first day after my arrival; I put it on and looked at myself in the mirror. It wouldn't do. It was definitely an afternoon dress, and Robert Thorn, no doubt, would be in a tuxedo.

Finally in desperation I pulled the dress Chase had given me from the hanger and held it up to me. It was perfect. Perhaps, I thought, I would wear it just this once, but after tonight I would have no need for it again. I slipped the dress on, along with my best crinoline petticoat, and I managed to get my hair up almost as perfectly as Babette had done it. I wore my best jewelry—a silver filigree necklace set with emeralds that had been my only inheritance from my mother.

I was glad I'd made the choice to wear the dress when I saw the look on Robert's face as he came to my door. I could tell he was pleased with what he saw. He himself was dressed in the most fashionable formal waistcoat with gleaming black boots and a fine beaver top hat.

"You grow more lovely with each passing hour," he said, picking up my hand and kissing it. "It's a shame to keep such beauty secluded in this godforsaken spot."

"I don't find it godforsaken actually," I said, gathering up my own wrap. It seemed odd to be doing that. The Shadows I had known as a child was full of servants who stood at the door, ready to help us all with our wraps and to watch over the house while we were gone.

"I suppose it's tolerable as long as you know it's only for a short time," Robert said.

I gave him a smile but said nothing, the thought crossing my mind that here was yet another person who seemed anxious for me to leave Galveston.

The gala ambience at the theater was as exciting as any opening night I could have imagined in New York. A crowd had gathered in the lobby, where champagne flowed freely. Men were all as elegantly dressed as Robert, and the women's gowns were a flower garden of silk and taffeta. I was more glad than ever that I'd had the beautiful black dress to wear. Robert introduced me to a number of people, many of whose names I remembered from my childhood and who remembered my father. Mr. Sealy and his wife were there, and I spent a few moments in cordial conversation with them. I could feel admiring eyes on me everywhere I turned—a new experience for me, and I was, I'll admit, enjoying it.

The sounds of the orchestra tuning up added even more to the atmosphere of anticipation, and that, along with two glasses of champagne, left me feeling giddy with the excitement of the evening. It was almost as if I were living in a fairy-tale world.

I was suddenly brought back to earth with a jolt, however, when the lights blinked to signal the beginning of the program, and I saw Chase Bradley a few feet away. An arrogant half smile played at his lips. I tried to look away, to pretend I hadn't seen him, but his eyes held mine for a brief moment, and then he gave me a formal bow. I grasped Robert's arm, hoping he would move more quickly toward our seats, but in the next instant I saw that Chase was moving toward us. He managed to work his way directly behind us, and then he leaned forward in the crush of the crowd so that he barely touched my bare shoulder with his arm, and I turned just enough to acknowledge the touch.

"Lovely dress," he murmured.

I glanced at Robert. He hadn't heard him and apparently didn't realize he was behind us. Chase knew I'd heard him, but I ignored him while I felt myself blush at the thought of him seeing me wearing the dress he'd paid for. Finally we came to the stairway that would lead us to our box seats, and I thought I had escaped the embarrassment Chase Bradley had caused me. To my chagrin, however, I saw that he was seated in the box next to ours. I half expected to see the beautiful blond woman he'd been with the first day I met him seated next to him, but he was alone in the gilded and velvet-curtained box. I tried not to look at him, to forget about him completely, but several times some magnetic force drew my eyes in his direction, and I saw that he was watching me.

Sometime in the middle of the second act, I glanced over and saw that the box was empty. Chase Bradley had disappeared.

Chapter 6

CHASE had managed to ruin the entire evening for me. I found that I couldn't even enjoy the candlelight dinner Robert had arranged in the fashionable restaurant overlooking the water. Finally, pleading a headache, I asked him to drive me home.

The ride back to Shadow Cove was less than pleasant. Wind had come sweeping in from the north, and it buffeted the carriage, causing it to rock precariously along the narrow ribbon of a road that followed the coastline. The sound of the wind whistling around the carriage and the lightning and thunder coming increasingly closer made the horses nervous, and the driver kept flicking his whip at their backs in an effort to keep them from shying and overturning the carriage as we raced across the flat, windswept coastal plain, now eerily lit by a pale and expiring moon.

By the time we arrived at the cove, the thunder and lightning had intensified, and it had begun to rain. Robert used his topcoat to shield me as he rushed me to the door.

"I feel uneasy leaving you here alone on a night like this." He was shouting against the sound of the wind and the roaring sea as I fumbled with the lock.

"I'll be perfectly safe!" I shouted. "The Shadows has weathered more than one storm like this."

When at last I got the door open, we both stepped inside. It was pitch black, and I groped my way toward the hall table to find the lamp. I had taken no more than two steps when I felt a hand on my arm. It startled me, coming out of the darkness like that, but I realized quickly enough as he pulled me toward him that it was Robert who had followed me inside.

"Laura, beautiful Laura," he whispered. I felt his breath on my cheek, and in the next instant he was kissing me. The kiss surprised me, coming as it did out of the darkness like that. But I might have been surprised anyway, since it had been more months than I could count since I'd been kissed. A spinster of twenty-eight doesn't have too many opportunities for a kiss, especially when she is kept busy earning her own living as I was, and when she is not afforded the social freedoms of the opposite sex.

Perhaps because it was so dark and the kiss had come as such a surprise, or perhaps because I was so unused to such things, the experience left me feeling unsettled. I managed to pull myself away and found the lamp at last. When I had it lit, I picked it up and turned to face Robert. What I saw on his face was unmistakably desire—or lust. His eyes held mine for a moment, then he glanced at the great stairway that led upstairs to the bedrooms. Then, just as quickly, he looked away.

"Good night, Laura," he murmured. "I shall miss you when you leave." With that he turned away into the night.

I stood alone in the great hall, holding my lamp, while shadows from the flame danced sensuously on the walls, caressing the cupped hands that still waited to be filled with candles. I had just been kissed by a handsome man, and I had just been treated to a lovely dinner and a night at the theater. Wonderful things were happening to me that I had never dreamed would happen, but I couldn't rid myself of that strange, unsettled feeling.

A loud crack of thunder startled me, and I felt suddenly chilled. Pulling my wrap tighter, I made my way up the stairs. Before I reached the top of the landing, I heard a haunting sound, like that of a door swinging on rusty hinges. I hesitated, unwilling for a moment to go any farther, but I reminded myself that I was a sensible woman quite used to taking care of myself and one who was not afraid of silly noises, and I continued to make my way up to my bedroom.

The creaking sound grew louder and more chilling the farther I ascended, and my steps became slower and slower. When I finally reached the top, I let out a sigh. The strange noise was nothing more than the door to my bedroom, slightly ajar and swinging back and forth in a draft. My relief was short-lived, though, when I realized that there was no reason for there to be a draft. I distinctly remembered closing my window. My steps slowed again as I approached the doorway. If my window was open now, then that meant someone had been in my room to open it. Or worse yet, he was still in there.

I stopped, unwilling to go any farther, but then I realized that if someone had been in my house, he could be anywhere, even lurking in the shadows of the very hallway I was in now. It could be that my room was safer than anywhere else. I walked toward the room at a faster pace and thrust the lamp in front of me as I stepped in the doorway to allow me to see all the dark corners of the room. I could see nothing except the eerily dancing shadows created by the lamp and the curtains of my window, reaching like ghostly arms into the room because of the wind blowing through the opening. The curtains were drenched, and a puddle of water stained the floor.

I set the lamp on the bureau and ran to the window to close it. As I did, a flash of blue lightning illuminated the night, and I saw below me, running along the foaming, wind-tossed sea, a white horse. On the back of the horse was a woman. Her white gown was wet and clinging to her, and her hair streamed behind her, blowing in the wet gale like a gossamer banner. The electrical flash had given the scene a strange phosphorescent glow, as if it were from another world or from a dream.

But the scene was real, I knew. The horse was Sir Blanco, and the woman was the same ghostly figure I'd seen before running along the beach. But why was she riding my horse? And why was she riding him so hard? Racing him against the wind like that would be hard on him, and certainly no human or beast should be out in that storm.

I was suddenly angry at the thought of anyone harming Sir Blanco, and I was determined to find out who was doing it. Grabbing my hooded cape from the wardrobe closet, I put it on over my dress. For a moment a sense of fear overcame me as I remembered the longshoreman's warnings and my own irrational fear that the creature was not a flesh-and-blood person. I hesitated, torn between fear and anger, but I pushed the fear aside and raced down the stairs and through the house to the back. Leaving the lamp on the table in the center of the kitchen, I hurried out the back door.

Rain pelted my face, and the wind forced my hood back, drenching my hair as I plodded through the wet overgrown garden at the back of the house. As I neared the beach, I called out to Sir Blanco, but the force of the wind swept my words away, making them sound distant and hollow, even to my own ears. I stopped and scanned the expanse of the beach, but there was nothing there except the black sea, foaming and raging back in anger to the wind, and the white sand, illuminated now and then with the wild flashes of lightning thrown from the sky by some unseen god. I called the horse's name again and whirled around, searching the area between the beach and the house, but still there was no Sir Blanco, no ghostly wraith of a woman. Fear gripped me again when I remembered having seen the woman walk into the sea. Could it be that she had ridden Sir Blanco into the black surf now? But Sir Blanco was flesh and blood, not a specter that could rise from the sea. He would balk at being forced into the water. No woman could have forced him, and I would see him running along the beach by now. An irrational sense of panic gripped me as I ran toward the stables. Maybe Sir Blanco was still in his stall. Maybe I had simply imagined it all.

The rain soaked me, and lightning flashed furiously all around me as I fumbled with the gate to the stable yard, but at last I had it unfastened, and I hurried toward the stalls. It was as dark as a crypt inside, and I was hesitant to enter the dark chamber. But it was only a stall, I told myself, not a crypt. I could smell the rich sweetness of the hay mixed with the distinctly pungent odor that means a horse is present, or has been present.

I took a tentative step into the darkness and then another and another. I heard a soft rustling, and I stood dead still, my heart pounding as if it were trying to escape my chest. Then the pounding seemed to stop, leaving a void in my chest as I looked down and saw two strange, unearthly red lights moving erratically on the floor. I sucked in my breath audibly, too frightened to cry out, and in the same instant another flash of lightning illuminated the stalls. A rat scurried across my feet, his red eyes dulled now by the greater light. I screamed aloud this time, and almost instantly the scream was answered with a startled neigh. It had to be Sir Blanco. I called his name again, and there was another answering neigh. It *was* Sir Blanco! He had recognized his name.

Slowly I groped my way toward his stall, holding out my hands in front of me to keep from stumbling. Finally I touched something—his wet nose—and I slid my hand up his bony forehead and felt his proud head toss in response. Another flash of lightning lit up the stalls briefly, and I saw his gleaming white coat. It was indeed Sir Blanco, safe in his stall.

Had I only imagined that I had seen him running on the beach? And had I only imagined the woman on his back? I ran my hands over his back and down his sides and felt the dampness. I had not imagined it. Sir Blanco was drenched. He had been out in the storm. He could not have gotten out into the storm by himself, though, because I distinctly remembered fastening the gate on his stall. A quick check with my hand told me it was fastened now. Whoever had ridden him had brought him back and put him up properly. But who was she, and where was she now?

Could it be that she was still in the stables? That she was waiting for me somewhere in the darkness? I whirled around suddenly at an imaginary noise, but there was nothing there except the darkness and the sounds of the storm. I felt an urgency to get back to the house where I could at least have a lamp to give faint illumination to the shadows. With the same groping movements that had gotten me into the darkened stables, I made my way out and ran through the rain to the house.

The lamp I had left burning in the kitchen was still there, sitting on the table in the center of the room, its faint light providing an eerie welcome. Picking it up, I started for the back stairs, but something made me stop, an apprehensive sensation that someone was watching me. I stood dead still, listening for sounds, but I heard nothing except the howling wind and the occasional rumble of thunder, growing less frequent and fainter now. I mounted the first step of the stairway, and the thought occurred to me that I should have gone around and taken the front stairs. They were wider and less steep and would have made it easier for me to see in the poor light of the single lamp whether or not anyone was lurking.

But I was being ridiculous, I told myself. I had locked the door when I left to look for Sir Blanco and had taken the key with me. There was no way anyone could have gotten into the house. And even if someone had—a vagrant or someone seeking refuge from the storm—there was no reason to believe anyone would want to harm me.

Armed with my forced courage, I began the climb up the steep staircase. I walked slowly, though, and with something less than determination. Suddenly I thought I heard a creaking sound, as if someone were with me on the staircase. I stopped, listening, but I heard nothing. My nerves were getting the best of me, and I feared I was becoming one of the "delicate weaker sex" Mr. Hienz so annoyingly referred to all the time.

But then it came flying at me from out of the darkness. I heard the whooshing sound and saw a gleam from my lantern reflecting on the cold steel, and in the same instant I screamed and pressed myself against the wall of the stairwell, barely managing to keep from dropping the burning lamp. The knife fell at my feet and clattered in a sloppy staccato down the stairs. I stared at it, paralyzed, unable to breathe, yet my heart raced with a wild, erratic drumbeat rhythm, and blood roared in my head. Then suddenly I turned my head and stared with even more fear into the darkness at the top of the stairs, knowing that whatever had hurled that knife at me was still up there.

With slow deliberation I crept down the stairs until I could reach the knife, and I stooped to grasp it in my right hand. I stared up the stairs again, slowly, cautiously, my breath coming in short, shallow gasps. I was terrified of what I might find up there, and I didn't know what made me want to try to find it. Fear had rendered me totally irrational.

Never in my life had I wished more that the Shadows had been closer to town so that we could have had electricity. It would have been a godsend to have been able to flood the hallway with illumination, but God, I was convinced, had nothing to do with any of this. Whatever was lurking for me in the shadows of the hallway was evil, and I had nothing but my flickering oil lamp to aid me and a kitchen knife with which to defend myself.

I walked slowly, holding the lamp in front of me and the knife in my other hand. I thrust the light into the darkness and left a wake of shadows behind me. As I passed each of the eight doorways leading to bedrooms and the little sitting room that Mama had used, I tried to open the doors. Each one was locked except for mine.

Lady of the Shadows

With all the caution I had used before, I searched every corner of my room, including under the bed and inside the wardrobe closet. No one was there. Whoever or whatever had hurled the knife at me had escaped, possibly down the front stairs. I started out of my room to have a look, but at last good sense returned to me, and I stepped back inside, slamming my door closed quickly. It took all of my strength to move the heavy bureau in front of it to barricade myself inside. I felt exhausted, both from the physical exertion and from my fright, when I finally got it positioned securely against the door.

I could do nothing more than sink to the bed and sit with my face in my hands and cry. When at last the tension was gone from me enough to stand, I removed my beautiful gown, ruined by mud and rain, and I fell into bed wearing nothing except my thin chemise. In spite of the night air that was closing in on me like a warm sticky sheet, I pulled the coverlet up to my chin and lay there shivering.

I couldn't imagine that I slept at all, but I must have because I was awakened quite suddenly. I wasn't sure what had awakened me—some noise, maybe, other than the storm? Some unseen presence? I lay wide awake staring into the darkness, and then I realized the bureau I had shoved in front of my door was moving. I shot up to a sitting position and pulled the covers to my chin, but just as quickly I recognized what futile protection a down comforter was. Throwing the covers back, I grabbed the knife I'd left on the bedside table and moved stealthily toward the door. I stood poised, holding the knife in both hands and raised above my head, waiting for whatever was about to enter my room.

The bureau, which had been moving by inches, lurched suddenly as the unseen presence rendered a powerful shove against the door. I saw a hulk in the darkness, filling my doorway, and instantaneously I brought the knife blade down.

A viselike grip on my wrist stopped the thrust and forced my arms behind my head, causing me to drop the knife, while a powerful arm around my waist pulled me forward against a hard chest.

"Let me go!" I screamed. "Let me go!"

"Damn you, settle down!" I recognized the voice. It was Chase Bradley.

I beat my hands against his chest. "Get out of my house. You have no right—"

"I said settle down. I'm not going to hurt you."

I flailed at him again and tried with all my strength to shove him toward the door, but he picked me up, as if I weighed no more than a feather pillow, and carried me to the bed. Rather than throw me on it and rape me, or kill me, as I feared he would do, he stood me against the bedpost and held me there while he removed his leather belt, and then to my horror and chagrin he strapped me to the post. He turned away from me, and I could sense him groping around the room.

"What are you doing? What do you want?" My voice was high-pitched with the mixture of anger and fear.

"I'm looking for the lamp, damn it." There was a thump and an "Oooh," and a muttered oath. He had stubbed his toe against the bureau, which he had pushed to the middle of the floor to force himself into my room. I might have laughed at his getting what he deserved, if I hadn't been so frightened.

Something crashed to the floor, and there was the sound of glass breaking and another oath.

"You're destroying my house!"

"Well, I can't find the lamp! Where is it?"

I didn't answer him.

"I said where is it!" He shouted at me, sounding annoyed.

"Do you think I'm going to tell you? Do you think I'm going to do anything to help you?" I might have saved my breath. He had found the lamp, and he had already struck a match and was holding the flame cupped in his hand while he guided it to the wick. The soft light washed away all but a thin film of darkness in the small room, and when he turned toward me and looked at me, I saw the scowling frown on his face melt away.

His gaze made me suddenly aware of how I looked, my thin shift barely covering my body, my breasts thrust forward by the awkward position of my hands strapped behind my back. He moved toward me, and my eyes widened, not in fear, I don't believe, but in uncertainty. He stopped directly in front of me, our bodies so close we were almost touching, and I could feel currents of electricity between us. My face was tilted upward toward his, and if he had made the slightest move, I would have swayed toward him in spite of myself. But he moved away. He walked behind me and began to work with the belt that held me tied to the bed.

"I'm going to unfasten you," he said. "But don't try anything. Don't do anything irrational."

My heart was pounding again, not from fear but from an emotion I wasn't sure I wanted to admit. I had to force myself to act and speak calmly.

"This is the second time you've forced yourself into my bedroom," I said, speaking over my shoulder, "and you're telling me to act rationally?"

"I suppose I owe you an apology." I felt the belt loosen and fall away, and I turned to face him, rubbing my wrists. A shutter somewhere flapped erratically in the wind, and I shivered again. Chase glanced down at me, his eyes stopping at the hardened nipples of my breasts showing through the thin cotton of my shift. I turned away quickly and retrieved my dressing gown from the back of a chair. I found it unsettling that Chase took it from me and held it while I put it on. "I *do* apologize," he said, "for breaking into your bedroom again, but I was worried when you didn't answer my knock at the door."

"I didn't hear a knock," I said, moving away from him as I tied my dressing gown around my waist. It was best to keep some distance between us.

"It must have been the noise of the storm that kept you from hearing me. I knocked and called your name several times."

Was he lying to me? Couldn't it have been he who was lurking on the back stairs waiting to throw a knife at me? But if it was, then why hadn't he finished the job now that he was in my room?

"What are you doing here?" I was feeling uneasy again and moved cautiously toward the doorway, only partially blocked now by the heavy bureau.

"I came out here to see about you."

I hesitated and gave him a questioning look.

"I was worried about you—being out here alone in the storm. Then when you didn't answer the door, I got even more worried."

"I've weathered many a storm here at the Shadows, Mr. Bradley." I watched his face for a sign that he was lying, something that would somehow give a hint as to the real reason he was here. What he said, however, caught me completely off guard.

"Don't you think we ought to call each other by our first names? Especially if I'm going to be frequenting your bedroom."

"Mr. Bradley!" I whirled toward him and saw his amused grin. "I have no intention of allowing you to frequent my bedroom, and I consider it highly improper that you would—"

"All right, Miss King," he said, holding up his hands as if to shield himself from my tirade. "Again I apologize. I was teasing you, but I should have known a spinster schoolmarm would have no sense of humor."

"Of course I have a sense of humor," I snapped. I looked at my hands fidgeting with the tie to my dressing gown and felt altogether miserable with the way he was confusing me. "And of course I appreciate your concern," I said, still without looking at him.

"I shouldn't have barged in here, I know," he said, taking a step toward me. "But when I saw that you were barricaded in here, I thought—"

"You thought what?" I glanced up at him, curious about what he was getting at.

"What frightened you, Laura?"

My mind whirled. How much should I tell him? Would he think I was just giving in to hysterics, as Mr. Hienz believed? Or was he somehow involved with the strange goings-on and only wanted to confirm that I was frightened?

"I thought I heard someone—some noise in the house."

"Did you see anything? Anyone?" There was an urgency to his voice.

"No, of course not," I said, deciding it was best not to reveal too much. After all, I still knew very little about this man, except that he kept breaking into my house. I was still edging my way toward the door, but before I could take more than a step, he grabbed my arm and pulled me toward him.

"Tell me the truth," he demanded. "You must have seen something. Did you see anyone? Did anyone try to hurt you?"

I hesitated, and my eyes moved to the knife still on the table next to my bed. "Of course not," I said, deciding it was best to be cautious. "Why would you ask a thing like that?"

He had seen the direction of my glance, and he looked at the knife, then back at me.

"Go back to bed," he said, dropping my arm suddenly.

"Thank you, but I don't need you to tell me—"

"I'll be downstairs." He moved toward the door and with one heave shoved the bureau away enough to open it wider.

"What—?"

"I'll sleep downstairs." With that he was gone. I ran to the door and followed him into the hallway.

"I don't need your protection. I'll be perfectly safe. I'm not afraid."

"Go to bed!" Chase flung the words at me from over his shoulder.

I watched him for a moment disappearing into the darkness, then I turned away and went back to my room. I was lying, of course. I was terribly afraid and wasn't at all certain that having Chase Bradley in my house was going to help any. I entered my room and locked the door from the inside before I realized what a futile gesture that was. Chase Bradley had the keys to unlock my door, and pushing the bureau in front of the door wasn't going to help either, obviously, since he had pushed it away with such ease before.

I got into bed thinking that at least I had the satisfaction of knowing that I was a light sleeper and that I had the knife close by so I could grab it the instant I was awakened. Besides, I rationalized as I lay awake, staring into the darkness once again, if Chase Bradley had meant to do me any harm, he would have done it by now.

I lay awake for a long time before sleep finally came, and once again I was awakened by the angle of sunlight spilling into my room. It was a slightly diffused stream of light because of the thick, moisture-laden air that hung over us as a result of the previous night's storm, but it was enough to make me open my eyes and to know that morning had come—that I had survived the storm and Chase Bradley in my house.

I got out of bed and dressed quickly in one of my practical blue serge frocks and hurried downstairs. I was anxious to see Chase because now in the light of day my mind was clearer, and I knew what I had to do. I'd decided that I was going to tell him everything I'd seen and force him to tell me what was going on; I was convinced he knew more than he was telling me. It was the very thing I should have done the night before had I not been so frightened and confused.

I hurried downstairs to the library, where I assumed he would be sleeping on a couch. He was not there, and neither was he in the parlor. I even ran outside to the stables and along the beach looking for him and calling his name, but he was nowhere to be found.

It wasn't until I reentered the front hall that I noticed the knife. It was the same knife I had placed beside my bed the night before. Now it was balanced in one of the cold marble hands that had once been candleholders, and the blade was stained with blood.

Chapter 7

I SCREAMED when I saw the knife, and I might have fled the house except that a dark spot staining the marble floor that I had not seen before caught my attention. When I moved closer, I saw that it was a drop of blood, and beyond it were other droplets marking a faint trail to the back of the house.

It certainly wasn't good sense, but some foolish compulsion to dig deeper into the mystery that surrounded Shadow Cove led me to follow the trail of blood. It led through the main salon, through the dining room and the hallway that separated the dining room from the indoor kitchen. I stopped when I got to the kitchen door and saw the trail of blood leading underneath it. Some sixth sense told me that the source of blood would be behind that closed door inside the kitchen, and I wasn't certain I wanted to see it.

I stood there for a moment, hesitating before I tentatively placed a hand on the door and pushed. The door opened just a little, the hinges squeaking a warning. I ignored it and pushed again, and this time the door opened enough that I could see inside. There was nothing there except the wood-burning range, the pump at the sink, the row of cabinets, and the wooden table in the center of the room. There was no person waiting inside as I had half expected, or half feared. There was nothing to greet me, not even a sound. The room was as quiet as a mausoleum. Yet as I took a step inside, I noticed something odd. It wasn't a presence I sensed, but a smell, the heavy aroma of the gulf.

As I stepped farther into the kitchen, I saw it—the gaping mouth, the beady eyes staring at me in death. It was the body of a large fish lying in the sink beneath the pump. Its middle had been slit to reveal bloody intestines and the source of the blood on the knife.

I could think of only one person who could possibly have done it, only one person besides myself who could get into my house—Chase Bradley. The melodramatic trick didn't seem to be his style, but obviously there was much about Chase Bradley I didn't know.

The longer I stood at the sink staring at the disgusting mess, the angrier I became. For some reason, Chase was determined to send me away from Galveston, and if he couldn't order me to leave, then he apparently thought he could frighten me away. Well, I was going to show him that neither would work, and furthermore I was determined to find out *why* he wanted me to go. Whatever the reason, it had something to do with Anton.

My fears disappeared in the face of cold logic, and I hurried upstairs for a hat and my riding boots. I was more determined now than ever to get to the bottom of these mysteries. I would ride to town to finish looking into Anton's papers and, if need be, to confront Chase Bradley.

As I rode into Galveston on Sir Blanco, I was once again aware of the stares and attention I attracted, but I resolved to ignore all of it. What did it matter to me if it was more fashionable for a lady to ride in a carriage or on a bicycle? I had more important things to consider.

I almost changed my mind about not caring about fashion when I saw Robert Thorn. He was seated in the office, pouring over a set of books. He had removed his jacket, but he looked roguishly handsome and fashionable in his shirtsleeves, particularly since the shirt was made of the finest China silk. He looked up when I entered, and his eyes widened.

"Laura!" He stood quickly. "Are you all right?"

"Of course I'm all right. Why shouldn't I be?"

"I was worried about you. Because of the storm, I mean. It can be so much worse out at the cove with no buildings to break the wind."

"I've weathered more than one storm at Shadow Cove."

"You keep saying that, but you're all alone now," he said, walking toward me. "Weren't you frightened?" he asked, taking my hat and shawl.

I hesitated a moment, not sure just how much I should say. "Of course not," I said finally. If I said anything, it would be to Chase Bradley. But I would wait to confront him until I delved further into Anton's papers and, I hoped, found some clue about Chase's association with him.

I turned away from Robert and went to my desk, flipping the riding crop against my leg nervously as I walked. To my chagrin, I found that all the accounts I'd been examining the day before had been cleared from my desk. I spun around to Robert.

"Where are the accounts I was working on?" I demanded.

He had gone back to his work, and he glanced up, wearing a look of surprise. "Oh, I assumed you were finished with those."

"Of course I wasn't finished," I said, unable to control my frustration. "I'll tell you when I'm finished."

"Laura, there is something wrong." I saw the look of concern on his face, and I was immediately embarrassed that I had shown such bad temper.

"There's nothing wrong." I turned away, unwilling to look at him until I collected myself. "Maybe the storm *did* make me a bit edgy. I apologize," I said when I was able to face him. "But if you would be so kind as to get the account books for me, I'll get back to work."

"Laura, are you sure—"

"I'm sure, Robert."

He held my eyes with his a moment longer. "Of course," he said and turned away to do my bidding.

I spent the entire morning going over the accounts, seeing how, over the past several years, King Enterprises had lost more and more money. As the price for exporting increased, it seemed the volume and profits decreased. When I questioned Robert, he said that other companies had undercut the price usually charged by the King company, and that the transcontinental rail lines had allowed cotton and other goods to move to other shipping ports.

The more time I spent on the accounts, the more obvious it became to me that if King Enterprises was to survive, something would have to be done about the way competition from other shipping companies and the railroad was cutting into our profits.

I asked Robert to provide me with a list of prices charged by the railroads as well as by our competitive companies on the waterfront. He was able to get them for me immediately, and I saw that he was right. King Enterprises was not competitive. I declined Robert's invitation to accompany him for luncheon. Instead I spent some time in the warehouse, talking with workers and with some of our customers, and I found them generally disgruntled. Shipping dates were seldom met, and our cost of damaged goods was far too high. By the end of the day I had a clear picture emerging of why King Enterprises was losing money. It had been inefficiently run with little or no attention paid to workers' needs.

I had been so immersed in the company that I hadn't even taken the time to read the mail a messenger brought to my desk. Nothing looked particularly interesting anyway, except for a small envelope that looked like an invitation to a party. I slipped it into my dress pocket and continued to work, planning to read it later. Right now I wanted to concentrate on King Enterprises.

It seemed obvious to me that if we improved our quality of service and maintained a more competitive price level as well as showed sensitivity to the workers, we could improve our business. I would also have to do something about the debts that were on the books. It would require some difficult decisions, perhaps even some layoffs, but if I could instill a sense of pride in being a part of King Enterprises, the way it had been when Papa was in charge, I could infuse more enthusiasm and more quality into the task. As for pricing, it would take some mathematical analysis to figure out just how low we could go. I was busy at my desk, doing just that when I looked up to see Robert standing in front of me.

"Once again I have to tell you you're working too late," he said.

I put my pen down for a moment and rubbed my throbbing temples. "I've found that I have a lot to learn about this business."

"Do you really think it's necessary to learn the business, Laura?" He had gone to the coatrack and brought me my hat and shawl. He was holding them for me, waiting for me to put them on. "After all, if you plan to sell and return to New York, what need is there?"

I realized then that I actually had stopped thinking in those terms. My thoughts had turned to revitalizing King Enterprises, making it the kind of company it had been, but instead of John King at the helm, it would be me, Laura King. Papa would have called me foolish for having such a dream, of course. He would say a woman wasn't suited to such things. But it was more than a dream, and I saw no reason why a woman couldn't build, or rebuild, an empire. In fact, I knew now that I wanted to try.

"You know, Robert, I've just been thinking—" I stood, letting him help me with my wrap. "I may not be so anxious to return to New York. After all, Galveston is my home."

"What about your job?" He handed me my hat and watched me while I walked to the mirror hanging near the rack and set the hat on my head.

"I have an indefinite leave of absence," I said. "The headmistress has already hired someone to finish out my term. And anyway, I've been thinking I ought to take over King Enterprises." I turned around in time to see the look on his face. "You're surprised."

"Why, yes," he said. "I must say I am."

"Well, so am I. I never thought it would be anything I'd be interested in. Oh, I'm going to give it time, of course, but I can see how it could get into a person's blood."

"Laura, I feel I must tell you this business is no place for a lady."

I laughed. "You sound like Papa. Or William Hienz."

"It's business, Laura, not a parlor game. Not a schoolroom exercise. It's tough, competitive business. Men don't always act like gentlemen. They're ruthless. Undercutting prices, manipulating sales, stealing away employees."

"I said I'd think about it, Robert. But ruthlessness never frightened me. My father, as you must have known, was king of the ruthless. Besides, I believe it's possible to be tough without being ruthless."

Robert laughed. "What a contrast you are to your brother. Not just in your business attitude, but in everything else as well. Anton could never stand to live at the Shadows the way you do, for one thing. He would only stay out there a few nights a month."

"Did Anton ever mention any particular reason why he

didn't like staying at Shadow Cove? Other than the isolation, I mean?"

"I'm not sure I understand. What sort of reasons?"

"Oh, strange goings-on—"

We had started toward the door, but Robert put his hand on my arm to stop me. "Laura, what are you getting at?"

"Oh, it's nothing." I felt suddenly embarrassed. "I just wondered if he was ever frightened by those silly stories."

"The ghost stories."

"Yes." I forced a laugh.

"Laura, there *is* something out there."

I turned to face him, feeling a queasy emptiness inside. He was the second person whom I considered to be sensible to say the same thing. Aunt Stella had been the first.

"You've seen it, haven't you?" Robert asked.

"I—I've seen something. I don't know what it is. Some woman, I think. She always seems to be crying. And once she—she rode my horse."

"There are vagrants, of course, but not women usually."

"No, she's not a vagrant. I thought she was at first, but I don't think so now. She's often well dressed. Always in white. But she does such strange things. Walks into the sea and—"

Robert took my arms and looked into my eyes, his own expression showing deep concern. "And what, Laura?"

"I'm not sure. She may have come into my house."

"My God! If you're serious, you can't stay out there alone. Move into town if you have to."

"That's out of the question, I'm afraid. You see, I haven't the money to rent anything. My only choice is to stay at the Shadows."

"Then Laura, my dear, my best advice to you, as your accountant and business manager, is to go back to New York. I can arrange to close the business for you."

"No!" I moved away from him. "No, I'm not ready to do that." I twisted the shawl in my hands. "You see, I'm not at all certain the person who came into my house was the woman."

"What?"

"It may have been someone else. Someone who has a key."

"The only person I know of who ever had a key was Chase Bradley and maybe that friend of his. Felix LeFeu."

There was a long silence.

"My God," Robert said. "Bradley! You don't think—"

"I don't know," I said, feeling miserable. "But I *do* know he was out there last night. I—I saw him." I couldn't tell him that he'd spent the night in my house. No matter how innocent it had been, it would be difficult to explain.

"Be careful of Bradley."

"Careful? Why?"

Robert laughed, more cynical than kindly this time. "He's your chief competitor, my dear. Sealy and Bradley Limited. The most ruthless competitors you could ever hope to encounter. You've heard of them, of course."

"Of course, but—"

"I know you know Thomas Sealy. I saw you talking to him at the opera. Don't let the kindly-old-gentleman act fool you. He'll steal your shirt while your back is turned and laugh in your face when you find it missing. He pales in comparison to Chase Bradley, though. Bradley's ruthless to the point of being dangerous. He even killed a man once, you know."

I felt the chill of shock in my bloodstream. "No," I said almost inaudibly. "I didn't know."

"Oh, my dear, please forgive me. You've gone white as a sheet. I forget sometimes that ladies of breeding have delicate sensibilities. I shouldn't have been so blunt. It's just that I think you should—"

"Nonsense!" I said quickly. "I was just surprised, that's all." I was truly embarrassed that he would think I was such a ninny. I hoped he'd tell me more about Chase Bradley killing someone.

"Of course you're surprised, and that's all the more reason you should be forewarned about Bradley," he said. "Especially if you're going to insist on staying out at the Shadows by yourself."

"But you can't be implying Mr. Bradley would try to kill me," I said, hoping to pull more information out of him. "I assume there's some explanation for why he killed before. Otherwise, he'd be a wanted man."

"He claims he was defending himself. That's all I know. A jury believed him, but there are those who think the jury was bought off. His reputation follows him all over the Gulf coast. If you value your life, don't cross him." He took both my hands in his and looked into my eyes. "Please don't go back to the Shadows. I personally don't want to see you leave Galveston, but Shadow Cove is no place for a woman alone."

"Robert, I—"

"No, please, let me finish. As your family accountant, I know your financial situation. I'll tell you again, my advice to you is to forget about this business. You can see yourself that it is not in good financial shape. You have your career in New York. And if you would allow me the pleasure of corresponding with you, then perhaps in time we could—"

"Robert," I interrupted again before he could go further. I knew he was about to suggest a courtship between us. I couldn't deny that the prospect of that pleased me, but I wasn't ready to think about it yet. And I certainly wasn't ready to think of forgetting about the business and of leaving Galveston. "I'm not certain yet what I will do, but I'm not the helpless delicate flower you think I am, so—"

"I never thought you were helpless, my dear, quite the contrary."

"There's a little of my father in me. I can't forget that I'm a King and that King Enterprises was once strong and profitable. I admit I've enjoyed learning about it."

"Laura, take my advice. Leave the shipping business to the men. You're not cut out for it."

"Why not? All this business needs is a little shrewdness and ingenuity. I think I'm rather well suited to this work."

He hesitated a moment, then smiled and brought both my hands to his lips. "You are truly your father's daughter. If you're that determined, all I can say is it will be interesting watching you. Can I drive you home?"

"Oh, no, I have Sir Blanco. I'll be fine."

"Dinner tonight, then. I'll send my carriage."

"Another time, Robert, please. I'm not quite up to it."

"Of course," he said, "but be careful out there, please."

I left after reassuring him that I would indeed be careful, but feeling none too reassured myself of my safety at Shadow Cove. As I walked along the waterfront on my way to the Strand to find a streetcar to take me to the stables, I remembered the small envelope I had shoved into my pocket. Opening it, I found that it was indeed an invitation, but not to a party, as

I had suspected. It was a note from Aunt Stella, inviting me to come by for tea. I was touched that she had asked me. In spite of my misgivings about Chase and in spite of the fact that I had made an excuse not to have dinner with Robert, I longed to see Johnny again, and the tone of the note made it impossible for me to refuse the invitation.

Little Johnnie talks of you constantly, the note said, *and is most eager for another baseball lesson from you. I explained to him, of course, that the weather is getting much too hot for ladies to be indulging in such exercise, but it would please us both if you would stop by for tea before you return home for the evening. I have taken the liberty of telling Johnny that if you agree to honor us with a social call, he will be allowed to give you his greetings and demonstrate his scholarly accomplishments. Sincerely, Miss Stella Beaufort.*

I smiled as I refolded the note, remembering that I had promised Aunt Stella that I would spend a few hours helping Johnny with his lessons. Her message, between the lines of her formal and cordial note, was to remind me of that promise.

When I arrived at the Bradley house, Babette answered the door, but Aunt Stella appeared quickly behind her. She was wearing an afternoon frock of soft lilac that made her plump face look fresh and glowing. Wisps of her silver and reddish hair curled around the edges of her old-fashioned cap in a slightly unruly manner that made her look like a mischievous child.

"Miss Laura! I am so delighted you could come! Do come in. Johnny and I both have been so eager to see you!"

Something bumped and crashed upstairs, followed by the sound of small feet running and Johnny's appearance at the top of the landing. He stopped and gave Aunt Stella a quick guilty look.

"Johnny!" I exclaimed, and held out my arms to him. His broad smile lit up his face as he bounded down the stairs into my arms. We hugged each other like mother and son, and he even gave me a kiss on the cheek.

"How's that baseball game coming?" I asked. "I hear you're in need of another lesson."

"Oh, no!" Johnny said with another quick glance in Aunt Stella's direction. "It's far too warm for ladies."

"Ladies?" I said, glancing around me. "I only see one lady

present. Aunt Stella, of course. Who else could you possibly mean?" I gave him a wink, and he rewarded me with a giggle.

"We don't have to use the rolling pin anymore," he said. "Papa bought us a real bat. A ball, too. Come on, I'll show you."

"Only if you allow me time for a little tea," I said. "It's very unladylike to be hungry, I know, but I'm starved."

"Oh, of course you are, dear," Aunt Stella said, moving about with her usual bustle. "Run along now, Johnny. Let the ladies have a chance to talk. And yes, we are *both* ladies," she insisted with a wink of her own in my direction.

"Oh, but you won't take too long, will you?" Johnny pleaded.

"Not if you give me another kiss," I said and bent down to receive it.

Johnny gave me a quick brush and dashed away. "I'll get everything ready," he called over his shoulder. "Don't be too long."

Aunt Stella laughed and led me to the parlor. "I think you've made a conquest, my dear. The boy has talked of nothing else except Miss Laura since the day he met you."

"He's a darling child. I've missed him."

"Well, we've all missed you, Laura." She poured the tea and handed me a cup. "And speaking of conquests, I don't think Johnny is the only one you've made."

I smiled at her, knowing gossip spreads fast in a small town. There would be talk of my having been seen with Robert.

Aunt Stella pretended to be interested in her teacup. "Chase is really quite smitten."

I almost choked on my tea, but I managed to swallow it and set my cup down carefully in spite of my hands, which had suddenly began to shake.

Aunt Stella glanced up at me. "Are you surprised?"

I cleared my throat uneasily. "I assure you, Mr. Bradley and I—"

"Oh, you can assure me of anything you want, Laura dear, but I know Chase Bradley. He hasn't looked at a woman the way he looks at you since—well, never mind. Anyway, it's more than the way he looks at you. I hear him asking Johnny when he thinks I'm not around. 'Did you see Miss

Laura today?' he asks, or 'Should we ask Miss Laura to have a look at your new bat?' And he was near worried sick about you in that storm."

I hardly knew what to say, but I managed some inane comment about his concern for me being no more than ordinary concern of a gentleman for a spinster alone. The truth was, though, that I wasn't at all sure Chase Bradley was a gentleman, and I couldn't help thinking about the bloody knife he'd used to frighten me, or the fact that Robert had said he was dangerous. I was very grateful to be saved by Johnny, who, at just the right moment, leaned his head mischievously around the corner of the door.

I gave him a tiny wave, and Aunt Stella turned around quickly, ready to scold him and send him away.

"Oh, please, let's invite Johnny to have tea with us," I said. "I do so miss having children around since I left my teaching position."

Aunt Stella, I soon saw, was more soft-hearted than her stern manner indicated, as well as more conniving. She relented with little or no coaxing and immediately pulled out a slate from a desk drawer. She had everything ready for me to hear Johnny's lessons, and she sat watching him like a proud mother hen as he read and did his sums. I dutifully gave him the required lesson in subtraction, and he tried hard to concentrate, but I could tell he was impatient to get on to more interesting things.

"Johnny!" I said, putting the slate away after we had worked for the three-quarters of an hour Aunt Stella had required of us, "I have forgotten my manners. I should have thanked you for the loan of your horse to me."

"Papa says I must let you ride Sir Blanco because you taught me to play baseball. Besides, I can't ride him anyway. Uncle Anton only gave him to me because he died."

"Johnny!" Aunt Stella scolded, appalled as adults often are at a child's candor. "You mustn't be so insensitive about the dead. I'm so sorry, Miss Laura," she said, giving me a frantic, worried look before she turned back to Johnny. "You must apologize, young man."

"It's quite all right," I assured her. "I'm not overly sensitive about my brother's death. We were never very close, and we'd grown apart even more over the years."

"But you don't understand, Miss Laura, Johnny is—Oh,

dear!" She busied herself, gathering up the tea things. "Johnny," she said, glancing up at him. "You must *not* speak ill of the dead."

"But I didn't, Aunt Stella," Johnny protested. "All I said was—"

"That's enough, John Bradley!" She spoke sharply, then started for the kitchen with the tray of tea things without bothering to call Babette. I watched her go with regret. There were several tea sandwiches still untouched on the tray that I had been looking forward to eating.

Aunt Stella's scolding had upset Johnny, and he sat in a pout, barely keeping back the tears as she left the room.

"Johnny," I said, hoping to distract him, "will you show me your new bat?"

He paid no attention to my overture. "I wasn't talking bad! I wasn't!" he insisted.

"Let's forget about all of that, what do you say?"

"She always says that. She always says I mustn't talk about Uncle Anton. But he's dead, ain't he? What's wrong with saying he's dead?"

"I don't know, Johnny," I said, and I managed not to correct his grammar. There was no point in adding insult to injury. "But how about that new bat?"

He smiled at me, just a little, but I took it as a sign he was giving up on his pouting at last.

"Is it a good one?" I coaxed.

"Do you really want to see it?"

"Of course I do."

He jumped out of his chair and ran for the door. "Papa says I have to grow into it, but I'm growing fast."

I'm not sure how long we practiced throwing and hitting the ball, but after a while I began to feel a definite weakness since I hadn't eaten all day, except for the one tiny watercress sandwich. I gave Johnny a hug and a promise to see him again soon. I bid Aunt Stella good evening and was on my way out when I met Chase face to face on the front porch.

"Good evening, Laura," he said, touching his hat. "To what do we owe the pleasure of your visit?"

"Aunt Stella invited me to tea," I said with cool cordiality. I tried to move away. There was something about this man that kept me off-balance, and now did not seem the time to confront him about the disgusting bloody knife. "I was just going. If you'll excuse me, please—"

"Just a minute." He put out his hand and held my arm. I turned to face him and once again was struck by his eyes. I'd seen the chilling glint of his winter-blue gaze before, and it left no doubt in my mind that he was capable of killing a man, just as Robert had said he had done. Now, though, the cold glint was gone, replaced by a smoky restlessness. "I'll see you home."

I was more than a little surprised at his offer. "Why, that's quite unnecessary, Mr.—"

At that moment Johnny burst from the door, and I saw Chase's eyes light up with delight. He bent down to embrace him, then lifted him up in his arms.

"I'm too big to be carried, Papa," Johnny said, but he clung to Chase's neck with affection for a moment before he wriggled himself free. Chase set him down and gave him his familiar tussle of his hair, which led to a playful sparring match between the two of them for a few seconds. They both seemed to have forgotten I was there, and I made a move toward the steps leading off the veranda to the front walk. I scarcely took one step, though, before Chase's hand was on my arm again, stopping me.

"I said I'll see you home." Again I tried to protest, but again he didn't give me a chance. "Sir Blanco is stabled?" he asked.

"Yes, but—"

"I'll tie him behind the carriage." He turned to Johnny and gave him an affectionate pat. "I'll be home in a little while, son. You may wait up for me, but have your supper first."

Chase had me by the arm, leading me to the carriage house in the back, and in the next moment he had me seated in the front with instructions to wait for the carriage to be brought out.

"Mr. Bradley. Chase!" I called after him, trying to stop him, but he continued walking away from me as if he hadn't heard me.

"Won't do no good, ma'am." The voice coming out of nowhere startled me, and I whirled around to see Felix LeFeu standing in front of me. He smiled at me in greeting. "Just do what he says. That makes things more simple for him."

"I'm not interested in making things simple for Mr. Bradley, and I have no intention of doing what he says unless it fits my purposes."

LeFeu responded to my haughtiness with a chuckle and turned his attention toward the carriage, which was now rolling through the double doors of the carriage house with Chase at the reins. Obviously the horse had not yet been unhitched since his arrival, or he would not have emerged so quickly. Chase nodded at LeFeu, more a signal, it seemed, than a greeting, and he spoke to him in what seemed to me to be the same unfamiliar language I had heard LeFeu singing the night he drove me home during the storm. LeFeu replied in English, "Sure thing, Chase." With that he turned to me, and with a formal bow and a look on his face of some secret mirth, he helped me into the carriage beside Chase.

I felt a moment of uncertainty, remembering the warning Robert Thorn had given me, but I realized I was being given an opportunity to confront Chase Bradley at last. I would ease into my prying under the cover of casual conversation.

"That language you spoke," I began. "I heard Felix singing in the same tongue. What is it?"

"Swahili. Felix's mother was brought here as a young girl from her native Africa and sold to a French trader just before the War Between the States. Felix is her son by her master, but she was the daughter of a king in her native land and didn't want her son to forget it. She taught him the language."

"I see," I said, "but the man calls you by your first name."

"Why shouldn't he?" Chase said without looking at me.

"But I thought—"

"You thought that because he is black he is my servant. And servants shouldn't address their masters by their first names."

"Well, of course I didn't—"

"Well, of course you *did*. This is the South. Your assumption is quite natural. But Felix LeFeu is my friend. Perhaps the best friend I've ever had, with the exception of John King."

"You knew my father?" I asked, startled.

"I knew him."

"You were business rivals."

"Not always. Besides, your father was a fair man. He didn't like injustice."

I'd never thought of my father as fair, certainly, but I didn't want to talk about that now. I could see that our conversation was getting me nowhere. I was going to have to try another tactic. I could sense Chase looking at me, though, and before I had a chance to think what to say next, he spoke to me.

"You're curious about what I said to him. Why don't you ask?" I could hear the teasing laughter hiding just under the surface of his words, and I could see the twinkle in his eye. He was having fun at my expense, and I turned away from him with my most practiced haughtiness.

"I'm not curious."

"Forgive me for second-guessing you."

"Unless it was something about a bloody knife and a dead fish," I blurted out, getting right to the point.

He turned to me with a small, puzzled laugh. "What?"

"A childish trick, your leaving that bloody knife and dead fish in my house the morning you left."

"I don't know what you're talking about." I saw his eyes, and God help me, I felt he was telling the truth. He did seem genuinely unaware of what I was talking about. That only made me more frightened and more confused. "Has someone been in your house?"

"I—I'm not sure. Yes, perhaps," I said, feeling foolish. "Vagrants along the beach, as you said."

"You're a fool to stay out there alone. Even Anton knew that." He flicked the reins at the horse's back, showing no signs of turning the carriage around, as if he knew he couldn't change a fool's mind.

There was another long silence before I spoke again. "Felix used to see after my brother when he did choose to stay at the Shadows," I said, still prying in spite of my confusion.

"Yes," Chase said. "Felix was a friend of Anton's as well. Anton used to call him the Magician."

"Felix told me."

"He *is* a magician. The man can work magic with anything mechanical. Always having to help Anton when he locked himself out of that big house."

"Johnny tells me he was fond of my brother as well."

I could sense a change, a tensing in Chase as he sat beside me, and he waited a little longer to answer than I expected. "Johnny was fond of him, yes, and he of Johnny. They were like two children together in many ways."

"But you didn't like my brother."

"You're wrong. I told you we were friends. I was as fond of Anton as Johnny was." He flicked the reins at the horse's back again, bringing the horse up to an even faster trot and causing the carriage to rock and sway enough to make conversation difficult after that. In spite of my blunt questions, I realized I had learned very little, and I was beginning to feel more frustrated than ever.

It was growing dark by the time we reached the Shadows, and Chase insisted upon seeing me into the house. I hadn't the energy to protest. My long day with nothing to eat had robbed me of all stamina, and in fact I was so hungry I felt quite light-headed as we walked up to the door. I used my key to open it and felt a moment of reluctance to enter as I remembered the horror of seeing the bloody knife in the candleholder that morning. But when I looked at the cold white hands, they were cupped and waiting and, to my relief, empty.

I felt another wave of hunger-driven light-headedness, and it was that, I'm sure, that made me sway toward Chase as I turned to face him. He reached for me, as if to steady me, and after that I was not quite sure what happened, except in the next moment I was in his arms, and his face was bending toward mine. I felt his lips on mine, and without realizing it, my arm went around his neck, whether to steady myself or out of some other instinct, I was not sure. His kiss was gentle at first, but I sensed his passion growing as his hand moved along the side of my body and barely touched the side of my breast, lingering there for a moment before moving to my back to press me closer to him. I knew I should stop him, but I didn't. I let him touch me and kiss me, and I kissed him back.

Chase was the one who broke the embrace finally. He pulled away and held both of my shoulders, looking into my eyes as we stood in the shadowy entrance hall.

"You're the one with the magic, Laura." His voice was maddeningly calm and steady, while I felt unable to speak at all. "But your magic won't be strong enough to save you. You've got to leave here."

I tried once again to speak to him, but he was gone, leaving me standing alone in the darkened hall.

Chapter 8

IN the stillness of the thick and salty night, I could hear the monotonous, plaintive song of the gulf through my open window. It was the kind of night I associated with the dreamless, untroubled sleep of childhood. Yet on this night I couldn't sleep. I got up several times and stood at my window, staring into the moonless night at the haze-blunted prickles of starlight and the heaving shadow that was the gulf. There was no apparition crying and walking along the beach, no frightened sounds from Sir Blanco's stable. There was only Chase—his words, his kiss—that haunted me.

Why had I let him kiss me? Why had I allowed him to touch me the way no man had touched me before? Why was his kiss so much more disturbing than Robert's or any other man's had been?

I got into bed and willed myself not to think about him, but he was still very much on my mind when I finally fell asleep. My sleep was short-lived, though. I was awakened suddenly with the uncanny feeling once again that someone was in the house. I listened carefully to the dead still of the night, but I could hear nothing except my own heart pounding so loud it seemed even to drown out the sound of the gulf. My nerves were alert, ready to pick up the noise of a squeaking floor, the soft shuffle of footsteps, any sound at all. Slowly the realization came to me that it was not a sound that had awakened me, but a sensation, an awareness of a presence.

I lay there rigid for several minutes trying to decide what to do. I could push the bureau in front of the door, as I'd done before, but that certainly hadn't been effective in keeping Chase out of my room, so it probably wouldn't be effective for anyone else either.

Was it Chase who had returned now? Was it for the same reason he'd claimed he'd come before—to assure himself of my safety? I'd tried to deny to myself that Chase could have had anything to do with the bloody knife, the frightening apparition, the accident at the wharves. But now, in the heavy, cloying darkness, I could imagine anything—that Chase could be trying to frighten me or kill me. At the very least he wanted me out of Galveston. Not knowing why only added to my fear.

I got out of bed and lit the lamp, as if the light would help me make sense of things. But I could only sit on the edge of the bed, feeling as disconcerted as ever while the feeling that I was not alone in the house persisted.

Without bothering to get a dressing gown or slippers, I picked up the lamp and my ring of keys and started through the house, opening all the doors. I checked all the upstairs rooms first, including the locked bedrooms, but as I held my light high, I could see nothing except the heavy hulking furniture that my mother had chosen to fill the rooms, as if the heavy presence of my father hadn't crowded her life enough. I went downstairs, using the servant's staircase, and made the rounds. Nothing was out of place. I went up again, using the front stairway to satisfy myself that I had searched every nook and cranny of the monstrous house. Still I found nothing.

I got back in bed feeling even more disturbed. Was I losing my mind? Had I only imagined all of it, including the ghostly woman and the bloody knife? I lay very still, hardly breathing, as I listened for sounds and stared at the shadows in my room. No shadow moved, and the sounds were those of the house settling, a shutter blowing in the wind, a night bird, and the ever-present keening of the gulf.

Finally morning came, and I got up in the stingiest light of dawn, anxious for the full light of day when I could think more clearly. By the time I'd had my breakfast and started my ride into town, I did in fact feel better. There'd been no bloody knife to greet me that morning, no dead fish in my kitchen, and I could convince myself now in the light of day that I could eventually find a logical explanation for everything.

I wondered if I could attribute my irrational behavior of the night before, including my reaction to Chase, to the fact that I'd foolishly deprived myself of food and rest. In any event, I was ready to face the day, and I was actually looking forward to the challenge of working more on my plan for turning King Enterprises around.

I arrived at the warehouse office quite early, even before Robert. It was at least an opportunity for me to spend more time with the most current account books that were often unavailable to me because he was working on them. I'd had only a little time that first day to see them at all. I had been going over the books only a short time when I made a puzzling and disturbing discovery. For the past three years Anton had been making regular payments to Chase Bradley. The account was labeled "loan debt." No one, neither Robert nor Chase, had ever mentioned that Anton had borrowed money from Chase. When I added up the amount that had been paid so far, it came to a staggering total of twelve thousand dollars. That was more than I expected to make in my entire lifetime as a teacher. The payments, I saw, had continued even after Anton's death. The money must have been a business loan since it was carried in the business account books rather than in Anton's personal accounts. Obviously it was one the courts hadn't been notified of, since it hadn't been mentioned in the probate proceedings. But why hadn't I been told about this debt either by Chase or Robert?

"You're here early!" Robert had just walked in the door, and he greeted me as he hung his hat and umbrella on the rack. "What a nice surprise to come into the office and find—" He looked at me and then at the books. His smile faded, and a muscle in his jaw tensed. "You've found the loan account."

"Yes." I struggled to keep my voice steady. "I've found the loan account. Why wasn't I told about it?"

Robert walked to his desk and sat down. "I thought it best you not know."

"Why on earth should I not know?"

"I knew it would only trouble you to see how deeply in debt your brother had gotten. I thought you would feel compelled to use your salary to pay the debt off. I was trying to protect you."

"Protect me? That's foolish, Robert. I don't need protecting. I need informing." Slamming my hand down hard on the desktop, I added, "I *must* know what's going on in this business. Everything!"

"I'm sorry, Laura, I only—"

"I appreciate your concern," I said, standing up and walking around my desk, trying to calm my frustration, "but I must have your confidence as well. Now tell me, why was the money borrowed from Chase Bradley and not the bank? Did the bank refuse him?"

"It had nothing to do with the bank refusing him. It was an arrangement between Chase and Anton." Robert wore a troubled expression, and I could see beads of perspiration on his face.

"An arrangement? What do you mean?"

"Go back to New York," Robert said. "Don't ask any more questions. Stay away from Chase Bradley. You saw what happened to your brother—" Robert looked stricken, as if he knew he'd said too much.

"What happened to my brother?" I was barely able to speak above a whisper. "What are you saying?"

"It wasn't an accident, Laura."

I felt a sudden void in my chest. "You're saying that he was murdered?"

"Laura—"

"Did it have something to do with this money Anton was paying to Chase?" I had regained my voice now, and I was all but screaming. "Was it some kind of blackmail?"

Robert shook his head and turned away from me.

"Why would anyone blackmail Anton?" I insisted. "Why doesn't someone tell me the truth?"

Robert turned around and came to my side and put his hand on my arm. I shook it off. I needed answers, not comfort now. "That doesn't make sense," I said. "Why would Chase murder him? That would only mean the extortion payments would stop. If that's what they were."

"Please sit down, Laura," Robert said, leading me to a chair. "I didn't want you to know the circumstances of your brother's death. I had hoped to spare you that pain." He sat on the edge of my desk and held my hand. "Yes," he continued, "there was some suspicion of murder. Anton drowned, yet he was a strong swimmer. It was never proved that he was murdered, though. There wasn't enough evidence to implicate Bradley or anybody for that matter, and the sheriff finally concluded that Anton must have been drunk. He had a reputation for overindulging from time to time, although there was no conclusive proof that he was drunk the night he died."

"But even if he was murdered, that still doesn't answer my question. Why would Chase do it? Why would he cut off his source of money?"

"I'd heard him threaten Anton before, threaten to take the business away from him. And there's no denying Sealy and Bradley has wanted to take over King Enterprises. It could be a profitable business in the right hands; you've seen that yourself. Bradley's the dangerous one, but old Sealy is a ruthless dog. He's always wanted to get his fangs into King Enterprises. When John King died, I think he and Bradley saw a chance to get it. I think they must have gotten Anton in debt to them somehow, although I don't know what Anton did with the money. But their plan must have been to weaken Anton by bleeding him dry, then take over the business. Only something made Bradley change his tactics. I don't know what. Maybe he just got greedy and wanted Anton out of the way sooner. But I think he killed him, thinking he could foreclose on the business. Except I've kept up the loan payments. There's no grounds for foreclosure. But now that you're here, Bradley and Sealy are going to try to get the business from you, one way or another. Get out now, Laura, before they hurt you. I'll keep the business running for you as long as I can, but I don't want you hurt."

"How can I leave?" I said, my voice shaking. "How can I leave without knowing what happened to my brother?"

"I warn you, Laura, don't stir up the past," Robert said.

I knew he was right—that I would be wiser to leave things alone, to go back to my old job, but I also knew that, in spite of my estranged relationship with my brother, he was my flesh and blood, and I couldn't leave the questions surrounding his death unanswered.

The outer office of Sealy and Bradley Ltd. was nicely furnished in mahogany and dark leather. A pale young man sat at the desk, his thin body looking as if it were held together by the suspender straps looped over his shoulders and the wire rims of his glasses. He gave a nervous start when he looked up and saw me. He stood up immediately and fidgeted with his jacket, which he'd snatched off the back of his chair. Apparently he was unable to think what he should say to me, so I took pity on the poor man and told him I was there to see Chase Bradley.

He was sorry that Mr. Bradley wasn't in, he said, but would I like to see Mr. Sealy instead. I was about to tell him I'd come back a little later in the hopes that Chase would be in when Thomas Sealy came out of his office. Seeing me, he greeted me with the same warmth he'd shown when I'd first met him on board ship.

"Miss Laura!" he exclaimed, holding out both his arms. He gave me a very proper embrace with a touch of his cheek to mine. "What a nice surprise to see you here! Come into my office, please, and tell me to what I owe this pleasure. Samuel, see that no one disturbs us, and if there are any of those little cakes my daughter Elizabeth sent over, bring a nice one for Miss Laura."

Before I could protest, he had ushered me into his office, and Samuel had handed me a plate with a tiny delicately iced cake on it. We passed pleasantries, and I had to assure him that I was doing well and that I wasn't too lonely at the Shadows. I didn't mention the strange goings-on, for the same reasons I was reluctant to mention them to anyone. I assumed that he would pass it off as "female hysteria" as William Hienz had done. I also agreed with him that *La Tosca* had been delightful. All the while my mind was whirling. Was this all a charade? Was Thomas Sealy as ruthless as Robert had suggested? He certainly didn't seem so to me. Perhaps it would be better if I waited until I could speak to Chase directly, if he was, as Robert implied, the force behind all the evil that had befallen Anton.

I didn't have a chance to ask any of those questions, though. Mr. Sealy had by then begun talking about a party he and his wife were planning.

"The missus and I would consider it an honor to have you attend, and our daughter is most eager to meet you. She's all excited about helping her mother plan this to-do. She and Mrs. Sealy will be disappointed, of course, that I've spilled the beans before you have the formal invitation, but you mustn't let on I've done it." He laughed and gave me a jovial wink. He seemed like such a pleasant fellow, not at all the "ruthless dog" Robert had described. "Now," he said, leaning back in his chair with a casual air. "Do tell me what has brought you here."

"I came to see Chase," I said, deciding just at that instant that truthfulness was the better plan. "There's a matter concerning Anton's affairs I need to discuss with him."

"The loan perhaps?"

I was too stunned to speak at first. I hadn't expected such an open acknowledgment. "Yes," I finally managed to say.

Mr. Sealy nodded. I could see that the congenial expression he'd worn when I first arrived had suddenly been replaced with a flinty-eyed seriousness. "Chase is in Houston. Company business. But I'm sure he'll be willing to talk to you about it when he returns."

"I am quite willing to discuss it with you if—"

"I know very little about the matter," Mr. Sealy said. "It was a private transaction between Chase and your brother."

"Very well," I said, setting the dessert plate aside and feeling more confused than ever. "Then I'll be going. I'm sorry to have disturbed you, Mr. Sealy, but would you be kind enough to tell Mr. Bradley when he returns that I wish to see him?"

"Please sit down, Miss King." The tone of his voice compelled me to look at him. "There's something I want to discuss with you. It's about King Enterprises."

I didn't move, not even my eyes, and I gave him my full attention.

"I'm interested in acquiring it."

Robert's warning flashed into my mind.

"What makes you think it's for sale?" I asked, although I was fully aware that Mr. Sealy had not said he wanted to *buy* the business. He had said simply that he wanted to acquire it.

His eyes seemed to chuckle. "Now, if that doesn't sound just like something old John King would have said. You really are your father's daughter. Please sit down, Miss Laura. If you don't, then good manners will compel me to stand, too, and at my age I find I prefer to sit."

I did sit down, although reluctantly. I feel a woman is at a disadvantage seated in front of a man behind a large executive desk, and I knew I needed every advantage I could manage.

"Now, you'll have to admit, Miss Laura, that King Enterprises is not on good standing. It's pretty well common knowledge in the business world, and if you've been going over the accounts, then you know it's true."

"I won't deny it's not the business it was when my father was alive," I said carefully. My breath was coming in short, shallow gasps, but I was doing my best to conceal it. If Robert had been right about Thomas Sealy, then I couldn't let him see any weakness in me.

"Yes, well, you mentioned to me recently that you're anxious to get back to New York. Nobody can blame you for that. Galveston has its rough edges, especially for a refined lady living alone, and heaven knows you wouldn't want to live at the Shadows alone."

"Why would you say that, Mr. Sealy?"

"Why, it's so desolate. And it's not safe, Miss Laura. It's not safe for a woman to be out there all alone. Chase has told me you've been frightened."

I was more than a little uncomfortable about the idea of the two of them discussing me, and I wondered just how much Chase had told him.

"Chase was concerned about me during the storm," I said, choosing my words carefully, "but there was no need. I've weathered them before." I wasn't about to tell him how frightened I had really been.

"In any event, Miss Laura," Mr. Sealy continued, "in light of the difficulties you're facing, I'm prepared to make you a reasonable offer for the business."

"Am I to understand, then, that you feel King Enterprises still has potential, Mr. Sealy? In spite of the current state of affairs?"

"In the right hands, yes."

"I quite agree with you."

His face lit up. "Wonderful! I will have my attorney draw up a proposal, and I think you'll find my offer quite generous. Of course you—"

"You don't understand, Mr. Sealy. I'm saying I believe King Enterprises is already in the right hands."

"But—"

"I have some ideas for getting the business back on track."

He looked at me with renewed interest, and there was a hint of surprise in his eyes. "Ah, yes, but Miss Laura, a woman—"

"A woman is as capable as a man."

"Perhaps so, my dear. In some areas at least. But you will need capital, and raising it can be difficult, especially for a lady in a man's world."

"You may be right," I said, standing and pulling on my gloves, "but as you said, I am John King's daughter, and I am going to try."

Thomas Sealy jumped to his feet. "Miss Laura." He hurried to my side to see me to the door. "You know I wish you only the best, but a woman—a lady of your position must follow certain conventions."

"I appreciate your good wishes, Mr. Sealy, and it's been a pleasure visiting with you," I said as I walked to the door.

"You will be at the party, won't you?" he called after me.

I hesitated. "Of course," I said, "but don't expect me to follow conventions. I'm coming without an escort." I was out the door before he had a chance to respond.

I was very unsettled as I rode Sir Blanco home. There were so many things to think about, not the least of which was Thomas Sealy's offer to buy King Enterprises. Although his offer seemed perfectly respectable, I couldn't get Robert's warning out of my head. But I also knew I couldn't make an intelligent judgment because I didn't have all the information I needed. Someone, maybe everyone, was hiding something from me, and all those ghostly appearances and bloody knives were not just vagrants playing tricks, but part of a plan to frighten me away, to keep me from finding out about that hidden truth.

Chapter 9

"ARE you all right?" Robert asked when I walked into the King Enterprises office the next day.

"Of course," I lied, although I was well aware that the strain was showing on my face. Robert must have seen it, too.

"What is it, Laura?" he persisted. "Has something else happened?"

"No. Nothing's happened." I removed my hat and gloves and refused to look at him.

"It's that house, isn't it?" he persisted. "I know you don't feel comfortable there, and after that story you told me about seeing someone—"

"I'm sure there's nothing wrong. Just vandals, as I said. I'm more careful now to keep the doors locked." I had to fight to keep my voice calm. I was feeling very agitated.

"You've got to leave that place, Laura. You can't let it do this to you!"

"Leave?" My voice was a shrill shout, and I knew my control had shattered. "Isn't that just what they want? Didn't you warn me this is what they'd do? Well, I'm not leaving and I'm not going to abandon my business."

As soon as I saw the look on Robert's face, I was sorry for my outburst. The tension and the lack of sleep had taken too much of a toll on me.

"I'm sorry," I said, turning away from him. I couldn't bear to face him after making such a fool of myself. "I shouldn't have snapped at you. I—"

"It's all right, Laura." He put his hands on my arms and turned me around. "Let's forget it, all right? Let's not even talk about the Shadows. How about something more pleasant? How about letting me take you to lunch?"

I looked up at him and managed a slight smile. He was offering an olive branch. The least I could do was accept it. "Of course," I said. "I'd be happy to."

"Good." He gave my arm a reassuring squeeze. "I know just the place."

Our luncheon was delightful. Robert knew the best places, and he was an amusing conversationalist, although by the time we had finished our rather long lunch, I couldn't think of anything of substance that we had talked about. Besides that, I was a little light-headed from having drunk more than my usual one glass of wine. The wine seemed to have an even stronger effect on me since I was still tired, and in fact I found I couldn't work at all that afternoon and had to leave early.

I still needed to shop for a dress for the Sealys' party, though. I was determined to attend. I had to let everyone know that I wasn't buckling under the strain of running a business, and I had to let Thomas Sealy and Chase Bradley know I wasn't going to be frightened or intimidated by cheap tricks. Furthermore, if Chase returned from Houston when Thomas Sealy said he would, then he would be sure to be at the party, and I still wanted to confront him about the loan.

To my dismay, I found nothing I could afford to wear to the party, and I went home emptyhanded. The next morning I came to town early with a plan to shop the one or two remaining stores I'd not gotten to the day before. I'd no sooner entered the first store than Aunt Stella came in, and she insisted on helping me shop.

"Why, none of these suits you," she said, glancing through the stock, "but I do have an idea. Let's make you a gown."

"Oh, but I don't have time. I couldn't possibly—"

"Nonsense!" she said. "There's plenty of time. Come along with me."

She took my arm and literally pulled me along to a dry-goods store where she picked out a length of ivory satin and matching lace. Before I could protest, it was cut from the bolt, wrapped in brown paper, and tucked under Aunt Stella's arm.

"But what about payment?" I asked as we walked out of the store.

"The bill will be sent in a day or two. I'll let you know, of course."

"Aunt Stella, please, you don't understand. I don't think I can afford—"

"Now, now, dear, let's not discuss it. It always gives me such a headache to talk of money. Come along now. We've got work to do."

Within a few minutes her carriage had delivered us to Chase Bradley's home, and I found myself standing on a chair while she draped the lovely satin around me. With her mouth full of pins, she told me to stand still or to hold this arm or that arm up while her fingers flew, sticking pins here and there.

In a little while Johnny came home, and the two of us sat on the floor in the sewing room playing games and reading and listening to the whir of Aunt Stella's sewing machine while I waited for fittings. It was wonderful to forget the shipping business for a while and to give no thought to the fear that engulfed me when I was at home. In fact, I can't think when I'd had a lovelier time, but by the time it was almost dusk and time for me to go home, I realized that yet another day had passed without my having even looked at the accounts of King Enterprises.

"Come by in the morning for a final fitting," Aunt Stella said as I prepared to leave. "It's going to be lovely. Chase is going to have the prettiest girl at the party."

I glanced at her. "Chase?"

"Yes. He told me before he left that he was planning to attend. So naturally I put two and two together."

"But I'm not going with him."

"Then who—" Aunt Stella's expression grew stern. "Not that Robert Thorn!"

"No, not Robert Thorn," I said, pulling on my gloves. "I'm going without an escort."

Aunt Stella gave me an indecipherable look, then with a clucking of her tongue, she turned away, leaving Johnny and Babette to see me out.

The dress was ready for the final fitting by noon the next day, and it was indeed lovely, every bit as pretty as the one Chase had bought. I was determined, though, that his money would not buy this one, and I made it a point of leaving some cash with Aunt Stella. She accepted it none too happily, but she was already in a gloomy mood anyway.

"It's a shame," she said, looking at me and shaking her head as I modeled the dress. "A shame that Chase would be such a fool. It's always business before pleasure with that man."

"Oh? From my observation that's not *always* the case." I hoped I didn't sound too eager, but I hoped Aunt Stella would take the bait and explain a little about Rachel without my having to pry.

"Well, naturally every man has his diversions," she said, sounding somewhat distracted as she stood back and tilted her head to one side to study the fit of the dress. "And of course there's Johnny. The light of his life, I tell you. I'm thankful for that!"

She had refused the bait, and I didn't quite have the courage to pry further about Rachel. I couldn't help wondering, though, if it was true that she was just a "diversion," as Aunt Stella had hinted. It also made me wonder if the kiss Chase and I shared that night he'd seen me home had been just another diversion for him. "Chase does seem awfully fond of Johnny," I said, changing the subject to what I thought was a safe topic. "In fact, he seems like an entirely different person around him."

"I expect that surprises you," Aunt Stella said. "I expect you've heard the gossip."

"Gossip?"

"About the man Chase killed."

I was momentarily taken off-guard and was unable to say anything. All I could manage was a confused and uncomfortable look.

"Oh, no need to feel guilty about the gossip," she said with a wave of her hand. "It's all around town. He killed the man all right, and it was self-defense, no matter what anyone says. It was before I came here to live, so I didn't know anything about it at the time, but I *do* know Chase. He's like a son to me. He wouldn't have killed him if he hadn't been forced into it." She leaned forward and pointed a finger at me for emphasis. "It wouldn't have changed him the way it did if he'd killed him in cold blood the way some say he did."

"There was a trial," I said. "He was found not guilty. Wasn't that enough?"

"Oh, there was a trial all right, but there's people believe the jury was bought. But it's just his enemies who say that. And there's enemies to be made in the business world. The man he killed was a business rival. A cotton merchant from Houston, claimed Chase was cheating. Pulled a gun on him. And Chase pulled his and killed him in self-defense."

"Weren't there any witnesses?"

"Of course. Felix LeFeu saw it all. And he testified in Chase's defense. But he's a black man, my child. Not all white men hold him credible. Chase's reputation for being tough with his competitors didn't help him either. Of course he's tough, but he's fair. He doesn't go around killing the competition. The jury failed to convict him, but like I say, there's still those that believe he killed in cold blood."

I felt a sudden chill. *Was* Chase Bradley capable of resorting to murder to get rid of his competition? Robert Thorn seemed to think he was. Aunt Stella didn't, but then, didn't Aunt Stella have a blind spot where Chase Bradley was concerned? After all, he was by her own admission like a son to her.

Aunt Stella had the dress finished the next day, and it was beautiful. Paying for it had left me in quite serious straits financially, but the dress was so perfect that I felt the sacrifice was worth it. Besides, if I was going to carry through with my plan to bring King Enterprises back, I would need to look right at this party. I remembered my father dressing in the best money could buy and insisting Anton and I do the same. Part of being successful, he always said, was looking the part.

I knew as I dressed myself for the evening that I looked the part. The ivory color of the dress was flattering to my complexion and hair, and in spite of the fact that I'd lost sleep recently, there was a glow to my skin. I could at least conceal the dark circles with a little powder. The truth was, the sea air seemed to agree with me, and I actually thought I'd gained a little weight. At least my bosom seemed fuller. Or was that the skillful cut of the dress Aunt Stella had managed that allowed just the hint of a full, soft curve to show above the ivory lace at the top?

I knew I couldn't be so frivolous as to get carried away with ivory satin and dipping necklines, though. Another part of success was careful attention to business—something King Enterprises had obviously lacked under Anton. But I was confident that I could turn things around, and I had to admit, I was enthusiastic about it. I knew without a doubt that my leave of absence from Mrs. Swathmore's Academy for Girls in New York was going to be extended indefinitely.

I looked at myself in the mirror one more time, checking the fit of the dress and the hairstyle I'd learned from Babette, when I heard a knock at the door. I knew it was the carriage I'd hired, and I hurried downstairs to open the door. My excitement about my new dress and the prospect of the party were marred slightly when I reached the bottom of the stairs and my eyes fell upon the marble hands. In my mind's eye I saw the bloody knife again, and once more I had the eerie sensation that I was not alone. I forced myself to try to forget it as I opened the door to the carriage driver.

It was amazing even to me how much a new dress and the thought of a party could brighten my mood. My spirits remained high on my ride to town, and I had forgotten the eerie atmosphere of my dark castle by the time the carriage arrived at the Sealys' grand mansion on Broadway.

The house was palatial with its sweeping marble staircase and deep, rich wood paneling and fine Oriental rugs. The tables were laden with delicacies, and the champagne flowed freely, all representative of the new wealth that was becoming a part of Galveston. Many of the guests showed off that wealth as well. There were men in formal tails, including Robert, who had not yet spotted me, and there were women in gowns of silk and satin that, if they hadn't come from the finest European markets, at least rivaled those that did. But there were also men in boots and rough-cut trousers with even rougher edges to their accents and grammar, as if to remind us all that Galveston was still a part of Texas, still a part of the frontier.

I was enjoying myself, talking with Aunt Stella and some of the women she introduced me to. Mr. Hienz walked over to give me his greeting and to apologize for the weather, and another gentleman in woolen trousers and black boots engaged me in conversation about his cotton plantation and the problems of shipping cotton from Galveston versus the cheaper system of rail and barge set up in Houston. As we talked, I saw Rachel Blackburn sweep past me on the dance floor in the arms of Robert Thorn. Rachel was radiantly beautiful in a satin dress the color of persimmons and overlaid with the most delicately etched lace I'd ever seen. She threw her head back and laughed at something Robert said, and her sparkling laughter made her seem even more beautiful.

As soon as the music stopped, men crowded around her, hoping for the next dance. She was definitely the belle of the ball. While I watched, Chase Bradley appeared from somewhere and bowed gallantly in front of her. She greeted him with an amused smile and a coquettish tilt of her head, and then, completely ignoring all her other admirers, she floated into his arms.

Chase was particularly handsome in his dark formal clothes, and Rachel looked like a delicate rose in his arms. As they danced passed me, Chase caught my eye. He smiled, an amused smile, I thought, and gave me a nod. I was embarrassed, of course, to have him see me watching him, but I tried to cover my embarrassment with a polite and proper nod of my own.

"You're John King's daughter, aren't you?" a voice said, seeming to come out of nowhere and giving me a jolt.

"I beg your pardon?" I turned quickly and saw a youngish gentleman in a clerical collar standing next to me.

"I'm Pastor Browning," he said with a formal bow. "Pastor of the Presbyterian Church. I understand your father was one of the founders of the church. Before I came, of course," he said, peering at me over his spectacles.

"I'm happy to meet you, Pastor," I said. "Aunt Stella speaks well of you. To hear her talk, when you speak, God himself listens."

His face colored slightly, but he looked pleased. "Well, you certainly have all the charm she attributes to you. Oh, and by the way," he said, offering me a chair and sitting down next to me, "I wanted to mention to you that the church is planning a dinner to serve the poor next Saturday night in St. John's Hall, and I need every able-bodied woman I can find—" Pastor Browning blushed again. "No, I didn't phrase that quite right," he said. "What I meant to say is . . . well, how are you at wielding a knife?"

My eyes widened, and the pastor appeared even more flustered. "Oh dear, I seem to be saying it all wrong," he said. "What I meant to say is, we need women in the kitchen. To cut up the chickens, you know—"

The pastor seemed so rattled I was glad for both our sakes when Robert came to my rescue. "I believe this is our dance," he said, pulling me to my feet. Pastor Browning immediately stood as well and bowed formally.

"I'll give your invitation some thought," I said as Robert whirled me away.

"And I'd be pleased to see you in services Sunday," the pastor called to me with a little wave.

Robert was a wonderful dancer, and although it had been years since I'd been on a dance floor, he made me feel completely at ease. As the music ended, I found myself face to face with Chase and Rachel.

"Good evening, Laura, Robert," Chase said. "You two ladies have met, I believe."

"Yes," I said. "Mr. Hienz introduced us, remember? How do you do, Miss Blackburn."

"Chase, darling," Rachel said, ignoring me, "I'd like some punch."

"Of course," Chase said, but there had been a moment of hesitancy in his voice. He turned to me and asked, "Can I get you some as well?"

I was about to refuse his offer, but Robert spoke up. "I'll get it, Laura." He was speaking to me, I assumed, but his eyes never left Rachel. She, however, didn't even glance at him. She had turned her attention to me.

"Lovely dress," I said, feeling a bit tense under her gaze. "The color becomes you."

I saw that slight, haughty smile again that I'd come to associate with her. "You're wise to wear ivory," she said. "It's such a safe color. Even the most sallow of complexions manages to look passable."

I was speechless for a moment, but then I remembered I was a King. I straightened my shoulders. "Certainly no lady of breeding would have uttered those words for any other reason than to compliment my wisdom. But I confess, in your case I don't know whether to say thank you or not."

This time it was she who was speechless while I held her firmly in my gaze. I saw her pretty mouth tremble for a moment, and I regretted my pettiness. But then that beautiful mouth hardened. "You think you're clever, Miss King," she said. "Your brother always thought he was clever, too. But he wasn't clever enough, was he? None of us, it seems, is clever enough to escape death." With that remark she walked away.

I was still watching her, feeling somewhat nonplussed when Chase returned, holding a cup of punch in each hand. I know he saw immediately that Rachel was gone, but he showed no surprise. Instead he set both the cups on a nearby table and bowed slightly.

"May I have this dance?" he asked, and without waiting for me to reply, he took me in his arms.

"But I should wait for Robert. He will be back with—"

"Robert be damned," Chase said as his arm tightened around my waist. "I've waited for this all night. You're by far the most beautiful woman here. You have all the other women seething with envy and the men, I would wager, waiting in line to dance with you."

I laughed, surprised that he was flirting. "That's where you're wrong, Mr. Bradley," I said, aware that he was leading us toward wide double doors that opened onto the veranda. "I'm afraid I've been a virtual wallflower. My time has been taken in conversations about housekeeping, dressmaking, and the cutting up of chickens for the Presbyterian Church."

"I find it hard to believe that the most beautiful and most desirable woman here would ever be a wallflower."

"You're very flattering, Mr. Bradley." By this time we were on the veranda, away from the sound of the crowd. Even the music seemed muted.

"I never flatter, Miss King," he said. "I always say exactly what I mean. That's a trait we share in common, I trust."

"What do you mean?"

He took my arm and led me to the railing. "Tom told me you were in to see me recently. He said you asked about the loan I made to Anton."

I had expected to have to broach the subject myself, and for one brief, irrational moment I was sorry that he had spoiled the mood. Chase Bradley hadn't brought me out onto the veranda because of the moonlight; he wanted to discuss business. All of his flirting and even the kiss a few days before had obviously been to soften me up for what was coming now. I couldn't let that matter to me, though. After all, I wanted to discuss business, too.

"Yes," I said, taking a step away. It seemed important to distance myself from him. "I did want to discuss the money you loaned to Anton. Could you give me some more information?

According to the account books Robert keeps, it was a rather large amount, and less than half of it has been paid, but if you could just tell me—"

"I consider the debt paid in full." He pulled a cigar from his pocket and lit it.

I turned toward him quickly. "I beg your pardon?"

"You owe me nothing," he said, studying the red fire at the end of the cheroot.

"Robert told me the loan was made to King Enterprises as a business loan, so of course I will repay—"

"The loan was not a business loan. It was a personal matter between Anton and me. And I gave Anton papers clearing him of the debt."

"But it's carried on the books as a business expense, and payments are still—"

"It doesn't matter how Anton carried it in his books. It was a personal loan. It had nothing to do with King Enterprises, and it was damned unwise of your brother even to discuss it with Robert Thorn."

"My brother was not known for his wisdom in business matters, obviously, Mr. Bradley, but—"

"I said the matter is closed, and why do you insist on calling me Mr. Bradley? I told you, my name is Chase." He dropped his freshly lit cigar to the wooden floor and crushed it with his heel as he moved toward me. "Look at that," he said. He was standing behind me, very close, and pointing over my shoulder.

I turned to look and saw a red crescent moon spewing out a long, undulating trail of starfire in the sky over the gulf. I'd forgotten how the ugly smoke belched from the smokestacks of steamships could be transformed at night into a comet shower of sparks dancing across the sky. And I'd forgotten how the haze could turn the moon red. I knew Broadway was too far away to allow me to hear the gulf, but I could sense it. I knew the long gray waves were whispering their song, eternal as a heartbeat. The heartbeat of the earth, I thought, the heartbeat of creation. The primitive, sensuous atmosphere of the night, the perfume of the oleanders, the kiss of the moist southern breeze combined into an intoxicating essence. I felt Chase move closer, or had I swayed involuntarily back against him?

"Beautiful, isn't it?" His voice was a hoarse whisper.

I moved, thinking I would break the spell, but when I turned toward him, I found myself looking up into his eyes. My face was very close to his, our lips almost touching.

"Yes," I whispered.

I know that he was about to kiss me, and I can't deny that at that moment I wanted him to, but something unexplainable happened, and I sensed the change in him even before he moved away.

"Enjoy it while you can," he said. He leaned forward, placing both hands on the railing for support as he gazed toward the fire-streaked horizon. "You won't have this kind of night once you get back to New York."

He'd broken the spell, and I felt shattered as well. "No, I don't suppose I would." My voice was breathy and unsteady as I fought to calm the churning turbulence inside me. "That is, if I choose to leave," I managed to add.

Chase straightened suddenly and turned toward me. "What do you mean, *if* you choose to leave?"

"Why do you and everybody else in this town keep insisting that I leave? Why is it anyone's business whether I choose to go back to New York or stay here?"

"My God, Laura, if you knew—"

"If I knew what?"

"It's for your own good," he said abruptly. "Haven't you realized that yet? You and others could be hurt, can't you see that?"

"No! I can't see anything, and I have no idea what you're getting at."

He took my arm without answering me and led me back toward the door to the ballroom.

"What are you doing?" I demanded.

"I'm taking you back to your escort."

I tried to pull my arm away from his grasp. "I have no escort."

"What do you mean, no escort?"

"What do *you* mean, I could get hurt?"

Chase's mouth had become a hard thin line, and his face had grown ashen, but he didn't answer my question. Instead he left me standing next to a group of women and strode away. I watched him winding his way through the sea of satin and silk and formal coats on the dance floor, but I was quickly distracted by Elizabeth Sealy, who wanted to ask my opinion about the development of a stretch of the beach for the purposes of swimming and recreation and to ask about styles for bathing wear for ladies I might have observed in New York.

"It seems to me that Galveston could prosper from tourism as much as from shipping, and wouldn't a line of swimming wear that was uniquely Galvestonian be interesting? Something comfortable, yet elegant. Just like our city."

The more she talked, the more I realized she was more than a vapid female interested only in the latest fashions, as her father had portrayed her. Given the chance, I knew she would be every bit as shrewd in business as her very shrewd father. I was interested in her ideas, but my attention was divided. I was still looking for Chase. He had left me feeling even more confused and troubled than I had been before.

"Laura, my dear!" Thomas Sealy waved to me from the refreshment table and began making his way toward me. "I've found you at last! You've been elusive, haven't you? All your time taken up with your admirers, no doubt. Ah, the two of you!" He extended both his arms as if to encompass Elizabeth and me as well. "Two of the most beautiful ladies present!"

Elizabeth laughed and gave her father an affectionate peck on the cheek. "I've caught on to your flattery, Papa. You think you can distract me with it, don't you? Well, I'm not going to let you off the hook. I'm still going to insist you talk to me about financing my proposal."

"You're a pretty little flibbertigibbet," he said, tweaking her cheek. "Wanting me to finance ladies' bloomers. The very idea!"

"Not bloomers, Papa. Bathing wear."

Thomas Sealy laughed, the hearty, jovial sound I'd come to associate with him. "My little girl," he said, giving her a one-armed hug as he winked at me. "Used to sew her own doll clothes when she was a child, and she never outgrew it."

I saw the look on Elizabeth's face and saw her frustration, but she never got the chance to express it aloud because her father had turned his attention away to signal the orchestra.

"May I have your attention, please," he said, his voice overriding the noise of the crowd. The orchestra now had obeyed his signal to stop the music, and he did indeed have everyone's attention. "Just a brief announcement," he said, "and a toast," he added as he picked up a champagne glass from the tray of a passing waiter. "I have the pleasure of introducing you all to a special guest, Miss Laura King, who has come to Galveston for the unhappy duty of settling her family estate after her brother's untimely death. This little gathering was planned long before her arrival, but it seemed a perfect opportunity to honor her. To you, Laura, the last of the Kings of Galveston."

The crowd erupted into a somber chorus of "Here, here," as glasses were raised, and I felt a moment of discomfort at being the center of attention.

"The last of the Kings!" someone shouted. "The sooner we're rid of all of you, the better. Old John King was a scoundrel!"

The crowd erupted again in a mixture of embarrassed murmurs and shouts—whether they were contradicting or agreeing with the heckler, I couldn't tell.

"You've not seen the last of the Kings yet," I said, unable to stand it any longer as my voice rose above the noise. The crowd grew quieter, and once again I felt a twinge of nervousness. "Your send-off for me may be a bit premature, I'm afraid." As I spoke, I spotted Chase standing near the front door with a small cluster of other guests. I kept my eyes locked on him as I spoke. "I've decided not to leave Galveston." A hushed murmur rippled through the crowd. Chase showed nothing on his face, not even the flinch of a muscle. "I have plans to revitalize King Enterprises," I continued, "including expansion to the port of Houston. I'm afraid it will be a while before you've seen the last of the Kings of Galveston."

It was impossible to miss the sense of surprise and excitement that swept through the crowd now. There were cheers and shouts of "Long live the Kings." Chase Bradley, however, didn't speak. Out of the corner of my eye I saw a flash of persimmon red as Rachel rushed out of the ballroom. And then, to my surprise, I saw Robert hurry after her. I had sensed Thomas Sealy's eyes on me the entire time, as if I were a performer he'd hired to amuse his guests, and when I glanced at him now, I saw that he was laughing.

Chapter 10

FOR a while guests crowded around me expressing polite and sometimes feigned enthusiasm that I would be staying in Galveston. Whoever had shouted the insult about my father had not made himself known. Underneath all the convention, though, I sensed an air of surprise.

"We'll be so pleased to have you stay in Galveston, ma'am," said one gentleman, "but you must know the shipping business is no place for a lady." He was, I knew, expressing what others were feeling.

"Why, sir, I don't know why not," I said, surprised at how my accent had slipped out to meet the occasion.

"Delicate flowers such as yourself can never see the dangers," he answered. "The rough characters along the wharves aren't the only thing. It will come down to you having to haggle over contracts and prices—you have no idea, my dear."

"You might be surprised at the ideas I have, sir," I said, giving him the most cordial smile I could manage. I glanced away and spotted Chase again. He was deep in conversation with Mr. Sealy. Judging from the expressions on their faces and their animated gestures, it appeared that they were arguing. When I saw Mr. Sealy gesture with his hand toward me, I sensed that the argument had something to do with me and possibly with the announcement I had just made. Perhaps, I thought, they were worried about competition. Or, if Robert had been right, perhaps they were worried that taking over King Enterprises wouldn't be so easy after all.

Whatever it was, I didn't want to think about it now, and I didn't want to have to defend myself for being a woman in business to one more person either. In fact, all I wanted to do at the moment was go home and rest—if rest was possible at the

Shadows. I was no "delicate flower," as so many men insisted, but I couldn't deny that I was tired. I knew, though, that it had more to do with the sleepless nights and the disturbing events at the Shadows than with running a business.

I made up my mind to slip away from the party as soon as possible. I would leave Thomas Sealy to argue with Chase Bradley and give Mrs. Sealy my thanks for the invitation. As I made my way toward her, I was intercepted by Elizabeth.

"I think it's wonderful!" she said, grasping my arm. "Did you see the way Papa's mouth flew open ? I thought he was going to have apoplexy, and then he acted amused, as if it were a joke. Papa doesn't take women seriously. He sees us as—well, as—"

"As fragile flowers, maybe? Ridiculous! There's nothing fragile about us, and you can tell your papa I said so. You can also tell him I think he's making a big mistake if he doesn't finance your business." I gave her hand an affectionate squeeze. "Excuse me, I see your mother over there, and I want to thank her for the invitation before I leave."

"You're leaving?"

"I'm a bit tired, Elizabeth, but I certainly don't want any of these men to know it."

She gave me an understanding smile. "I won't tell a soul," she said. "But I'm glad you came. Perhaps we could meet again, and I could ask your advice."

"My advice?"

"About starting my own business."

I agreed to meet her for luncheon and give her the benefit of my limited experience, and I knew I was looking forward to it. I saw in her a woman of similar interests to mine with whom I could be friends. Perhaps my life in Galveston would not be so dreary after all.

As I rode home in the carriage after taking my leave, I couldn't help but think about how complicated my life had become. I had expected to settle the estate quickly and return to my old life in New York. But Galveston had seduced me and awakened desires in me I had long suppressed. I'd denied to myself over the years how much I loved the island and the smell and the sound of the gulf, the feel of the damp salty air on my skin. Now that I was back, I had succumbed to its seduction. Beyond that, though, was another seduction—

King Enterprises. My father had made it forbidden territory to me because I was female, and that had made it even more seductive. Now that I'd entered that territory, however, I knew I'd found my true home. The exotic cargo, the busy hum of the wharves, the romantic vision of ships in the harbor still attracted me, just as they had when I was a child. But the challenge of the business, of running it, of making it successful, was just as seductive. I was determined to turn it around, to make it what it had been under John King and more. I was equally as determined that I wasn't going to be frightened away. I would uncover the threatening secrets of Shadow Cove as well.

I felt my resolve weaken as we drew nearer to the Shadows and I saw the house, decaying, dark, and sinister in the moonlight. My driver pulled the carriage up to the gate. I waited a few seconds for him to come down from his seat and open my door, but all he did was shout to me.

"We're here, ma'am. Shadows."

Obviously he was anxious to get away, so I opened my own door and stepped out. The wind was blowing, and it caught at my skirt and pulled it tight against me, making me shiver where it swept over my bare arms. I pulled my shawl up around me and reached into my reticule for the cash I had put there to pay the driver. Behind me the wind moaned with the voice of a crying woman as it did battle with the house, pushing against the corners and spires. The driver scarcely took the time to bend down to snatch the money from my hands before he slashed his whip at the horse and sped away into the darkness.

I turned with dread toward the house. I could make out the white blur of marble hands as I stepped inside, and behind me the heavy front door slammed with a sound of dead finality.

I moved forward, my hands held in front of me, trying to find the table and the lamp I kept on top of it. I bumped into it, and the table legs scooting across the marble floor made a screeching sound. Feeling along the table for the lamp, I soon discovered that the table was empty except for something I brushed with my hand that fell with the sound of dry bones hitting the floor. The box of matches. I dropped to my knees until I found one and picked it up, then felt along the wall until I touched cold lifeless fingers, and finally the long taper

I had placed in their grasp. I lit the candle, and the flame cast undulating shadows across the entry hall. It wasn't much of a light, but I could at least see as far as the foot of the stairs. There, on a table several feet away, next to the curving banister, I saw the lamp. But I had not placed it there! Or had I? I stared at it a moment, trying to calm myself. Trying to convince myself that there was a logical answer, that perhaps in my haste to leave for the party I had forgotten that I had moved the lamp.

I lit the lamp and carried it with me upstairs to my room to prepare for bed, glancing out the window just as I blew out the flame. I half expected to see the woman again, but she was not there. The fire-spouting steamships, too, were gone, having slipped over the horizon, and the red moon had fallen into the sea, leaving nothing but dim icy stars.

As I lay in my bed, Chase kept slipping into my thoughts— the way he made me feel, the way he had kissed me, the way he had made me want . . . I had to stop thinking such thoughts! I only had to remember how I distrusted him. I felt he had lied to me about the money he loaned Anton. Why had he said it was a personal loan when my company accounts listed it as a business loan? And why had he decided on the spur of the moment to forgive the balance? Was it to keep me from digging further and finding out something he didn't want me to know? I was more determined than ever to find the answers. I would keep my promise to Pastor Browning and attend the church my father had helped establish, but Sabbath or not I had work to do.

When I got to town the next morning, there was still an hour left before church services would begin, so I headed straight for the offices of King Enterprises. I had just pulled the books from the shelf behind Robert's desk when I heard a noise at the door and looked up to see Robert himself walking in. He was unshaven and red-eyed, looking as if he had not slept at all, and he seemed just as surprised to see me as I was to see him.

"Laura! My God, what are you doing here?"

"I might ask you the same thing, Robert. Surely you weren't planning to work today."

"No, I—well, as a matter of fact I was. I thought it would be quiet today, that I could work undisturbed."

"But there can't be that much work to do. Not with business down the way it is."

"Laura, my dear." His tone was solicitous. "Is that what's worrying you? The business being down? You must stop thinking about it. You have your career, quite apart from this. And I have other prospects. Businesses are always in need of a good accountant."

"Did you miss my announcement last night, Robert? I'm giving up my career and my old life. I'm going to stay in Galveston."

"Of course I heard you, and it made such a good show for you to look so courageous, so much the strong woman." He laughed. "You'll have all the women in Galveston exerting their rights. Organizing female suffrage rallies. Why, at the party all of them were saying how clever you were to stand up to old Tom Sealy. Some of the women were jealous of all the attention you got, too."

"I wasn't just trying to be clever, Robert, and I wasn't seeking attention. I'm dead serious about this. I thought I'd convinced you of that. Didn't you say yourself I'm like my father?"

"Well, of course you have that stubborn streak, but I thought once you came to your senses—"

"I have come to my senses, Robert. I know what I want. But before I go much further, I have to get to the bottom of a few things, and I'm going to need you to help me."

He threw up his hands in a gesture of mock defeat. "Of course I'll help. I'll help all I can, but there's not much I can do except tell you the debt is enormous and the income is—"

"What about those loan payments to Chase Bradley?"

"That's only part of it. There's also—"

"He claims the loan has been forgiven."

"He what?"

"He says he gave Anton papers freeing him from any debt."

"He's lying, Laura. There were never any such papers. The money is deposited into Chase Bradley's account as payment for the loan. Several thousand dollars a year. More than most men make in a—"

"I saw the entries," I said, tapping the books I still held next to my chest. "I know the amount."

"Then you know he's lying. He threatened Anton, Laura. Threatened to take the business away from him if the loan payments weren't kept up. I didn't want to tell you about it. I didn't want to worry you, but that's why I've continued to meet the loan payments. It is a legitimate debt owed by King Enterprises, but Chase Bradley is an unforgiving creditor. He'll take the business away from you in the blink of an eye if you falter on the loan payments."

"You just advised me to leave, to let the business falter. What you're saying, then, is that King Enterprises is as good as lost to Sealy and Bradley. Why have you bothered to keep up the payments this long?"

"I hate to see it lost as much as you do, Laura, especially to Sealy and Bradley. I kept up the payments out of loyalty to the family. But now I can see that it's a losing battle and that you can be hurt."

I looked away from him, feeling confused, not knowing what to say. I wanted to believe that he was a loyal friend. I didn't want to think that he was lying to me. But I didn't want to think Chase would lie to me either.

"I'm not sure what to do," I said finally, feeling miserable, "except that I can't leave the business. I want to learn all I can about it, and I want to make it strong again, the way it was when my father was alive."

"Of course you do, Laura, and that's admirable, but you have to know when to retreat."

"I think I will," I said, "but now is not the time. Have faith in me, Robert. Trust me at least as much as you did Anton. Now, if you'll excuse me, I've got to hurry to get to church. We'll talk more about this later. I don't want to upset Pastor Browning by walking in late."

I left, taking the ledger with me, stored in a saddlebag. I planned to go over the entries later at home. As I rode my stallion across the Strand and all the way to the Presbyterian Church, I was again keenly aware of all the eyes staring at me. A woman riding a horse into town on a weekday was unusual enough, but the sight of a spinster going to church on a white stallion was enough to turn all heads and set tongues to wagging. I know they thought me to be eccentric, and the fact that I had taken over the family business only added to my aura of eccentricity. I hadn't set out to be eccentric—circumstances had forced me to be so. All I could do now was hold my head high and pretend not to notice the curious stares, pretend not to care that a real lady would be more conventional and arrive in a carriage.

When I pulled Sir Blanco to a halt in front of the church, no less than five gentlemen hurried toward me to help me dismount. I accepted their help as graciously as I could, then, still aware of dozens of pairs of curious eyes trained on me, I kept my head high and walked toward the church. Out of the corner of my eye I saw Chase Bradley watching me and knew that he had done so from the moment I arrived. I was surprised to see him, since I had not known him to be a churchgoing man at all.

His gaze made me feel uneasy, but I only held my head higher and entered the church.

Light filtered through the stained-glass windows and left mottled patterns on the backs of parishioners like the mark of the beast of Revelations. But the beast, if he existed, would have been calmed by the rose and blue hue of the light as well as the droning strains of the organ. As I walked up the aisle, I saw the backs of Aunt Stella and Johnny in front of me. Johnny, who was wiggling around in his seat, saw me also and gave me a broad grin and an animated wave. Aunt Stella stopped his gesture with a touch of her hand, but she couldn't resist turning around herself to see what had attracted Johnny's attention. I gave them both a smile and a nod and slid into a pew two rows back from them.

The organ music rose to a high crescendo, signaling that the services would begin soon and that the congregation was to rise for the processional hymn. I reached for a hymnal, and as I opened it, I was aware of someone stepping into the pew and moving next to me. I turned to offer to share my hymnbook and, to my surprise, met Chase Bradley's cool gray eyes. I was too stunned to react for a moment, since he was the last person I expected to share a pew with me. I had expected him to sit with his family.

He gave me an infuriatingly innocent smile as he took the hymnbook from me and began to sing in a strong but curiously off-key voice. He glanced back at me and piously pointed out the place in the hymn I should be singing.

I grasped the side of the hymnbook and tried to sing. It wasn't easy. He kept pulling me off-key with him. He brushed my arm ever so slightly with his, and I felt my voice falter. Somehow I managed to get through the first scripture reading and the Apostles' Creed and the Gloria Patri, but when we sat down for the sermon, he moved even closer. Of course, there were other people in the pew now, but there was still plenty of room. It hadn't really been necessary for him to move so close that his thigh was pressed against mine, nor that his arm be placed behind me across the pew.

I tried to lean away from him, but that did no good. I could still feel the pressure of his thigh against mine, and I could smell the mixture of shaving soap and—what was it? Musk?

God knows I tried to concentrate on the sermon and to keep my eyes on Pastor Browning. I distinctly heard him recite "lead us not into temptation," but I was thinking of Chase's firm, demanding mouth as it had claimed mine. I was thinking of the way his fingertips brushed my breast, of the way his body felt next to mine.

I glanced at Chase and saw a little half smile on his face—as if he were reading my thoughts. I coughed and tried to move away again. Chase moved his arm from behind me, shifted in his seat and moved away from me, but he still wore that knowing little smile.

"Too warm?" he whispered.

"I'm fine," I whispered back.

"Then be still. You're attracting attention."

I opened my mouth and tried to think of something to say. But the words that came to mind were not suitable for a lady and certainly not suitable to be uttered in church.

"And you're very good at attracting attention, I might add," he whispered, leaning close to my ear. "Riding into town on a white stallion. Why, you rival Lady Godiva. And that announcement you made last night. You made sure you were the center of attention with that. You had every woman in the place envying you."

I felt my face flush again, but I wasn't certain whether it was more from the embarrassment of being compared to Lady Godiva or from the anger at his impertinence.

"I assure you that neither my riding Sir Blanco nor the announcement had anything to do with attracting attention,"

I whispered. "I ride the stallion because it is my only means of transportation. And I mentioned expanding King Enterprises because I was tired of having everyone assume I would just give up and leave."

"Shhh!" he said and smiled at an elderly woman who had turned around in her pew, obviously disturbed by our whispers.

Somehow I got through the sermon, and when it was over, I turned to Chase, but he never gave me a chance to speak.

"I never assumed you would up and leave," he said. "At least, not after I got to know you. I was afraid of something like this. All I can say is, don't be surprised if you get more than you bargained for."

"What do you mean?" I could see that his flirtatious mood was gone, but the dark anger I'd associated with him when I first met him was missing as well.

"I'm afraid you'll find out soon enough, Laura, and God help us all."

He moved away from me then, leaving me more disturbed than ever. What did he mean that I would get more than I bargained for? Was that a threat? Was he going to try to stop me somehow?

I became aware of Johnny tugging at my skirt and calling me with exuberant excitement.

"Miss Laura! Miss Laura! You did come! Did an angel bring you?"

"An angel?" I asked with a laugh.

"When I said my prayers last night, I asked God to let me see you today. You're here! Maybe an angel brought you."

"Why, that was very sweet of you, Johnny," I said, giving him a hug.

"It was just a test, sort of."

"A test?" I asked, amused. "What do you mean?"

"Well, I thought if I got this prayer answered, I'd try for a bigger one."

"Oh?"

He nodded his head, then signaled that I was to bend down so he could whisper. "What I really want is for you to come live with us."

"Johnny," I said, straightening, "that's not possible, I—"

"Oh, but it is!" His eyes were wide with excitement. "You could marry Papa. He's sure to be against it at first, of course, but we could talk him into it. Just like I did when I got my puppy. He was against that at first. Said it was too much trouble. But you're not a lot of trouble, are you, Miss Laura?"

"I feel quite certain your papa would say I was," I said dryly.

"Well, if he won't marry you, then you could be my aunty and live with us. Just like Aunt Stella. It would be nice to have two."

"I'm sure it would be very nice for me, too—to be your aunty, I mean." I caressed his face briefly. "But I can't come live with you. My home is at Shadow Cove, and your home is in town. We can be friends, though, and we can visit each other often."

I saw his little mouth harden into a thin stubborn line that for a moment left me feeling vaguely uncomfortable. "If you're going to be stubborn, Miss Laura, then I'll get Aunt Stella to pray. She's much better at it than I am."

"I'm sure you're very good at it, too, Johnny," I said. His eyes had clouded over, and his little mouth had lost its stern look now and had begun to tremble. He was about to cry, and I knew that if he cried, I would, too. It wouldn't do, though, for him to see me cry. I gave him another hug and added as I walked away, "Some things just aren't meant to be, but we can always be friends. And I would like for you to call me Aunty Laura."

"But being friends and living apart is only second best," he called after me. "Why does God only give second best?"

I didn't know how to answer him and couldn't bear to turn around and look at him to face his disillusionment, no matter how temporary it might be. Instead I made my way toward the hitching post where I had secured Sir Blanco. Before I could untie the reins, however, Thomas Sealy approached me, calling my name excitedly.

"Miss Laura! Just a minute, I want to talk to you." He was red-faced and puffing from having run to catch up with me.

"Mr. Sealy," I said, turning to greet him. "I hope your wife and daughter told you how delightful I thought the party was last night and how grateful I was that you invited me. You were busy when I left, so I—"

"Oh, never mind all that rot," he said with a wave of his hand. "They told me, of course. But I don't want to talk about the party. I want to talk about that proposal you made."

"Proposal, Mr. Sealy?"

"Of course. You know what I'm talking about. Expanding to the port of Houston."

"Mr. Sealy, don't try to talk me out of it. I *am* staying in Galveston. I can't for the life of me understand why everyone is so dead set against it. But I am a King. I own King Enterprises. I'm staying, and I'm determined to make the business prosper."

Mr. Sealy laughed heartily. "You're a King all right. Every bit as regal, not to mention as shrewd, as your father. Why, I'll bet you're a damn—excuse me," he said with a glance over his shoulder toward the church. "I mean, I'll bet you're an excellent businesswoman. Just the kind of person who'd make a good partner."

"What?" I felt stunned and confused.

"I want to talk to you about merging our two firms."

Now I was even more stunned. "You want to talk about—" Thoughts spun in my head. A merger would provide the capital I needed. It would provide something for Sealy and Bradley, too—ships and warehouse space. But would it work? Was it some kind of a trick Chase Bradley was behind, or would he be as shocked at the idea as I was? I needed time to think. "Mr. Sealy, this is the Sabbath. One doesn't discuss business on the Sabbath."

A slow grin crept across his face, and I got the feeling he was reading my thoughts. He knew I was stalling for time. In the next moment he would be pressuring me to make a decision, telling me time was running out. But I was wrong.

"Take your time, Laura. Think it through."

Was he giving me time because he knew he could take over the business anyway if the debt to Chase wasn't paid?

"Does Chase know about your offer?"

His face took on a look of wariness, and I saw him glance away briefly. "We'll talk about that later," he said. "After the Sabbath." He bowed toward me slightly and tipped his hat. "In my office at nine."

I watched him walk away, but I knew my last question had made him nervous. Either Chase didn't know about his offer, or he did know and he disagreed with the proposal. Anyway, Thomas Sealy obviously had a reason to be evasive.

My Sunday morning had been anything but comforting and inspirational, and I felt quite disturbed as I rode Sir Blanco away from the church down the long road along the coast to Shadow Cove. Sir Blanco seemed to sense my mood. He anticipated, I think, that I wanted to run, to feel the power of his muscles bunching and lengthening and the freedom of my own spirit let loose with the wind that rushed past me. I let him go, hoping that it would clear my mind as I had imagined it did when I was a child.

I had ridden no more than a quarter of a mile when I felt myself suddenly separated from Blanco, and I was flying through the air, over his head, while the saddle slipped out from under me. Sir Blanco screamed and reared, then ran away, just as I hit the ground. Hot arrows of pain shot along my arm and up my neck into my jaw. For a moment I was too stunned to realize what had happened. Then I heard Sir Blanco cry out again and saw him dance on his hind legs, and saw the saddle lying in the sand beside me with a severed strap lying carelessly across the seat. Someone had tried to kill me. The saddle cinch had been cut. I reached for it to examine it closer, but just before I touched it, another arrow of pain pierced my arm, and I remembered Chase coming late into the church after everyone else was in, and I remembered his veiled threat. *"You're going to get more than you bargained for."*

Chapter 11

I WAS shaking so hard I couldn't stand. It wasn't the pain in my wrist so much as fear and anger that affected me. All I could do was stare at the saddle and wonder what the secret link between Anton and Chase was that could make Chase want me dead. I was certain that was what he wanted. A fall from a horse could certainly be fatal, and often was. It was sheer chance that had made me ride away from the road and ride along the beach. Falling in the sand had saved me. Had I fallen on hard-packed earth, I could certainly have been killed, or at best seriously injured.

I felt a wave of nausea sweep over me. It was more than the pain in my arm that made me sick, though; it was the knowledge that Chase would stage my death to make it look like an accident. Had the same thing happened to Anton? Did that explain why my brother, an excellent swimmer, had drowned? The more I thought about it, the more upset I became, and the more I knew I had to find out the secret of my brother's death and life that was now stalking me.

I moved to try to stand and found myself suddenly drenched in perspiration. The pain and the heavy oppressive heat were working together against me. Only my mouth felt dry—a sticky dryness that worsened my nausea, and I felt myself surrounded by a strange red glow that moved about me in circles. I closed my eyes again and became acutely aware of the pain in my hand and arm and the hot sand pressing against my cheek. I didn't remember lying down. But perhaps I hadn't. Perhaps I had fallen over.

I tried to sit up but felt a searing, throbbing pain in my hand when I tried to put my weight on it. I lay still for a moment, waiting for the pain to subside. Finally I managed to bring myself up to a sitting position, but I held my injured wrist carefully to my side. I noticed then that there was a strange, ominous quietness all around me. No sound at all, except for the muted, sullen sound of the blackening sea.

Sir Blanco had disappeared completely. Next to me lay the saddle with its broken strap, and a few feet away I saw my account book, its leather back sprawled open and the pages sticking up like some odd plant, motionless on the windless beach. I started to crawl toward the book to pick it up, but every movement made my wrist hurt. I finally managed to retrieve it, though, and I cradled it in my right arm and got to my feet. The pain in my left wrist was even more intense now, and I supposed, much to my annoyance, that I would need to see a doctor.

I glanced up and down the stretch of beach I'd been riding along and saw Sir Blanco's hoofprints in the sand, leading away from town toward Shadow Cove. I called his name several times, in spite of the fact that I knew it was futile. Even if the horse had heard my voice, he'd be more likely to heed his instincts and return to the source of his food.

I gave up calling for him and began the walk back to Galveston. I had walked for almost an hour and was already on the outskirts of the town before I met a couple in a buggy who stopped to ask if I needed help. I explained that I had fallen from my horse, and when they saw my swollen wrist, they insisted upon driving me to the home of a doctor they knew. I was glad to have the ride since the wind had by now begun to stir the air, and the clouds overhead were thickening and threatening rain.

The doctor, whose name was Terrance McCarty, had his office at a side entrance to his house. He was mildly disgruntled at having been awakened from his Sunday afternoon nap to have to come downstairs to tend to something as uninteresting as a wrist.

"It's just a sprain," he said as he wound a bandage around my arm. "Nothing serious. You'll need to carry your arm in a sling, of course, but it should heal in time. How is it you came to do this?"

"I fell. From my horse."

"From your horse. Yes, of course. Interesting." He disappeared for a moment and returned carrying a large white square of cloth, which he folded into a triangle. "Here we go," he said, tying my arm into the sling. "You're lucky it's your left arm. Not left-handed, are we? No, I didn't think so. Have any children, do we?"

"I'm a spinster."

"Ah, yes. Fortunate. Caring for the little ones with an arm in a sling could be a burden." He patted my head. "A fall from a horse you say? Hmmm. Curious activity for a maiden lady. Well, just stick around for a little while and let me keep an eye on you in case there's a concussion. You'll be fortunate if there's not. I'll be back to check in a bit."

"How long—"

I never got to ask my question. Dr. McCarty was already out the door. It was just as well. I was tired of hearing how fortunate I was. I looked around the office for something to read while I waited, but there was nothing except a shelf full of medical books. I found the drawings of body parts uninspiring and the text even more so. Even my ledger was more interesting, I thought, opening the book.

I glanced at the numbers. As dull and boring as numbers had always been to me, I knew these were not. The history of King Enterprises could be told with these seemingly lifeless figures, and perhaps the secret to Anton's past as well, if I was only clever enough to find it.

There was nothing there, though. Nothing except figures that showed profits dropping, costs rising. Costs for fuel, maintenance and upkeep of the ships, harbor taxes and wharf fees, Robert's modest salary, and of course the haunting debt payment to Chase Bradley. Chase was bleeding King Enterprises dry and refusing to admit it, refusing even to talk to me about it, preferring instead to put on a flirtatious act. After today I was convinced he was also trying to kill me. All I was doing was running up against a brick wall. I still didn't know the real story. Disgusted and distressed, I slammed the book closed. Thickening clouds were robbing the waiting room of enough light to read by, anyway.

I paced the floor, trying to ignore the throbbing pain in my arm. Several times I glanced toward the stairs, looking for Dr. McCarty. I wanted him to come release me so I could find a way to get back home. Raindrops had by now begun to pellet the windows, and I could hear thunder rumbling in the distance. I needed to see about Sir Blanco.

If I could only have found a telephone, I could have rung up Robert and asked him to drive me home in his carriage. But there was no telephone available to me.

I knocked on the door leading to the front of the house several times, but no one responded. Apparently the doctor had forgotten about me and had gone back to his nap.

Finally, when I could stand it no longer, I left a few dollars on the doctor's desk and let myself out. Fortunately I was not far from the wharf area. I could walk to the King offices and use the telephone there to call Robert. It had begun to rain a little harder now, and I pulled my shawl over my head and hurried, account book still in hand, toward the wharves.

Lightning tore the sky open as I ran, and I heard its crack almost instantaneously with the clap of thunder. The very air seemed to be charged with electricity. I was soaked by the time I got to the King warehouse, and I had to fumble awkwardly with the key with my uninjured hand while I held my account book under my arm.

The building was deathly quiet and dark. In the old days, even the Sabbath had been a busy day for King Enterprises, and I remember my father going down to the wharves after church. Sometimes he even skipped services to come down here.

When my eyes had adjusted to the darkness, I took a cautious step farther into the warehouse, being careful to avoid the bales of cotton, boxes of cargo, and winches and lines that cluttered the floor. I had taken only a few steps when the sound of the wide warehouse door slamming shut startled me. I sucked in my breath to stifle a scream and swung around, half expecting, half afraid, to see someone behind me. But there was no one. The door had been pushed closed by the wind.

It was even more difficult to see with the only light coming in from the windows high over head. That light was diffused more than usual because of the clouds and the rain, becoming heavier by the minute. I finally made my way to the back of the warehouse where the office was located and once again used my key to let myself in. We had not yet had our building equipped with the new electric lights that many of the homes had, but I soon had the gas lamp lit. Its odd blue glow only added to the anxiety I felt because of the storm, and I was anxious to get to the telephone to call Robert.

Lady of the Shadows

A dramatic crack of thunder startled me just as I lay the account book on Robert's desk, and my sudden jump caused me to knock the telephone to the floor. I picked it up and held it to my ear. It had gone completely dead, either from the storm or from the blow I had dealt it. I felt another moment of panic and seemed unable to think what to do next. But I forced myself to be calm, to try to think rationally. I would wait out the storm and then walk the few blocks to the stables and hire a carriage.

I walked with exaggerated calmness toward the washroom to find a towel, since I had gotten damp enough in the rain to feel uncomfortable. I willed myself not to think about the storm and the fact that winds often whipped up to hurricane force, sending high waves to lash at the shore. I tried not to dwell upon the fact that I was on the wharf, dangerously close to the sea.

When I pulled at the door of the washroom, I met with stiff resistance. It was locked. Robert always locked it before he left, and he kept the key in his desk. I turned back to the desk, still working at remaining calm, but I could feel my heart racing, and I had begun to perspire enough to feel more uncomfortable. My hand shook as I reached to pull open the desk drawer. It was locked, too, but I tugged at it harder, as if that would somehow unlock it.

When I still met with resistance, my facade of calm broke, and I pounded the drawer with my fist and shook it even harder. I pounded and shook again and again and muttered an oath I'd heard on the wharves and knew would never be heard from the mouth of a true lady. It wasn't vitally important that I have the key to the washroom, of course. I could certainly survive with a little rain on my clothes. But I wasn't thinking rationally at the moment, and my anxiety had built to an intolerable level. I had taken the easiest means of venting it. With one final pull at the drawer with my good hand, I heard the wood crack, and the drawer fell, dangling like a broken bone from the desk front.

I came to my senses then, suddenly embarrassed. I would have to explain my irrational behavior to Robert come Monday morning and would have the uncomfortable duty of apologizing for destroying his desk. I did the best I could to push the drawer back to a less precarious level, but to my chagrin it fell with a crash to the floor. When I stooped to pick up the contents, my eyes fell upon a small leather book that had fallen face-up. I picked it up and glanced at it and saw Robert's name on it. Undoubtedly it was some personal account book. I was about to close it and put it back in the drawer when I noticed the figures in one of the columns. It was a series of numbers that were very familiar to me. I looked closer and realized that the book was indeed a personal account book of the type people used to record bank account transactions. The familiar series of numbers matched exactly the loan payments that had supposedly been made to Chase.

In spite of the heavy, humid heat that choked the room, I felt a sudden chill. Robert had been embezzling money from King Enterprises! I had allowed myself to be suspicious of Chase, but not of Robert, because Robert had been hired by my father. And my father, the indomitable John King, did not make mistakes—at least, that's what I had been led to believe since childhood. He certainly wouldn't make the mistake of hiring an embezzler to do the accounting. But if Robert Thorn was an embezzler, then he had good reason to want me to leave Galveston, and he had a reason to kill me if I didn't. That also meant he could have had reason to kill Anton, if my brother had found out about the embezzlement, too. But what about Chase? Maybe he hadn't been lying about the debt, but he'd made no secret of the fact that he, too, wanted me out of Galveston. Was he aligned somehow with Robert? Had they both been trying to kill me? And what, if anything, did they have to do with the strange woman I'd seen haunting the beach around Shadow Cove?

For a moment it was all too confusing, and I couldn't think what I should do. It could very well be dangerous for me to return to Shadow Cove. But I couldn't stay away. I had to get there somehow to see that Sir Blanco was safe. Perhaps I could hire a carriage to take me there and ask the driver to wait until I made sure Sir Blanco was stabled. But what then? Ask him to return me to town? What good would that do? I had no place to stay.

Without realizing I'd done it, I found myself staring at the portrait of my father that hung over the safe. I saw his intense blue stare, his hard shrewd mouth, his eternal youth, captured forever in the painting. He would have known what to do. He would not have whimpered and fretted and broken things with frightened tantrums. He would have acted decisively with a care for no one except himself and with no romantic notions.

Perhaps that was where I had gone wrong. Perhaps I'd had romantic notions and let my heart rule my head. I'd been flattered by the attention I'd gotten from the two men. The truth was I'd felt more than flattered when I was with Chase. I'd felt drawn to him by the unmistakable excitement I felt when I was with him, by the electricity that seemed to flow between us, and equally so by the kind gentle side I thought I'd seen in him through his obvious love for Johnny. I'd felt all of those things, while at the same time I'd felt confused and frightened and distrustful. John King, I knew, would never feel so confused.

Suddenly my thoughts of my father and of Chase Bradley were interrupted by an indescribable yet unmistakable sense of another presence in the room. I whirled around and felt my scream stick in my throat when I saw the dark ghost. In almost the same instant I knew it was not a ghost but Felix LeFeu who stared at me.

"Don't be scared, missy," he said in his odd accent. He stood ramrod straight, holding a damp raincoat across his arm. At least that let me know he'd come in from the outside and had not just materialized out of nowhere, as it seemed he might have.

"What do you want? How did you get in here?"

"Chase send me."

"Chase? But how did you know I was here?"

"I see you, missy. I watch you. I even stay in your house at night, just like Chase say for me to do."

"So it was you who—"

"He say watch you, but I ain't able to be with you all the time," he said, dropping his eyes to my arm. "You got to be mo' careful, missy. Chase send me now to tell you—"

"Now, look here," I said, letting my anger overtake my fright. "I won't take any bullying from Chase Bradley. He's not going to scare me away from my own business no matter what kind of scheme he's got going, and you can tell him I said so. You can—"

"I come to tell you Master Johnny gone, ma'am."

"What?"

"Little Johnny. Gone. Maybe lost in the storm."

"Oh, my God, no!"

"He think maybe Master Johnny took by someone. He think maybe you be next."

A coldness gripped me, as if my blood had congealed. "I know someone's after me," I said, my voice barely more than a whisper. "But why Johnny?"

"Chase say I must take you to Miss Stella."

"Of course," I said, coming to my senses somewhat. "I must see her. She must be frantic with worry. But, please, can you explain—"

"I got my wagon," he said, handing me the raincoat. "Ain't gonna keep no rain off of you, but it get you to Miss Stella."

He was balking at answering my questions, but before I could press further, he was holding my good arm, ushering me out of the office and into the warehouse.

"You must be careful, miss," LeFeu said. "You leave yo' warehouse doors unlocked. I walk right in. Chase, he right, you a danger to yo'self." With that remark he gently placed the raincoat over my head and ushered me out through the rain to the wagon.

Rain and wind lashed us all the way to the Bradley house, and I pulled the raincoat tighter around me in a futile attempt to stay dry. When we got there, LeFeu helped me down from the wagon and, with his arm protectively around me, helped me to the front door. Before we could knock, Chase opened the door.

"Laura!" he said. I thought I could hear relief in the way he had said my name, and I thought for a moment he was about to embrace me, but he made no move toward me. "What happened to your arm?" he asked.

"I—fell from Sir Blanco," I said and immediately regretted volunteering the information. He already thought I was an awkward, bumbling idiot, according to LeFeu, and besides, with Johnny missing and in danger, I knew he had more pressing concerns. But he wasn't going to let the moment pass.

"You? Fall from a horse?"

"Yes, I—"

"Master Johnny," LeFeu said, interrupting to speak to Chase. "You find him? You come back because you find him?"

"No," Chase answered. I saw a look on LeFeu's face that was part concern, part relief, and I knew that he had feared that Johnny had been found dead. "I came back for another mount," Chase said. "If the storm gets worse, the little mare won't be able to take it. I had to get the gelding. I'm going to saddle him now."

"I kin do that," LeFeu said and was suddenly gone.

Chase glanced at me again, and I saw the unmistakable anguish in his face.

"Aunt Stella," I said. "How is she?"

"Go to her," he said, gesturing with his head toward the parlor. "She needs you."

I brushed past him and hurried into the front parlor where Aunt Stella sat staring with red and swollen eyes at the storm. Two women, neighbors who had come to offer support, sat like birds on a fence on the horsehair sofa, one of them twisting a handkerchief in her hands, and the other with her head bowed, resting on her hand as if she were praying. Babette sat in another chair, crying into a handkerchief, her usually crisp uniform a crumpled mass of black and white. Another woman was stooped over Aunt Stella holding a glass of water. She glanced at me when I entered.

"Aunt Stella," I said quietly, walking toward her. She looked at me with dulled eyes, and I thought for a moment that she hadn't recognized me, but I soon realized that anguish had robbed her of all vitality. She knew who I was, and she held a trembling hand toward me. I took it and kissed it as I knelt beside her. She placed her other hand on my bowed head.

"You've been injured, my child," she said, glancing at my arm. "What happened to you?"

"It's nothing," I said, not wanting to worry her. "Just a careless fall."

"He wandered off," she said, her mind skipping back to her grief. "He was playing out in the back with his baseball. He's got to where he can hit it right well, you know. Always having to chase after it. I saw the storm coming, and I called for him to come in. When I looked again, he was gone. Chasing after that ball, I guess. He knows better. He knows these storms can be dangerous. Needs a paddling, he does," she said, although I knew she could never paddle him. She was letting her anger substitute for the grief. If she truly thought he had wandered off, then Chase hadn't told her his suspicion that Johnny had been kidnapped. I took that as a signal that I wasn't to mention it either. I had hoped I could ask her, though, and that she could tell me why Chase would think such a thing.

"He knows how a storm can whip up the waves, how the wind can tear down buildings," Aunt Stella continued. "Think what it can do to a small boy. He knows better. Why did he do it?"

"I don't know," I whispered. "Try not to worry. Men are looking for him."

She caressed my rain-dampened head again and turned her eyes back to the window. "They'll find him," she said in her slow, lifeless voice. "Chase will find him."

"Yes," I assured her, "Chase will find him."

"Not dead," she said. "Please, God, don't let them find him dead."

"No." I found I couldn't speak above a whisper. I watched her a moment and saw her eyes close and her head nod.

"I gave her a smidgin of laudanum," the woman standing beside her with the water glass said. " 'Twill make her sleep. It's what she needs."

I nodded.

"And the French gal," the woman said with a glance toward Babette, who was still weeping. "I've a mind to give her a dose, too. Poor thing loved him like he was her own little brother."

I stood up, fighting the fear and frustration that was welling up inside me. I loved him, too. I loved him more like a son than a brother. I loved him as if he were my own flesh and blood, and I knew I had to do all I could to keep him from harm. Aunt Stella would be sedated and well cared for, and Johnny needed me more. I picked up the raincoat Felix had brought me and headed for the door, hoping I wasn't too late to tell Chase I was going with him on the search.

I ran through the rain to the corral and saw Chase just as he mounted a gelding and rode him toward the gate.

"Wait!" I called. Chase saw me and reined the gelding in. I saw the question in his eyes. "I'm going with you!" I said, shouting to be heard above the wind.

"Don't be foolish!" he shouted back. "The storm's going to get worse."

"I'll be all right," I said. "I can ride as well as anyone."

"Not with that broken arm!"

"It's not broken. Just a sprain," I said, shaking myself free of the sling. "I can ride. I'll show you." I started toward the stalls. "I'll saddle the other horse, and I'll stay up as well as you."

"Damn it, you can't ride the other horse. She's a mare in foal. You can't take her out in this."

"Then I'll ride with you." I had already started moving toward his gelding, ready to get myself up in the saddle with him however I could.

"You'll do nothing of the kind," Chase said. He wheeled the horse toward the gate again.

I pulled the coat close around my body and followed him out of the gate. I was going to look for Johnny, and nothing—no storm and no stubborn man—was going to stop me. I would go on foot if I had to, and I would go to the school first. Perhaps he'd gone there to play in the schoolyard and was afraid to come home in the storm. I'd gotten only a few steps beyond the gate when Chase turned his horse around again and shouted at me.

"Where do you think you're going?"

"I told you. I'm going to look for Johnny."

Even through the rain I could see his jaw stiffen and the muscles of his face contort into a frown. He spurred the horse and cantered toward me. For one insane moment I thought he meant to do me harm, to run me down, but he slowed as he drew nearer and with a quick movement leaned out of the saddle and swooped me off my feet. In the next second I was seated in front of him while he held me securely around the waist, the powerful muscles of his upper arm pressing against my breasts while he held me close to him.

"There's no getting rid of you, is there?" he asked. "Once you get your mind made up, you don't let go. Well, you may be in for quite a ride, my darling. I'm not going to stop until I find him."

"I have no intention of stopping either." I was acutely aware of the way my body rubbed against his with each step the horse made.

"Just keep in mind I won't have time to mollycoddle you. I'm taking you along to help search. With the three of us searching—you, me, Felix—that should increase our chances of finding him before it's too late."

"Don't worry," I said. "I have no desire to be mollycoddled, as you call it. I expected to be treated as your equal."

His only reply was to tighten his grip around me, pulling my body even closer to his. He headed the horse east, toward the beach and away from the schoolyard, where I had planned to look first.

"You're going toward the gulf," I said.

"Yes," he answered. "That's the way Felix thinks he went. He says he saw footprints in the mud before the rain got so heavy they washed them out."

"Felix says you think someone took him." I found I had to turn my head slightly to make him hear me above the sound of the rain.

He didn't answer but kept his eyes straight ahead.

"Tell me what's going on, Chase," I insisted. "Felix said you thought I might be in danger, too. I know someone wants me harmed or out of Galveston or both. And I know it has something to do with my family or the family business. What possible reason would the same people have for wanting to harm a child?"

"Evil never makes sense, Laura. And it's best you don't question it."

I wanted to argue with him, to tell him I had every right to question threats on my life, and to find out if I could somehow be causing the danger to Johnny, but he had spurred the horse, quickening the pace enough to make conversation virtually impossible. We rode until we reached a cluster of houses that sat a little way back from the beach, and Chase reined the horse to a stop. He lifted me down first and then dismounted.

"Go to each of those houses," Chase said. "I'll take the ones on the other side of the street. Ask if anyone saw him. Ask if he was alone."

"Chase, you've got to talk to me." I felt almost sick with worry. "You've got to tell me what connection I have with this."

"You have nothing to do with this, Laura," he said. He'd already started to walk away from me, leading his horse.

"Why do we have to be enemies?" I called to him. "Will it help if I apologize for suspecting you were trying to cheat me?"

Still he just kept walking away from me. I called to him again. "It was Robert Thorn."

Chase turned around. "Thorn?" He made it sound as much like an oath as a question.

"He's been embezzling from the company for some time. I think he's been trying to scare me away from Galveston to keep me from learning the truth."

"He's desperate, then," Chase said angrily. "That explains a lot of things. And you're the one who set it off."

"But you just said I had nothing to do with it. I don't understand. And none of this explains that creature—that woman I see crying on the beach."

"It explains a lot of things, Laura," he said, walking toward me. "But there are things you're better off not knowing." He grabbed my arm and pulled me along with him.

"What are you doing?" I demanded.

"I changed my mind about leaving you on your own. You're coming with me."

"Look, I'm in no more danger than I ever was," I said, thinking of the severed saddle strap. I realized now that it must have been Robert who had staged my accident. It didn't matter, though. Looking for Johnny was what mattered.

"Just the same, you're coming with me," Chase said. He took my arm, but instead of pulling me roughly along as I half expected him to do, he put his own arm protectively around me and guided me from house to house.

Our inquiries produced dubious results. No one was certain they'd seen Johnny, although a couple of women thought they might have. Both said they saw a child who appeared to be alone, walking in the rain toward the beach road. Several men volunteered to aid in the search, and Chase turned no one down.

We rode toward the shore. The gulf was now dark and angry, whirling and churning in a deadly dance as if it were bringing the storm up from somewhere deep in its innards. It had exchanged its mournful cry for a mad roar to announce its dangerous power. Chase dismounted and led the horse, walking along the black gulf. Others walked ahead of us and behind us. Although none of us dared say it, we were all watching for the same thing—Johnny's small body washing up on the shore.

We searched for what seemed like hours but was in fact no more than two hours at the most. All of us were drenched, and the rain had gotten heavier. The wind intensified, too, forcing us to bend over to walk into it.

I fell to my knees in the sand and tried twice to stand, only to be thrown down again. I heard a voice behind me, but I couldn't make out the words. Chase stepped in front of me and pulled me to my feet.

"You've got to get out of the storm," he said. His voice was all but drowned out by the sound of the wind and the black, roaring sea.

I tried to tell him that I would be all right, that I wanted to stay and search for Johnny, but he insisted.

"The storm's getting worse," he said. "You take the horse and go back to my house."

"But what about you?" I was also shouting to be heard, and I was having difficulty standing up, so great was the force of the gale. "If it's not safe for me, it's not safe for any of you."

His answer was to pick me up and carry me to the horse and to set me in the saddle. "Go home!" he said. "I'll search until dark, and then I'll ride home with Felix." With that he gave the horse a slap on the rump, and the gelding started away at a trot.

The storm was worsening by the minute, and I knew it was not fit weather for either human or beast. As I watched the gelding, his head down, shoulders hunched and twitching with nervousness, I thought of Sir Blanco. Had he ever made it back to the stables after I fell? Was he trapped somewhere in the storm? Even if he had made it back to Shadow Cove, there was no one there to put him away. He would still be out in the dreadful weather. I knew I would have to go see about him. I was still a few miles away, and it would be hard going in the wind and rain, but I felt I had no other choice. I couldn't let the poor beast die in the storm.

If I could make it to the Shadows, I could wait out the storm there and ride back to town when it was over. I would ride along the coast road, and on the way I could continue to search for Johnny.

An eerie brightness had accompanied the storm, but the wind fought it and forced me to close my eyes. That only made the roar of the wind and the mad trashing of the sea seem even more violent. A small tree branch, sailing on the wind, slashed my forehead and startled me enough to force me to open my eyes. I saw red drops of blood mingling with the rain where it fell on my hands, but I ignored it and the sting of the wound on my forehead and let the rain wash the blood away as I rode on, calling Johnny's name over and over.

The gelding sensed my determination and plodded on, head down, withers tense and twitching. It seemed an eternity before I could see the dark mass that I knew was the house at Shadow Cove. The spires and towers thrusting into the storm gave the house a defiant look, as if it were daring the wind and rain and sea to destroy it. When I drew closer, I saw that the ground was littered with broken branches and leaves and a few shingles. The storm was taking the dare.

I rode first to the stables, and my heart sank when I saw no sign of Sir Blanco standing outside, waiting to be put away. That meant he hadn't made it, that he, like Johnny, was lost somewhere in the storm.

Then I heard a faint sound, barely audible above the roar of the wind, but I knew it came from somewhere inside the stables. The gelding I had been riding heard it, too, and lifted his ears and answered with a nicker. We had both heard the neighing of a horse!

I pulled the gelding by the reins, leading him inside the stables, and the first thing I saw was the beautiful, proud, white head of Sir Blanco. He neighed again, scolding me for leaving him alone.

"Sir Blanco!" I cried, running to him. "Who put you away? How did you get in here?"

He shook my hand away when I tried to rub his nose, showing he was still peeved at me, and lunged his head aggressively at the gelding. I felt a sudden chill as I realized that whoever had put him in the stable could still be here. I whirled around, glancing in all directions, trying to see into the dark corners of the stalls.

"Who's here?" I asked aloud, my voice trembling. "Is anyone in here?"

There was no answer except the storm and the gelding, blowing and nickering as he tried to back away from Sir Blanco.

I moved cautiously toward the gelding and placed a hand on his neck to guide him toward one of the stalls, all the while searching the area with my eyes. I would put the horse away and go to the house to wait out the storm, just as I had planned.

When I had given the horse food and water and placed a blanket over his wet back, I gave Sir Blanco another unwelcome pat on the nose and went back into the storm toward the house. I had decided that it had to be Felix who had seen Sir Blanco waiting near the stables and had taken pity on him and put him away. He had admitted he'd been out here watching out for me at Chase's behest in the past. He must have been here today, also, and he'd gone back to town looking for me when he saw Sir Blanco approach without me. It was odd, though, that he hadn't mentioned it when he saw me.

I entered the house through the back door. In spite of the fact that it was not yet late enough to be dark, the storm robbed the house of light, and the cold, unearthly feeling enveloped me as soon as I entered. I tried to ignore it and headed straight for the back stairway, anxious to get to my room and put on dry clothes.

As soon as I got to the top landing, I saw the thin stream of light coming from beneath the door that led to the upstairs sitting room. I had not seen the light as I approached because the room was on the opposite side of the house, but there was no doubt that a lamp burned in there now. I stopped, dead still, and at first I could hear nothing except my heart pounding and the blood rushing in my head—loud enough that even the storm seemed distant. I took one cautious step forward, toward the door, and thought then that I'd heard another sound—a faint rustling inside the room.

I took a few more steps, slowly, quietly, and touched my hand to the door, pushing it open. The hinges, so infrequently used now, cried out in anguish, and when I peered inside I saw nothing except the yellow glow of the lamp. But when I gave the door another slow push and took a step inside, I saw her.

She was dressed in white, and I knew she had been walking along the beach. She clutched a child next to her body, and I recognized the thin, bloodless face of Johnny Bradley.

Chapter 12

I WAS too stunned to realize at first that the woman was Rachel. She had a wild, frightened look in her eyes, and she had a gun pointed at me while she gripped Johnny, pale with fright, with her other arm.

Johnny called out to me in a small frightened voice, calling me Aunty Laura. Then with a frantic jerk he freed himself of her grip and started toward me, but she caught him by the arm and pulled him back. I made a move toward him, and in the same instant she swung the gun toward me.

"Stay back!" she said. "Don't touch him! I don't want him hurt."

"I won't hurt him, Rachel. I only want—"

"I said stay back!" She raised the gun higher, and I heard it click as she cocked it, ready to fire. I stopped and took a step backward. Johnny began to cry, and he called my name again.

"He calls you Aunty!" Rachel said. "Chase taught him to do that, didn't he? What right did he have to tell you? What are you trying to do to me? Why do you want to hurt me?" She was ranting nonsense and waving the gun dangerously.

"I don't want to hurt you, Rachel, and I don't want to hurt Johnny either. If you'll just let me—"

Johnny jerked himself free of her again and made another lunge toward me. In the same blinding moment I heard the loud explosion and felt a sudden disturbance of the air as the bullet sped past my face. Johnny stopped, dead still, halfway between Rachel and me, his eyes like wide brown disks in his white, white face. The mind plays odd tricks in moments of stress, and a vision of Anton in a long-forgotten scene from our childhood flashed in my mind—Papa catching Anton stealing tobacco from the canister he kept in the library, and Anton facing his accuser with dark, frightened eyes.

The odd, disconnected memory evaporated quickly when I saw Rachel drop to her knees, crying, with the gun dangling at her side. I saw her weak moment as an opportunity to reach out to Johnny, but she was more alert than I thought. As soon as she sensed a movement from me, she came to life and leveled the gun at me again and at the same time grabbed for Johnny.

"Get away from us!" she sobbed. "Get away! I won't miss next time, I swear!"

"Aunty Laura! Get back!" Johnny screamed.

"It's all right, darling," I said, backing away. "It's all right. Don't cry. I'm going back, see?"

Johnny continued to sob convulsively, but he nodded his head and locked his wide frightened eyes on mine, wanting to believe I was telling the truth—that everything was going to be all right. Rachel, in the meantime, continued to hold the gun pointed at me. She was shaking so hard I was afraid she was going to pull the trigger accidently. I was even more afraid that Johnny would make another impulsive lunge for me and the bullet would strike him. My only hope was to force myself to remain calm and to pray that any serenity I could muster would transfer to Rachel. I tried to think of something to say, something soothing, something that would belie the terror I felt, but no inspiration came. Rachel gave me no opportunity anyway. She continued to rant.

"I wouldn't have come here if it hadn't been for the storm. I had no choice, you know. I had to protect Johnny. And you. The careless one! You let Anton's poor Sir Blanco out in the storm. I had to put him away. And now I have to protect Johnny."

"Of course," I said. "I understand. You didn't want Johnny out in the storm. You must have seen him out playing when the wind and rain began, and you wanted to protect—"

"No!" she said with cold, calm fury. "You don't understand. You don't understand at all. If you did, you wouldn't be talking to me that way. In that tone of voice—like I'm a crazy person."

Her unexpected turn toward rationality was equally as unsettling to me as her raving had been a few seconds earlier.

Instinct told me to be even more careful. "I'm sorry, Rachel, I—"

"You're sorry? You're sorry for what? For coming here with your high and mighty ways? Why did you have to come back in the first place? Anton always said you were going to be a problem one day. Anton was a problem, you know. All of you Kings are the same, aren't you? Noble fools. Even Anton in the end tried to be noble. Why couldn't he see that he was being foolish?"

"What are you talking about, Rachel?" I tried not to show the emotion in my voice. I was afraid she might take another wild shot at me, but I also sensed that she knew something about Anton that I needed to know.

"I couldn't let him ruin me, could I? Could I?" she demanded, waving the gun at me.

"I don't know, Rachel—"

"That's right, you don't know. You don't know me at all. Nobody does. Especially not Robert Thorn. He couldn't see that I couldn't let him hurt Johnny."

"Robert? Hurt Johnny?"

"Oh, yes, Robert," she said with a cynical laugh. "You're still unwilling to believe the worst about your dear, sweet, oh-so-attentive Robert, aren't you? Even now that you've found out he's been bleeding you dry with his embezzlement scheme, you still don't want to believe it. It only shows what a fool you are, doesn't it? I'm no fool, though. I knew what he was doing. He's very clever, you know. Only he went too far, and now I'm the only one smart enough to stop him." She laughed, a high-pitched hysterical sound. "He was going to kidnap Johnny and use him to lure you and Chase out to the beach, and he was going to kill you both. Then he could have all of King Enterprises."

"But that's ridiculous, Rachel. There's no way Robert could get King Enterprises."

She laughed her cynical laugh again. "Of course he could. With you out of the way he could fix the books so it looked as if the company owed him enough that he could claim all the assets. He even stole Anton's will so there would be no one to claim any of the property. No one except you. 'But I can handle the little old maid,' he said. But he couldn't handle you as well as he thought. Oh, yes, you're shocked, I can see. But you should know, Robert is very clever. That's why I agreed to marry him. Agreed to all of his schemes because I knew he would be rich one day with all his cleverness." Her cold, cynical tone changed abruptly as she reached to touch Johnny's head and said softly, "But I couldn't let him harm my son."

"Your son?" She was raving again, talking like a madwoman.

"Don't pretend you don't know," she said, angry again. "I know Chase told you everything. I know he told you Anton was Johnny's father."

I felt quite unbalanced for a moment, but there was something about the tone of her voice, something about the way she looked at me that made me think she wasn't mad at all, that she was telling the cold stark truth. Johnny, young and innocent as he was, stared at her as if he knew she was saying something that would affect his life forever.

"Anton," I whispered when I was finally able to speak at all. I had the sudden flash of memory again—of Anton looking frightened, Anton with a happy smile, Anton as a child—and now it all made sense. In spite of the fact that the resemblance was faint, there was an expression in Johnny's eyes that was exactly like my brother's.

"Yes, Anton," Rachel said. "He even named the boy for his father." Her voice had softened somewhat again. "Johnny was conceived here in this very room." I was shocked that she would be speaking so bluntly in front of Johnny, but I didn't dare risk crossing her by trying to silence her. "It was here on a night when the warm breeze from the gulf came through the window there and made love to us while we made love to each other," she continued shamelessly. "We were up here while everyone else was downstairs at one of Anton's marvelously wild parties. I was full of champagne. I didn't take the proper precautions. Just that one time I wasn't careful."

She saw the shocked expression on my face and laughed. "Am I embarrassing you?" she asked. "Does it shock you to hear about the things a man and a woman do?"

"Not in front of Johnny, Rachel, please—"

"What does it hurt a child to know the ways of the world? What good does it do to let him become an ignorant, noble fool?"

"There will be a time to tell him the ways of the world, Rachel. But not now. Not like this. It's not right—"

"Enough!" she said, brandishing the gun again. "Spare me your lectures on right and wrong. Don't you think I had enough of that from your brother? And anyway, it won't do you any good to lecture me. I'm only telling you this because I know you won't be around to tell anyone. Don't you see I'm going to have to kill you? I know you won't keep my secret."

"Rachel, please, if you don't wish it known, of course I wouldn't—"

"I don't want your empty promises!" she cried. "Anton made empty promises. He was going to keep our secret. Said it was best for both of us. But he changed his mind. He turned into the noble fool, and we had to kill him."

I felt quite numb with shock and revulsion, but Rachel continued to talk, and I forced myself to listen. "It wasn't that I didn't love Johnny," she said, touching his head gently again. "I always did. It's just that I couldn't afford the scandal. And neither could Anton. After all, we couldn't marry, could we? We didn't love each other. It was just a lark. A night of champagne and gaiety and the warm gulf breeze." She sighed. "I can't say I regretted the night. Just that I was so careless. Anton said, and I quite agreed with him, that it would ruin us both socially if the truth came out. That's why he got Chase to help us."

"Chase?"

"Oh, yes, Chase knows the truth. But he's the only one. He and Felix LeFeu. Anton went to Chase for help. Poor Anton, always so helpless, always dependent on Chase to tell him what to do. It was Chase who arranged for Felix to drive me in his carriage to Houston. I stayed there until after my baby was born. Everyone thought I was visiting relatives. Relatives!" She laughed, a bitter sound. "None of them thinks I'm good enough for them. No one ever did except Papa, and now all the money he left me is almost gone, and I'm almost as old as you are. I have to do something, don't I? Robert was my best hope! He's so clever. I know he's going to be rich."

I was hardly listening to her now. I was looking at Johnny. I really was his aunty. He was my very own flesh and blood. Knowing that only strengthened the bond I'd felt all along, and I was determined now to make certain I got him out of this situation safely, even if it meant risking my own life, even if it wasn't yet clear to me how I was going to do it. In fact, I felt quite unclear about a lot of things, including why Chase had gotten involved.

"Chase knew the truth. Why didn't he tell me?"

I hadn't realized I'd spoken out loud until Rachel answered. "Of course he knew the truth," she said. "He's the only person Anton and I could trust. We knew we could trust him to protect Anton and Johnny because of his loyalty to old John King."

"My father?"

Rachel laughed again. "My, my, you are a naive fool, aren't you? Didn't you know your father saved Chase Bradley's life? No, I don't suppose you did. You were busy being the privileged little rich girl. Away at school. Protected from harsh reality. It was after Chase killed that man. He was working for your father then. John King hired the best lawyer in Texas to defend him. He could afford it, though. Your father was a rich and clever businessman. Too bad your brother wasn't as clever."

"I want Papa to come help us!" Johnny cried suddenly, as if he'd taken in all he could bear. "No one will hurt Papa, will they, Aunty?"

He had obviously heard and understood everything, and my heart went out to him, but I hardly knew what to say. I wouldn't be telling the truth if I told him Chase would not be hurt. I was desperately afraid myself that Robert Thorn could have killed him by now.

"Tell him!" I said to Rachel. My voice was a harsh, hissing whisper that I hardly recognized. "Tell him Chase will be all right."

Her cold stare faltered, and she glanced at Johnny, then back at me. I sensed her confusion and saw the tormented look in her eyes. "I can't," she said.

"Why are you doing this? Why didn't you try to stop Robert from harming Chase, too? Don't you know what it will do to Johnny if Chase is killed? He's the only father the boy's ever known!"

"Don't do that to me!" she screamed. "Don't try to make me feel guilty the way Anton did. It was Chase's idea to take Johnny as his ward. Is it my fault he did that? It would have been better for all of us if he hadn't!"

"You should be grateful that Chase took him in. How can you be so callous?"

"Callous?" she shrieked. "I'm realistic, not callous. I didn't mind who took the boy. I just wanted him to have a good home. It was Anton who couldn't let well enough alone. Oh, at first he was perfectly content to have Chase care for him, and he eased his conscience with that money he gave to Chase to help pay for Johnny's keep." She laughed again, the same odd, empty sound as before. "Oh, I knew what those so-called loan payments were. Anton told me, and I was clever enough to tell Robert. That's the way he was able to conceal the money he embezzled."

"The money was meant for Johnny. It wasn't a loan! I should have—"

"You should have kept your nose out of it! You should have stayed in New York where you belong. There was never any loan. Never any reason for you to go snooping around. Robert said you'd never find out. Said you weren't smart enough. But you were too smart for your own good, weren't you? And look where it got you. You couldn't let well enough alone. Just like Anton couldn't. He let his damnable conscience get the best of him. Started to feel guilty about Johnny. Providing money wasn't enough, he said. He was going to claim him as his own. He said I should own up to my responsibility, too. But how could I do that? How could I let the truth be known and have it ruin me?"

"Rachel, listen to me. No one has to know. If you'll just put that gun away—"

"Don't try to trick me. Don't tell me no one will know!" Her voice was frantic and high-pitched, and she waved the gun at me again. "You'll tell everyone. You'll ruin me! You'll say it's the right thing to do. Just like Anton did. It all started about a year ago—this awful streak of conscience and responsibility Anton developed. Poor fool. He even started taking more of an interest in the business. That's when he discovered Robert's embezzlement scheme. Found out more than he was smart enough to handle. He was going to ruin us both. We had to get rid of him. We had to destroy his will, too. Because he left everything to Johnny. Don't you see? We had no choice."

It had all been done with cold-blooded calculation. That meant she was even more dangerous than I had imagined. But there was another side to her as well—a side that had allowed those protective maternal instincts to surface and made her want to save Johnny. I knew I had to use that somehow to save us both now. Holding her gaze steadily with my own, I asked again, "What do you think will happen to Johnny if Chase is killed?"

Again I saw the confused look in her eyes. I knew it could easily lead to her becoming irrational again and firing the gun, as she had done before, and this time she might not miss. I watched as she raised the gun and saw it waving in her shaking hand. Bringing her left hand up, she used it to steady her right hand as she held the pistol, still pointed at me. When she spoke again, her voice was as unsteady as her hands.

"I'm taking Johnny with me," she said. "We're going away together."

"I want my papa," Johnny cried. "Aunty Laura, tell her. I want my papa!"

The terrified look on Johnny's face was almost more than I could bear. "Rachel, please!" I said. "Can't you see what you're doing to him?"

She made another attempt to steady the shaking gun with both hands as she shouted at me. "Stay back! I know what I'm doing."

"Please!" My voice sounded almost as frantic as hers. "Please tell me what you're going to do with Johnny."

"I—I can't let the scandal ruin us both," she said, her voice faltering again. The gun bobbed dangerously. "I know a good orphanage in Houston. I can visit him regularly. I—" She glanced at Johnny, who had begun to cry, and the sight of it obviously disturbed her. "It wouldn't have come to this if you had gone home after a week or two like you were supposed to do," she said, her voice rising to an even higher pitch. "Robert said you would. He said you wouldn't be any problem. Then when you didn't go, he said we could scare you away. But he wasn't as clever as I thought. All those tricks he planned—me making those ghostly appearances along the beach, leaving the bloody knife in your house—none of it worked." Her laugh sounded reckless, tormented. "I was so upset there were times I thought I would just walk into the sea, but Robert kept coming back with more schemes. When that bloody knife didn't scare you away, I told him I wanted no more tricks, though. I'd already been almost caught once—by Felix."

"Felix?"

"Oh, yes, I saw him out here all the time. He even slept in your house. I suppose Chase sent him out here to make sure you were safe. It was too dangerous for me to be here when Felix was around. That Felix LeFeu is too smart. He would have figured out soon enough what we were up to. That's why I told Robert we'd have to find another way to get rid of you."

"Rachel," I said, forcing myself to keep my voice calm. "Whatever it is you think you have to do to me, you can't do it in front of Johnny."

"Johnny is a child," she said. "In time he will forget."

I wanted to tell her she was wrong, that children don't forget, that witnessing the murder of another person could wound his spirit for life. But I never got the chance. I saw her grip tighten on the gun. I saw her finger move slowly, squeezing the trigger. At the last minute she turned toward Johnny, and that's when the gun fired.

Chapter 13

Johnny hit the floor at the same time that he cried out, "Run, Aunty Laura!" He had slammed himself into Rachel and lost his balance in the process. She had turned toward him when she sensed him lunging at her, and because of the jarring blow Johnny had dealt her, had accidently fired the gun at the ceiling. Pieces of plaster and molding were still raining down on our heads. "Run, Aunty!" Johnny cried again. But instead of running, I made a grab for Rachel.

Everything had happened too fast for her, and she was caught totally by surprise. She hardly knew what had transpired, hardly knew, in fact, when I took the gun from her hand. I pulled Johnny toward me and forced him behind me.

"Stay where you are, Rachel," I said, leveling the gun at her, just as she had at me. The look on her face was a mixture of fright and confusion. "Stay where you are," I repeated, "and you won't be hurt." I was backing toward the door, and Johnny, standing behind me, sensed what I was doing, and was backing up, also. "Hurry, Johnny," I said, turning toward him slightly. I prayed that he would run out the door and all the way downstairs and out of the house, but he didn't. He stayed very close to me, moving only when I moved.

"You'll never get away with this!" Rachel cried. "I won't let you. I won't let you ruin me. We'll both die first! You'll see!"

I continued to back toward the door, fearing with each step that she would lunge at me. I was uncertain what I would do, not at all sure that I would have the courage to pull the trigger should she do anything wrong. I could have cried with relief when I heard Johnny turn the doorknob, and in the next second we were both out the door. Rachel was still screaming threats at me as I slammed the door closed, and we could hear her pounding the door with her fists, demanding to be let out. My hands shook as I took the key from my pocket and turned the lock.

"Hurry, Johnny!" I cried. "To the stables! We'll ride Sir Blanco to find your papa." We both scrambled down the back stairs and through the kitchen to the back door.

Wind and rain lashed at us as we ran across the grounds toward the stables. Johnny stumbled twice, pushed down by the force of the gale. Finally I picked him up and carried him the last few steps. Sir Blanco was dancing about restlessly in his stall, tossing his head and throwing himself against the gate.

"Why is he doing that?" Johnny asked, holding back. "Why is he scaring me like that?"

"He doesn't mean to scare you, Johnny," I said. "He's doing it because the storm makes him nervous. But he won't hurt you. Come on. You must help me saddle him."

Still Johnny held back, staring with uncertainty at the big white stallion.

"Come on, Johnny," I said. "You were a very brave boy to help us get away from Rachel. Now you have to keep being brave."

"She said she was my mother," Johnny said, turning his wide, innocent eyes on me. "Aunty Stella said my mother is a beautiful princess and the angels took her to heaven. She's *not* my mother, is she?"

I looked at him, uncertain of what I should say. I didn't know whether a lie or the truth would be more unkind. "I don't know, Johnny," I said at last, knowing I was retreating into cowardice. "Maybe someday you'll know who your mother is."

"Yes," he said with a seriousness and longing that almost broke my heart. "Yes, someday I will know." Then, without changing his serious expression, he asked, "Was I really brave, Aunty Laura?"

"You were very brave," I said. "And you must continue to be brave. You must be brave enough to ride with me through the storm to find your papa, but first you must help me saddle Sir Blanco."

He nodded his head solemnly and turned cautiously toward the horse.

"I'm going to put a rope over his head," I told Johnny. "Then I will put the rope over the rails of his stall so you can help hold him still."

Johnny nodded his head again, never showing fear except in his eyes, and when I saw it there, I knew how very brave he was to follow my instructions. I did manage to get the horse saddled with his help, and this time I used a traditional saddle. I would have to straddle the horse, but I had no inclination to worry about the impropriety of that now. My only thought was that it would be easier to ride double that way.

Sir Blanco was in no mood for the unfamiliar sensation of two humans on his back, and he was in even less of a mood to be taken out into the storm. He bowed his back and kicked his hind legs, trying to throw us off. I heard Johnny suck in his breath, but he never uttered a cry as I held him close to me with my weak arm, while I pulled the reins tight with my other hand, all the while clamping my thighs tight against the saddle. Sir Blanco danced around some more, then reared up on his hind legs, pawing his front feet at the air in defiance of everything. Johnny turned his face sideways in an attempt to bury it against me.

"Don't be frightened, Johnny," I said. "We just have to show him who's boss."

"I'm not frightened," Johnny said, but his voice belied his statement, and his arms were locked against mine as if it were his only means of clinging to life, sending waves of pain along my wrist. I didn't pull my arm away, though, for fear of unnerving Johnny even more. "Papa says he's never seen a woman sit a horse as fine as you," Johnny said, sounding a little calmer. "He says you look ignorant and you expect the world to stop when you ride by. Does that mean the storm will stop, too?"

"I'm afraid your papa was exaggerating," I said. *Ignorant?* I thought. What did he mean by that? And what right did Chase Bradley have saying such things about me to a child? I had no time to think of such petty things now, though. "Hang on, Johnny. Here we go."

I had gained control of Sir Blanco now, and we headed out into the storm and along the coastal road. The wind howled mercilessly, like a banshee heralding death, and Sir Blanco reacted as if he had heard the warning and feared for his own life. He reared up on his hind legs again, crying out in fear and anger, and it was all I could do to bring him under control. Finally I got him to walk with a slow steadiness, obeying my commands, but I sensed his edginess in the toss of his head and in the tension of his body. Johnny clung to my arm with as much force as ever and kept his head down, too. Neither of us bothered to talk. We couldn't have heard each other anyway above the howling of the wind. To add to our discomfort, we were both drenched, since in our haste to escape the house I'd not taken the time to find even so much as a shawl to cover us.

We had ridden only a short distance when I saw the shadowy form moving toward us through the storm—a man on horseback. My heart leapt. It had to be Chase. He was still looking for Johnny. I spurred Sir Blanco to a faster pace and rode toward him. It was already too late before I realized my mistake. The lone rider was not Chase, but Robert Thorn. He had seen us, too, and he rode toward us at a gallop.

Wheeling Sir Blanco around, I prodded him with my heels, urging him to run, urging him I knew not where, except that I knew I had to escape the man who had murdered my brother and who now felt he had the same reason to kill me. Riding into the wind and the rain was even more difficult than it had been when our backs were to the storm. Even though neither Johnny nor I was heavy, our two bodies made for an awkward balance that Sir Blanco was unaccustomed to, and that slowed him down enough to allow Robert to gain on us.

I pulled Johnny closer to me and leaned forward in the saddle, rising in the stirrups, hoping to minimize the imbalance, but I only made things worse. My skirts, billowing against the wind like a sail, held us back even more. Robert was close enough that I could hear the frantic pounding of his horse's hooves, and in the next second he was beside us, leaning out of his saddle, reaching for us. I tried to veer away, but the sudden movement frightened Johnny, and his desperate spasm as he grabbed for me almost cost us both our balance.

Robert grasped the reins above my hands and pulled on them, forcing Sir Blanco to a stop. The brush of his horse's flank against Sir Blanco frightened him, and he reared up, pawing at the intruder. Johnny screamed and tried to grab my arm, but the rain had made our skin slippery and his grip failed.

I felt him slipping away, falling out of the saddle. I tightened my grip, trying to hold him close while pain shooting through my injured wrist weakened me and left me swimming in waves of nausea.

It was too much for me. I couldn't control Sir Blanco and hang on to Johnny as well, and suddenly Johnny was out of my grasp and on the ground.

In one instinctive movement I pulled the horse into obedience and backed him away so Johnny wouldn't be trampled, then I jumped from the saddle. My skirts were sodden weights hindering my every movement. I stooped over him, barely able to see him through the wet ribbons of my hair that clung to my face, but there were his wide eyes staring up at me, showing more surprise than pain. Scooping him up in my arms, I held him close to me, forgetting for a moment that Robert Thorn loomed over us.

Robert's hand, placed roughly on my arm, brought me back to reality. I jerked away, but he only laughed and grabbed me again. "You make it easy for me," he said. "God, if I'd known it was going to be this easy, I could have saved myself a lot of worry."

"Are you mad, Robert? You can't get away with this." I said, trying to free myself from him. He held me fast, though, and was pulling me, with Johnny in my arms, toward the frenzied sea.

"Why not? They'll simply find that you drowned in the storm. A coincidence, isn't it, that you'll meet your death in the same way your brother did? Only instead of disgracing yourself by being drunk, you'll be a heroine. They'll know you died trying to save the little bastard here. You escaped death twice before—once in the warehouse and once falling from your horse, but I won't mess up this time."

I let Johnny slip from my arms. "Run!" I cried. "Ride Sir Blanco. Hurry!"

Johnny, frightened as he was of the big horse, tried to run toward him, but Robert lunged for him, stopping him. Johnny fell to the wet sand, and Robert fell with him, bogged down by the damp, sticky expanse. I recognized it as the only opportunity I was likely to have, and I jumped on top of Robert, catching him by surprise, so that he lost his grip on Johnny. I hardly knew what I was doing, except that I was vaguely aware of pounding him with my fist, and out of the corner of my eye seeing Johnny slogging through the wet sand toward the horses. I never got a chance to see what happened next because Robert's arm slammed against my face, and my head jerked backward. For a moment I saw dozens of lights dancing in front of my eyes.

The sensation lasted only a moment, and in the next instant I was aware of being jerked to my feet and my arms flailing, trying to keep Robert back. I was losing, though, and I felt his hands encircling my throat and felt him cutting off my air with the force of his thumbs. I foolishly tried to cry out, but no sound would come. I grasped at his hands with my own, trying to pull them away, to free my clogged throat, but his grip was too strong. I had the sensation of my body moving, of being dragged closer and closer to the screaming, thrashing water. It reached for us, raging, vomiting fury, trying to pull us into itself.

Somehow, in the midst of my rising panic, I was possessed with a moment of cold rationality. I knew it would do no good to try to move his hands. I would have to force him to move them himself. I reached for his eyes, scratching and clawing, while at the same time my knee came up through my torn skirt and met his groin in just the same way I'd seen the sailor do it on the wharf. With an agonizing cry, Robert backed away and fell to his knees, bent over with pain. Then, like an animal maddened with fear, I attacked him again and pushed him down. Just as he went down, a mighty wave reached for us both and pulled us into the roiling gulf, covering us with foaming, swirling water. I never let go of him but held him fast until the wave receded, knowing I would never be fast enough or strong enough to run away from him. I had to best him now, or die trying. The blow I had dealt to his groin had weakened him, but not enough. He lunged for my throat again, and we flailed about in water up to my thighs. Again I pushed him, forcing him down under the water. He arose like a thundering, sodden phoenix and this time forced me down until I was covered with the entire swirling, thrashing, roaring ocean.

I couldn't see. I couldn't breathe. I couldn't think. All I could do was follow my animal instincts and try to fight my way to the top. I grasped at nothing but water and felt myself being pulled downward by my heavy skirts, but still I kept fighting. My lungs seemed about to burst in my chest, and my eyes burned with sand and salt. My knees struck something solid and unyielding, and then, as I fell forward, my hands touched the same thing.

Wet sand beneath the water! I stood, and fell, and stood again, but somehow I managed to drag myself to the sodden shore, and as far away from the sea as I could get before I vomited, then collapsed and lay face down in the wet sand while the rain poured itself over me and the sea raged behind me.

I lay there for several minutes until I felt something pushing at my side. I was too numbed with exhaustion to be frightened, but I sat up, resigned to whatever Robert Thorn would deal out to me. It wasn't Robert Thorn's eyes that met mine, though, but Sir Blanco's aristocratic and impatient gaze. He pushed at me again with his nose, demanding that I stand and get him to shelter.

"Johnny!" I cried, scrambling to my feet. "What have you done with Johnny?"

His only answer was an arrogant stare, and I sagged against him, sobbing uncontrollably. Johnny, obviously, had fallen from his back, and was now undoubtedly lost or injured or dead somewhere in the storm. I had feared the big stallion would be too much for him, but it had been my only hope to send him home that way. Now I saw how foolish I had been to have left the Shadows. My concern had been to get Johnny away from Rachel and back to Chase, but my judgment had been poor, and Johnny had paid with his life for it.

One small glimmer of hope lit up my soul. Johnny undoubtedly had not been able to control Sir Blanco, and the big horse would have gone wherever he wanted. If I mounted him now and allowed him to do the same thing, then perhaps he would retrace his steps and lead me to wherever Johnny had fallen. It was a small hope, but it was all I had.

I pulled myself up into the saddle and nudged Sir Blanco's sides with my heels, then, with no guidance from the reins, let him go his own way. Not surprisingly, he started toward Shadow Cove. My eyes searched every inch of the rain-soaked ground, and I called out Johnny's name until I was hoarse, but there was no sight of him and no answer to my call. Sir Blanco kept walking through the storm and didn't stop until he reached the stable door at Shadow Cove.

I dismounted and took the time to pull the saddle from his back and to throw a blanket over him before I ran to the house. One small flame of hope still flickered within me—that Johnny had gotten this far and had taken shelter inside the house. I burst inside calling his name.

There was no answer. Nothing but cold, dark silence.

I ran through all the downstairs rooms calling his name again and again, and finally I went up the stairs. I felt a sudden paralyzing numbness when I reached the top of the landing and saw the open door at the end of the hall. It was the door to the room where I had left Rachel locked inside. For a moment I felt too frightened to investigate, but my concern for Johnny overcame all my fear, and I ran recklessly down the hall and into the room.

It was empty. An andiron from the fireplace lay on the floor next to the door where Rachel had dropped it after she had shattered the lock. I stood there, taking it all in, trying to decide what I should do next.

Suddenly I heard a sudden rush of noise as if the front door had blown open. I started to hurry downstairs to close it, but I stopped just as I reached the hallway. I had just heard the solid thud of the door closing. The wind hadn't blown the door open. That sound meant someone or something had closed it. I strained to listen and felt a sickening void in my chest when I heard the sound of footsteps on the marble staircase.

Quickly I picked up the andiron and entered the room. I didn't dare close the door, for fear the sound of creaking hinges would alert the intruder to where I was. Instead I pressed myself against the wall next to the door, hardly daring to breathe.

The sound of the footsteps grew closer. The unseen presence had reached the top of the landing and now was advancing down the hall.

I felt as if I had stopped breathing, but my heart pounded thunderously in my chest while I waited. The footsteps advanced with measured steadiness, closer and closer, coming as if directed by some magical force all the way down the hall to the room where I waited with the andiron raised above my head. I took a step forward to meet it as it stepped into the room, and in the same moment brought the andiron down with as much force as I could muster.

I felt a lightning bolt of pain shoot through my arm and permeate my body as a firm hand gripped my sprained wrist and stopped the andiron from hitting its mark. I sucked in my breath to squelch a scream and found myself face to face with Chase Bradley.

"Laura! Thank God!" He let go of my arm and pulled me toward him, holding me close to his chest.

"Chase!" I whispered, wanting badly to let him hold me, to feel his hands on me, to believe that everything was going to be all right now that he was here. But I knew everything would never be all right as long as Johnny was missing. I had to tell Chase what had happened. But how could I do it? How could I tell him the person he loved most was probably dead?

"Chase," I said again. "Johnny . . . Johnny is . . ." I found I couldn't speak the unthinkable, and I felt tears of despair blinding me.

"Johnny is safe."

"No," I said. "No, you have to know the truth. It's my fault. He tried to ride Sir Blanco. But I shouldn't have told him—I mean, it's my fault we left. Because she was here, and I was afraid for Johnny, but I only led us both into trouble, and now he's out there. Oh, Chase, how can I ever bear it ? We've got to go look. We must find—"

"Wait a minute," Chase said. He gripped both of my arms and was staring intently into my face. "What are you talking about? You're not making sense. I told you, Johnny is safe."

"What?"

"He's safe at home with Aunt Stella."

"What?" I said again, unable to take in what he was telling me.

"Felix found him. He was riding along the coastal road, headed toward town."

"Riding? But—"

"Felix said it was Robert Thorn's horse he rode, and poor Johnny was frightened out of his wits. Said you told him to find me while you fought off some wicked man. Felix and I both knew the wicked man he was talking about had to be Robert. I sent Felix back to town with Johnny, and I came looking for you. Only it took me a hell of a long time riding through that storm. When I couldn't find any sign of you or Robert anywhere along the coast, I damned near died of worry."

"Riding Robert's horse?" I tried to sort it all out. Of course he wouldn't take Sir Blanco. He probably couldn't have mounted him anyway. He was too small. But he was smart. Smart enough to take the smaller horse. And he was safe! *Safe!* I could have sung for joy. "He's alive, then?" I asked, wanting to be reassured. "Johnny is alive?"

Chase laughed. "I just told you. He's alive. And safe."

"I know who he is," I said.

"You know—what do you mean?"

"Rachel told me. She was here. She told me he's Anton's son."

Chase stared at me for a moment, not speaking. "Why?" he said at last. "Why would she tell you? And what was she doing here?"

"She brought Johnny here."

"Rachel? But why—"

"To protect him from Robert. It was Robert who kidnapped him, Chase. To use him as bait to get us out to look for him. He was going to kill us both because we knew the truth about his embezzlement. And because he knew I had figured out he was the one who had killed Anton."

"My God, Laura, are you sure?"

"I'm sure. Rachel told me everything. Anton had found out about Robert's embezzlement, too, and that's why they killed him. She and Robert had been trying to frighten me away from here, and she was the one who had been in my house and on the beach. All those tricks. Leaving a bloody knife in my house. Ghostly appearances. It was Rachel."

"Rachel? Then she's smarter than I thought. Even Felix didn't figure that out."

"You had him staying out here watching out for me. Why didn't you tell me?"

"Because I knew you'd never allow it if you knew. You're so damned independent."

"If you knew how many times I lay awake because I had an uncanny sensation that someone was in my house! But that's not all you haven't told me, is it? Rachel told me how you helped her when the baby was born, and how you took Johnny to live with you and how Anton paid you. That's what those so-called loan payments were. Why didn't you tell me, Chase? Why didn't you tell me Johnny was my nephew? Is that what I overheard you telling someone I was not to know?"

Chase took a step away from me. "It was Felix I was arguing with that day at the waterfront. He thought we should tell you. Said you were smart enough to find out anyway. Just like Aunt Stella figured it out, only she never let on she knew. I said no. I didn't want to risk anything getting out to hurt Johnny— or his mother." He had spoken without looking at me, as if remembering the details was hurtful to him. "I thought it would just complicate things for everybody. For Johnny. For Rachel. For you. I thought it was best to let sleeping dogs lie."

"That's why you kept trying to get me to leave Galveston, wasn't it? Because you thought I would uncover the truth. Awaken those sleeping dogs."

"Yes," he said, turning back to look at me. "That's what I was afraid of. And you've done a damned good job of it, too."

"I never meant to hurt anybody, Chase, I—"

"Where's Rachel?" he asked. "Is she going to cause me trouble? Is she going to want him back? I never thought she would, but I should have known. A mother's instincts—"

"Don't worry about her instincts," I said. "She wanted to protect him from Robert, but she was going to put him in an orphanage in Houston. She couldn't let the truth about having an illegitimate son ruin her socially, she said."

"Oh, God," Chase said, shaking his head. "The poor woman. She could never grow up. Never face reality. Where is she now?"

I told him how I had locked her in the room after she'd acted irrationally with the gun, how I'd set out to find someone to take her into custody, and how I'd found the room empty when I returned.

"She's out in the storm, then," Chase said grimly. "She'll never make it. The storm has washed out all the roads. Some houses have already been swept into the gulf. The Shadows could be next, Laura."

"I know," I said, turning to the window. "I've seen how it's worsening."

"I wasn't even sure I was going to make it here," he said. "I followed the road as far as I could, but it's washed out part of the way. I was scared to death of what I might find when I got here. I half expected it to be Thorn here, not you. But I should have known if you could keep a horse under you, you'd ride through the fires of hell and survive."

At his mention of Robert, I had a sudden flash of memory of Robert in the water, of how I had seen him go under and not come up again.

"What the hell happened to Thorn?" Chase continued. "How'd you get away from him?"

I had started to shiver.

"Laura? Are you all right?"

"I—I have to tell you something."

"What—"

"It's about Robert. I—I think I killed him."

Shock and disbelief covered his face like a shroud.

"I pushed him into the sea. No, I don't remember if I pushed him, but I—"

Chase distracted me by going to the bed and pulling the coverlet off with one quick jerk, then he wrapped it around me, covering my rain-soaked clothes and hair to control my shivering. "Johnny told me what Robert was doing to you," Chase said, his arms still around me, holding the coverlet. He turned me around to face him. "He was frantic with worry that Robert was going to kill you."

"It was so confusing, so terrifying—"

"You were fighting for your life. Be thankful you were strong enough to do that." I saw the tension and agony on his face. "Are you sure he's dead?" he asked. "Did you see him drown?"

"We fell into the sea. There was a struggle, and he let go of me. I thought I was going to die—to drown—all that water—the storm. I came out of it, finally, but he wasn't there. I never saw him again."

I was still shaking, and Chase placed his hand under my chin, lifting my face to look at him. "It was an accident. You were fighting for your life. You've got to remember that. It's the only way you can hold on to your sanity." The gentleness of his gesture touched me as much as his words. I knew that he was telling me that he'd had to find a way to hang on to his own sanity after he'd killed a man. "Look at you," he said. "We've got to get you out of those wet clothes before you catch cold."

Suddenly a strong gust of wind shattered the glass in the window, and a torrent of rain flooded the room. I screamed, then instinctively pulled the coverlet from my shoulders and started toward the window to cover the void. Chase took my arm, stopping me.

"Let it go," he said. "It's useless. The storm is stronger than the house. It's only a matter of time for this house now, Laura."

I turned to look at him, knowing he was right. Was it only a matter of time for us, too?

"Go on. Do as I say and find yourself some dry clothes," Chase said. "I'll heat some water so you can get some of that mud off."

The wind howled and whistled through the window so loudly I could hardly hear him, and I could feel the house swaying under its force. It occurred to me that bathing and changing clothes wouldn't make any difference now if we were destined to be killed by the storm. But I was too tired to protest.

Chase stared down the back stairs, leaving me alone in the hallway. What an infuriating man he was, always ordering me around, even to what could be my last living minute, even telling me when I needed a bath. Not that he was wrong. A bath, no matter how impractical it might seem in the face of death, still sounded good. I took a dressing gown and a few toiletries from my room, then went to another room, away from the broken window, to remove my clothes, letting them fall in a soggy, tattered heap to the floor. By the time I had toweled away some of the mud and tied my dressing gown around me, I was already feeling better. The next task was to try to do something with my hair. All of the pins were gone, and the hair stuck to my head and face in a tangled, matted mass. I started with a wide-toothed bone comb, pulling it through a few strands at a time and graduated to a bristle brush. I'd spent several minutes and made a little progress when I heard a soft knock at the door.

I glanced up and saw Chase standing in the doorway. It was an awkward moment. In polite society, a man doesn't go in a lady's bedroom, especially when she is wearing only a dressing gown, and for just a second I felt uncomfortable. Then I recognized the ludicrousness of my false modesty. Chase Bradley had made a habit of bursting into my bedroom since the first day I met him. That was all the more reason why the fleeting look of uncertainty and vulnerability I saw on his face was so puzzling. Was he worried about the propriety, too? Whatever the reason, it didn't last long.

"Your bathwater's ready," he said, moving with his customary swagger into my room. "What's taking you so long?"

The gall of this man! Before I could speak my fury, he was behind me, reaching over my shoulder, taking the brush from my hand. "Let me help," he said, and he started with long, gentle strokes to brush my hair. He followed each stroke of the brush with a movement of his hand down the length of my hair—a long slow caress. I could feel the cool dampness of my hair through the back of my dressing gown, and his hand, by contrast, felt warm, dry, and soothing. He kept up the slow gentle strokes until my very blood warmed and throbbed through my veins, awakening all my senses. All the while I was vaguely aware of the room growing darker and of wild, erratic flashes of lightning illuminating everything.

One of his fingers moved to the side of my face to explore the wispy curls at my temples. Gently he worked his finger inside the curl, and then pulled it out, and then reinserted it and pulled it out again. I felt the house shake in the storm and heard a crashing sound as if another window had broken, or a piece of the roof had blown away, but I ignored it. I could concentrate on nothing except the warm stirring deep inside my groin, and I turned slightly toward Chase. The movement caused a strand of hair to fall over my shoulder. Chase moved in front of me to touch the strand with the brush, bringing the long stroke down as the lock of hair followed the curve of my breast, following with his gently stroking hand. My breath caught in my throat, and I all but stopped breathing when he repeated the movement, his hand moving slowly, cupping to conform to the shape of my body, lingering only slightly over my hardened nipple.

I hardly knew when he dropped the brush and pulled me to my feet and toward him until I was crushed against him and his mouth was on mine. His kiss was urgent, demanding, passionate, and I felt him enter me with a thrust of his tongue. I was literally losing my balance, and I clung to him, afraid that he would go further. Or that he would stop. I felt his hand loosen the ties on my dressing gown and slip inside, to touch my flesh, to massage a taut nipple with his thumb and forefinger, to move downward along the sensitive flesh of my stomach to the spot that no one had ever touched, but that now throbbed for the want of him. My own hand moved to cover his, and he mistook my action for protest.

"No," he whispered hoarsely. "Don't stop me. I want you. I love you."

He loved me! His words were a breathless staccato as he spoke. "I love you," I whispered. Both of us looked at each other, knowing the unspoken words that hung between us. That this could be our only night left. Our only night to love. I let him pick me up and carry me to the bed. He lay me down gently, and his eyes never left me while he removed his shirt. I could feel the awesome pounding of my pulse as I watched. His shoulders and chest were broad and muscular, and a mass of hair on his chest gathered itself into a thin line on his stomach that moved downward. The thumping in my veins became an erratic stutter as he loosened his trousers, and I saw the place where the seductive line of hair ended.

Lightning and thunder crashed, and the wind pushed at the house, sending it into a shudder as he lay down beside me and, with his hand behind my head, lifted my face to his to kiss me, gently this time, but oh, so seductively exploring, sucking, and teasing me to take him in.

Neither of us was thinking of the storm now. Neither of us was thinking of death. We could think of nothing except the feel of flesh against flesh, of the warm moistness inside me that he was now exploring with his fingers, of the hard shaft throbbing against my thigh.

He continued to explore with his fingers, his mouth, his tongue, moving over my body, down, down, making me arch for him brazenly, unashamedly wanting him. He raised himself above me, lean and hungry. My breath caught in my throat in a little shriek as he pushed inside me, and he hesitated.

"I don't want to hurt you," he said.

"Don't stop," I whispered, my hands on his back, trying to pull him into me. Another thrust. Another shriek. And there was no stopping him now. He took me soaring out of the storm so that I no longer heard the wind tearing away pieces of the house and of my old life. Chase was taking me into another dimension I'd never known before. I lifted myself to him, moving with his rhythm, calling his name to follow me into the explosive cataclysm I'd never known.

Slowly I opened my eyes and saw him above me, and I knew he had held back for me. But there was no holding back now as the muscles in his arms tightened and sweat glistened on his tight jaw. He pressed harder, faster. I heard him groan, felt his tremor, and knew that he had filled me with his love.

When it was over, he lay beside me, let out a heavy sigh with a little laugh, and threw his arm across me, pulling me toward him until our sweat-slickened bodies touched. "I love you, Laura," he whispered. "God, I love you more than I ever knew a man could love a woman."

"Chase," I whispered. "I never knew—"

"Never knew what?"

I wanted to tell him I never knew it could be like this. I wanted to ask him why we had wasted so much time, why we hadn't been doing this all along. But I couldn't say any of it. In spite of the fact that I knew we might never survive the storm, I was still too much the shy spinster to say it.

"Never knew what?" he asked again.

"Never knew how much I loved you," I said.

He laughed and stood up, pulling me up with him. I felt shy all over again, standing there naked with him naked in front of me. "Come on," he said, taking my hand and leading me toward the doorway.

"Come on where?" I resisted a little, pulling back on his hand.

"That bathwater is getting cold."

"Bathwater? No!" I said with an uneasy laugh.

"Why not?"

"We can't. I mean, we're naked."

"Isn't that the way most people take baths?"

"But we have to go all the way downstairs. We can't go down there like this."

"Afraid somebody's going to see us?"

"Chase, for heaven's sake," I said, reaching for the coverlet and wrapping it around me.

He laughed, then he picked me up, coverlet and all, and carried me down the back stairs to the kitchen. He set me down in front of the long, high-backed tub, then stuck a hand in to test the water temperature. "Just right," he said with a wink. "It's too muggy for a hot bath anyway. Get in," he said, motioning toward the tub.

I looked at him, holding the coverlet close around me, remembering how it had felt to have him inside me. I could still feel the sticky moistness he had left between my legs, and I knew then what I wanted more than anything. With my eyes locked on his, I dropped the coverlet from my shoulders and let it slide to my waist over my hips to the floor. His eyes swept over my body, and I found to my surprise that I enjoyed it, that I wanted him to look at me. His eyes came back to meet mine, and then, surprising me even more, he reached for me, lifting me under my armpits. He was going to get into the tub with me!

Instinctively, brazenly, I wrapped my legs around his waist while he stepped into the tub and lowered us both into the water, making it splash over the edges. My legs were still spread and floated upward when he moved me toward him, pressing my breasts close to his chest, and he brushed my lips with his, teasing me with his tongue while another part of him teased me beneath the water. I soon could no longer be described as a shy spinster, I thought. Chase Bradley was taking away every trace of shyness.

"That wasn't so bad, was it?" he asked, his lips against mine.

"What wasn't so bad?" I moved my head and tasted the salty skin on his shoulder

"What we did upstairs."

"Not so bad," I said, nuzzling his neck.

"I hope I didn't hurt you."

"It didn't hurt. It felt good."

"That's one good thing about women who ride horses."

I sat up suddenly to look at him, making the water splash over the edge of the tub again. He had a wicked smile on his lips, and I knew what he was talking about. I hadn't led so protected a life that I hadn't heard of the delicate membrane that could be broken under more than one condition.

"You're being crass," I said.

"I'm being truthful. I wanted you to enjoy it. I didn't want to have to hurt you. I'm glad you're such a good horsewoman."

I cupped two palms full of water into my hands and splashed it in his face. He sputtered and coughed, caught by surprise.

"What the hell was that for?" he asked, wiping his eyes.

"For telling Johnny I was an ignorant horsewoman," I said, splashing another double handful at his face again.

This time Chase dodged it and threw back his head and laughed. "Ignorant? I didn't say ignorant. I said arrogant."

"Arrogant?"

"That's right. Arrogant. Riding into town on that big stallion with your head held high just like old man King used to look. And sitting that sidesaddle with all the skill of a circus performer. Do you have any idea how beautiful, how desirable, you looked? How you made every man in town who saw you want you? Every woman envy you?"

He was embarrassing me, and I dropped my eyes. "Chase—"

Suddenly my face was soaked with water, and I looked up to see him grinning at me. "That's for being arrogant enough to soak me."

I laughed and splashed him back, then reached to cup more water, but he grabbed my wrists, laughing, too. "You're more than arrogant," he said. "You're—" He stopped speaking when he saw me wince involuntarily at the grip he had on my sore wrist. "Oh, God, I didn't mean to hurt you."

"It's all right."

He kissed my wrist and dipped it under the water, then, with his eyes still on me, reached over the edge of the tub for the soap. He began to rub it over me, acquainting himself with every contour of my body, then shared the soap with me, and I did the same with him. We pleasured each other until I felt a new fire burning that no water could chase away. What would the headmistress at Mrs. Swathmore's Academy think if she could see me now? But I had no time to think of Mrs. Swathmore's or headmistresses, not when Chase was doing what he was doing. I began to move slowly, rhythmically, wanting more.

He stood up and pulled me up with him, then lifted me from the tub and dried us both on the coverlet. Then he carried me, wrapped in the coverlet, to the big parlor at the front of the house, and he began again to make love to me. When it was over the second time, he held me in his arms.

"Two rooms and twenty-eight to go," I said, nuzzling his neck.

He turned to give me a questioning look.

"I want to make love to you in every room in this house." I laughed, giddy with love and passion for him. "But we've got to hurry. The way this storm sounds, there may not be any rooms left soon."

He pulled me closer. "Don't laugh," he said. "You know this is serious. These storms can kill."

"I know," I said, letting him hold me for a moment before I pulled away. Suddenly another great blast of wind shook the house with the sound of a loud explosion, and in the next moment the parlor was flooded. We both looked up and saw that a section of the wall had caved in, and rain was pouring through.

"Get dressed!" Chase said, pushing me away from him. "We may have to abandon this place."

I did as I was told and raced upstairs to find my clothes. Before I finished dressing, Chase came in, fully clothed. "Go downstairs," he ordered, pulling on his boots and shirt. "It's not safe up here." I hesitated, not wanting to leave him. "Go on!" he shouted. "Do as I say. Go to the library. Stay away from the damaged side."

With one last hesitant glance at him, I hurried out of the room and down the stairs. I let myself into the library and started to close the door, but I stopped. I didn't want any doors closed until Chase was downstairs, even if I did have to listen to the deafening sound of the wind and rain blowing through the hole in the parlor. But it was odd, I thought, that the sound was not as loud and frightening as it had been before. Perhaps the storm was over. And we had survived!

Yes, I was sure of it, the wind and rain were subsiding. By the time Chase came into the library, it had calmed even more. He glanced at me and stopped before he reached my side. It was quiet. Eerily quiet.

"The eye," Chase said. He turned away, walking toward the grand entry hall, staring out one of the windows at the side of the wide front door. Of course! I should have remembered. The calm meant we were in the eye of the storm. In a few minutes the wind and rain would return with a vengeful fury. Chase stood at the window with his hands in his pockets, his shoulders slightly stooped as he looked into the menacing calm of the night. "It'll come back," he said. "Worse."

"I know."

"If I thought we could make it to town—"

"It wouldn't make any difference. The whole island is in danger."

"No, the danger's greater here. You're too close to the sea here. My house is built farther inland. Built to withstand these storms. But we'd never make it on foot. Our only chance is the horses."

"Chase—" I tried to call him back, but he was already out the door and moving through waist-high water in the darkness. I tried to follow, but the water was too high, and it was beginning to roll into the house. In a little while Chase came back, soaked.

"They're gone," he said.

"You mean Sir Blanco—"

"Gone. And my horses as well."

I felt painful tears in my throat for the loss of the beautiful white stallion that had been my brother's and that he had meant to give to his son. But the tears remained unshed. For the moment I had the more pressing problem of my own survival. And it seemed unpromising. The eye would pass soon, and it was obvious that the house at Shadow Cove couldn't stand much more.

I glanced at Chase, wanting to say something—something to voice my fear, but he took my hand and led me back inside. I let him lead me to the library and watched while he made a fire, then he sat down on the sofa in front, pulling me down next to him. In a little while we lay down together, clinging to each other on the narrow sofa. We didn't speak. We didn't move. We listened to the sounds of the returning storm and to the sound of our breathing, and I knew that if I had to die, this was the way I chose to go. I went to sleep in Chase's arms, listening to the fury of the returning winds.

I thought I was dreaming when I heard the distant sound of the purring gulf, and the gentle suck and seep of a tidal pool. But I opened my eyes and saw the sun shining through a broken window. I sat up suddenly, and my feet touched dampness. It was no tidal pool I'd heard, but the floor of my own house, flooded from the storm. Most of my furniture was ruined, except for the sofa I'd slept on with Chase.

I looked up and saw him standing in the arched doorway, knee-deep in water. We had survived!

"Good morning," he said. "I've been inspecting the damage."

"And—?"

"It's bad. I don't think you can save the house. But don't worry. We'll live in my house in town."

"We'll—"

"And there's no need to worry about King Enterprises either. Sealy and Bradley is doing well. Mrs. Bradley will always be taken care of."

"Wait just a minute," I said, standing and sloshing through the water. "Are you trying to tell me—"

"I'm trying to ask you to marry me. I'm trying to ask you to be the mother of my children. Including Johnny. I'm trying—"

"I accept," I said, interrupting him. "But there's something you need to know about me—"

"I'm looking forward to a hundred years of finding out things about you."

"And the first thing is that if you marry me, I'll be your partner in more ways than one."

"What?" He sounded surprised. And amused.

"You've taught me about lovemaking. I can teach you about business."

"You can teach me about—" His tone expressed disbelief, but I interrupted again before he could finish.

"I have my own ideas about King Enterprises."

"Now, look here!"

Before he could say more, a small voice cried out, "Papa! Papa!" We both turned to see Johnny in Felix LeFeu's arms in the doorway. "I knew you'd be all right!" he cried. "I told Uncle Felix you would. I made him take me here. Didn't I, Uncle Felix?"

I waded through the water, pushing its weight ahead of me with each step until I reached Johnny, and I took him in my arms.

"Aunty Laura!" he exclaimed, hugging me.

"How would you like to call her Mama?" Chase asked. I turned to look at him. "She's going to be your mama," he said, smiling at me. There was a moment of silence between us before Chase added, "And my partner—in more ways than one."

"Mama?" Johnny asked. "Are you going to be my real mama?"

"I'm going to be as real as I can possibly be," I said, hugging him.

Within a few minutes Felix had us all loaded into the wagon, and we were making our way toward Galveston through water, belly-deep on the horse. I never looked back once. I was leaving it all behind me—the Shadows, now in ruins, with all its memories of unhappiness. It would be three days before Robert Thorn's body would be found, washed up on the beach, and Rachel's would never be found. It would be assumed that the sea had claimed her. But I wasn't thinking of either of them as we drove away from the tattered house that day. I was coming out of the shadows and into the light, toward a new dream, and all the hopes that I carried with me seemed to be symbolized in what happened next.

We had gone only a short distance when Johnny shouted with excitement. "Look!" he said, pointing to something in front of us. In the distance on a rise of high ground stood a white stallion, his mane blowing like satin ribbons in the breeze.

"A consummate storyteller."
—Mary Higgins Clark

BARBARA MICHAELS

NEW YORK TIMES BESTSELLING
AUTHOR OF
SOMEONE IN THE HOUSE
AND *INTO THE DARKNESS*

BE SURE TO READ BARBARA MICHAELS'
BESTSELLERS

__INTO THE DARKNESS 0-425-12892-X/$5.50
__PRINCE OF DARKNESS 0-425-10853-8/$3.95
__THE CRYING CHILD 0-425-11584-4/$4.95
__SOMEONE IN THE HOUSE 0-425-11389-2/$4.95
__SEARCH THE SHADOWS 0-425-11183-0/$5.50
__SHATTERED SILK 0-425-10476-1/$5.50
__BE BURIED IN THE RAIN 0-425-09634-3/$4.95
__AMMIE, COME HOME 0-425-09949-0/$4.99
__SMOKE AND MIRRORS 0-425-11911-4/$4.95
__WAIT FOR WHAT WILL COME 0-425-12005-8/$3.95
__WINGS OF THE FALCON 0-425-11045-1/$4.99
__SONS OF THE WOLF 0-425-11687-5/$4.95
__THE SEA KING'S DAUGHTER 0-425-11306-X/$4.99
__THE DARK ON THE OTHER SIDE 0-425-10928-3/$4.50

For Visa, MasterCard and American Express orders ($10 minimum) call: 1-800-631-8571

FOR MAIL ORDERS: CHECK BOOK(S). FILL
OUT COUPON. SEND TO:

BERKLEY PUBLISHING GROUP
390 Murray Hill Pkwy., Dept. B
East Rutherford, NJ 07073

NAME_____

ADDRESS_____

CITY_____

STATE_____ZIP_____

PLEASE ALLOW 6 WEEKS FOR DELIVERY.
PRICES ARE SUBJECT TO CHANGE WITHOUT NOTICE.

POSTAGE AND HANDLING:
$1.50 for one book, 50¢ for each additional. Do not exceed $4.50.

BOOK TOTAL $ _____

POSTAGE & HANDLING $ _____

APPLICABLE SALES TAX $ _____
(CA, NJ, NY, PA)

TOTAL AMOUNT DUE $ _____

PAYABLE IN US FUNDS.
(No cash orders accepted.)

JILL MARIE LANDIS

The nationally bestselling author of <u>Rose</u> and <u>Sunflower</u>

___JADE 0-515-10591-0/$4.95

A determined young woman of exotic beauty returned to San Francisco to unveil the secrets behind her father's death. But her bold venture would lead her to recover a family fortune—and discover a perilous love....

___ROSE 0-515-10346-2/$4.50

"A gentle romance that will warm your soul."—**Heartland Critiques**
When Rosa set out from Italy to join her husband in Wyoming, her heart was filled with love and longing to see him again. Little did she know that fate held heartbreak ahead. Suddenly a woman alone, the challenge seemed as vast as the prairies.

___SUNFLOWER 0-515-10659-3/$4.95

"A winning novel!"—**Publishers Weekly**
Analisa was strong and independent, Caleb had a brutal heritage that challenged every feeling in her heart. Yet their love was as inevitable as the sunrise...

___WILDFLOWER 0-515-10102-8/$4.95

"A delight from start to finish!"—**Rendezvous**
From the great peaks of the West to the lush seclusion of a Caribbean jungle, Dani and Troy discovered the deepest treasures of the heart.

For Visa, MasterCard and American Express orders ($10 minimum) call: 1-800-631-8571

| FOR MAIL ORDERS: CHECK BOOK(S). FILL OUT COUPON. SEND TO:
BERKLEY PUBLISHING GROUP
390 Murray Hill Pkwy., Dept. B
East Rutherford, NJ 07073

NAME_____
ADDRESS_____
CITY_____
STATE_____ZIP_____
PLEASE ALLOW 6 WEEKS FOR DELIVERY.
PRICES ARE SUBJECT TO CHANGE WITHOUT NOTICE. | POSTAGE AND HANDLING:
$1.50 for one book, 50¢ for each additional. Do not exceed $4.50.

BOOK TOTAL $____
POSTAGE & HANDLING $____
APPLICABLE SALES TAX $____
(CA, NJ, NY, PA)
TOTAL AMOUNT DUE $____
PAYABLE IN US FUNDS.
(No cash orders accepted.) |